ADAM

NICHOLAS JAMES DARLING
WITH ANDREW MICHAEL ARROYO

Published in La Jolla, California, by AAI Books, an imprint of AAI Media.

Scripture quotations marked (NLT) are taken from the Holy Bible, New Living Translation, copyright © 1996, 2004, 2015 by Tyndale House Foundation. Used by permission of Tyndale House Publishers, a division of Tyndale House Ministries, Carol Stream, Illinois 60188. All rights reserved.

Scripture quotations marked (NIV) are taken from the Holy Bible, New International Version®, NIV®. Copyright © 1973, 1978, 1984, 2011 by Biblica, Inc.™ Used by permission of Zondervan. All rights reserved worldwide. www.zondervan.com. The "NIV" and "New International Version" are trademarks registered in the United States Patent and Trademark Office by Biblica, Inc.™

Scripture quotations marked (KJ21) are taken from the 21st Century King James Version®, copyright © 1994. Used by permission of Deuel Enterprises, Inc., Gary, SD 57237. All rights reserved.

Scripture quotations marked (NKJV) are taken from the New King James Version ®. Copyright © 1982 by Thomas Nelson. Used by permission. All rights reserved.

Any internet addresses, phone numbers, or company or product information printed in this book are offered as a resource and are not intended in any way to be or to imply an endorsement by AAI Media, nor does AAI Media vouch for the existence, content, or services of these sites, phone numbers, companies, or products beyond the life of this book.

Cover design: Deranged Doctor Design
Cover elements: Shutterstock®
Cover illustration: Guilherme Krol Lins
Interior design: Champagne Book Design
Editing: Megan Ryan

Requests for information:
AAI Books
P.O. Box 2789
La Jolla, CA 92038
ISBN: 978-1-952945-22-9(Hardcover)
ISBN: 978-1-952945-23-6(Paperback)
ISBN: 978-1-952945-08-3 (E-book)
ISBN: 978-1-952945-21-2 (Audio Book)

Printed in the USA

Library of Congress Control Number: 2022939774

This foundational part of human history was delivered to us as a gift of forty three verses of Scripture (Genesis 2:7-3:24). Anywhere this story deviates from Scripture, understand the deviation as fiction, because that is what it is. While the intimate details of Eden remain a mystery, we are confident that the Spirit of the Uncreated One will unveil the truth of Adam's story as well as your own (1 John 2:27).

CONTENTS

THE LETTER

PROLOGUE

MY STORY ISN'T ABOUT A FALL. IT'S A STORY OF the love between a father and his son and the world's first broken heart. Nothing is quite what it seems. The human heart is fragile. The human heart is powerful. Winds blow and the leaves of interpretation change with the seasons of our existence. I'm not here to change your mind. Our father who breathes life into all and breathed the first breath into my lungs: he alone reveals. I have no authority to tread that sacred space between you and him. Its ground is far too holy for me to set foot on. He alone can speak directly to your spirit. He will do so at a time of his choosing.

Some have said I was cursed from the beginning of time; others have thought of my life on Earth as mere myth or legend. My voice has been silenced, my story untold, like in nightmares when spirits steal your breath. The time has come for you to know my story and what really happened. I will tell you as much as I know, as much as I can remember.

I unleashed death from her iron chains and into our world.

I had sought safety, power, and protection within her promises. I lusted after her. With a seductive kiss, she looked into my eyes as she plunged her thirsty dagger into my longing heart. She turned it like a key into Pandora's box. A skeleton key that in time would give her access to every heart. A part of me died that day, a part lived on. The simple truth was I couldn't look away from her gaze or the stories her eyes began to tell. I ended up giving her everything, every key to our kingdom. When her infiltration was complete, she took everything and gave only death in return. Death to faith, hope, and love. Distortion for beauty. Lies for truth. Death to you and me. She had nothing else to give.

I ran as hard as I could. I wanted to escape the memories of my past, the obligations of my present, and the fear I had of my future. In despair, I attempted to outrun my sins, but the spirit of the Uncreated One caught up to me. With my next breath, he filled my lungs. In an instant, time itself collapsed in front of me and I could run no more. The moon and the sun rose and fell hundreds, then thousands, of times. My mind spun as he led my spirit across continents, generations, the rise and fall of civilizations, and the birth and death of empires. I watched the seasons accelerate, and my heart began to burn bright with a holy anger. I watched days, weeks, months, and years turn into decades and centuries as they streamed by in mere seconds.

Enraged and breathless, I came to see how deep our collective bondage had become. Violence and bloodshed flourished under our reign. Under a powerful delusion, we claimed the right to the blood of our brothers and sisters. We sacrificed our sons and daughters to worship fallen gods. We pursued prosperity but only found paranoia and pain. Our sins demanded sacrifice, and so we practiced witchcraft inside of our submission to its constant impulses. Some blindly and ignorantly followed the spirit of the air. Others knowingly partnered with evil. The authority of heaven was ignored. We became lawless. Each exalted their own perceptions above that of their creator. The rulers who we elevated from among us were the ones we deserved. The Earth was filled with tyrants, not good and just kings, for we were not good and just. We died unknown. We died unloved. We died and were forgotten.

I could take no more. I was a broken man. Soon I was enveloped by a white mist. In my despair, I began to hear a deep cry that echoed from the heart of eternity itself. It filled all of space and time. The mourning of my father continued as all of heaven grieved. Hell reveled in the lot we chose for ourselves. If you could feel the entirety of all the pain that filled your life collapsed into a single moment, the gravity of that moment would crush you. It is the slow but crushing weight I feel now. This burden is far too much for me to bear.

Whether I was in the flesh or the spirit, I could not discern. But the moments that followed were more real to me than anything I had yet to experience in my life. As the mist dissipated, I realized I was just a few feet from my father's throne. The crown that belonged to me was at my feet. I struggled with all my might but quickly realized I did not possess the strength to lift it up or lower it on my head.

As I looked around, I saw the guardians who were there with me in the garden at the very beginning of time. Their eyes were bright and filled with an intensity that made me want to look away. Pensive and unsure of myself, I slowly looked up into my father's golden-brown eyes. I expected wrath but found none. There was a gentleness there that beckoned me to come closer. I approached and sank into his arms. I put my head on his chest. He held me as we both wept. My body trembled as he softly kissed my forehead. In that moment, I felt the weight of both our hearts breaking.

As he held me in his arms, I felt once again that I was his son. I belonged to him. Gradually, he pulled back the curtain of time and gave me a vision of you. I cannot tell you why. I do not know. I can only say that when I saw you, my breath was taken away. You were beautiful beyond words. I traveled with you across the entire span of your life on Earth. In awe, I witnessed your creation. I could feel the beating of your heart as you dreamed within your mother's womb. I even witnessed your very last day and how you would pass into eternity. I saw everything in between, even this moment now when you'd read this letter of mine.

As I took in the years of your life on Earth, I was captivated as visions of joys, defeats, trauma, and the deep pain you've experienced violently cascaded into the very depths of my soul. Every molecule in my being harmonized to the emotions you felt. I was undone by all the suffering you endured. Immediately, I knew what I wanted. I begged and pleaded until my eyes emptied all their tears and my heart grew hard as stone.

I shouted with demands as my fists flailed against his chest. I lost all control. I implored him. I wanted him to let me walk through the veil that separates my past from your present.

I wanted to step into this moment right now. This place where you read these words of mine. If you'd let me, I'd wrap my arms around you and hold you. You could beat my chest in rage and anger. You could weep in anguish. You could ask any question you wanted. I'd wipe the many tears that stream down your cheeks. Perhaps tears from pain endured so long ago you've put it out of your memory. I could tell you how sorry I am for the brokenness of your world, the brokenness in your heart.

I heaved in anguish. As I looked to pound my fists against his chest yet again, they flew through the air instead. Startled, I looked around and saw nothing but the mist that once again had enveloped me. I no longer saw the eyes of my father. Fearful of his reaction, a part of me was relieved I no longer found myself in his presence. Another part of me was terrified. The throne room had vanished just as quickly as it had appeared.

Slowly, the mist transported me into yet another world. A world without him. Cold, hard stone was beneath my feet. Iron bars were in front of me. I knew where I was. It is where I write this letter to you from. I am a prisoner within the depths of Sheol. A place without hope. Beyond the iron bars, I saw the cruel eyes of the demon called Futility. A familiar spirit. One with whom I had walked closely after my time in Eden. He approached my cell. He said nothing. He didn't need to. As he breathed on me, I grew in despair. In the silence, his accusations wrapped around me like a cool blanket, and I realized I was a slave. I belonged to him.

Beyond the bars of Sheol, I looked to my left at a familiar golden orb of light. Its soft brilliance grew until it rivaled the sun. I saw Futility flee in horror at the approaching luminosity.

I raised my hands to shield my eyes from the brightness that filled my prison cell. As the light dissipated, I saw him, and thousands of eyes emerged from the edges of his angelic wings. Though I expected Menakiel to speak, he spoke not a word, but in his presence, I knew what must be done. The time had finally come. I must write you this letter. I must tell you my story. With these words, I hope that once you fully understand, you might be able to forgive me. But more importantly, I hope this will reach you in time so that your fate might be different from mine. My son, my daughter: it is time you knew your history and what really happened. Few things are what they seem.

– Adam

ACT ONE

IN THE BEGINNING

DUST & LIGHT

I

MEMORIES FADE, BUT THE BEGINNING, OR AT least my beginning, is different. My beginning is not like something you remember in the natural course of things. It's not a memory I can conjure up by will. It's more like something I fall into. It's as if the memory itself springs to life and remembers me at its will, pulling me back into its world.

There is nothing beneath me. The air is thin. Only a dark void, an inky blackness dragging me under. Even now, I can feel my descent. I am falling faster. The fog of time is now being pierced as I am pulled into the memory of the Uncreated One. I'm being taken back to those moments. I will never forget them. If you decide to come with me, I will share with you many things, secrets meant to be revealed only at this time. I can't promise that you'll understand everything. There are many things here I don't understand.

4004 B.C.

Past the sweeping treetops of the jungle canopy, I looked into an endless sea of stars. Like millions of eyes returning my gaze, they peered down from their place in the heavens. Their starlight carried a certain dignity and composure. Their presence provided a comfort that stood in stark contrast to the pitch blackness of the jungle I found myself in. A covenant they were committed to honoring had drawn them here. There was an intention to their noble presence, a deliberate narrowing of their focus to this very moment.

Flickering light from thousands of fireflies flashed all around. As the fireflies rose off the jungle floor, particles of dust rose from the ground as if magnetized to the individual movements of each firefly. A small cloud of dust and light rose around me. The sound of various animals hidden behind the thick jungle brush and a steady chorus of cicadas slowly cascaded into my conscious mind.

Before my ears were opened, I could hear. Before my eyes were given their color, I could see. Before my tongue was formed from the dust, I could taste the sweetness of the earth in my mouth. My senses were different back then. They were heightened and able to apprehend more of the world around me. My mind was clearer and more capable. It had abilities that were never meant to be forfeited. Through a simple thought, I could cast my vision into any living creature, any animal moving within the jungle or any bird flying miles above the Earth.

I was a participant of all the life around me, and the ability to see through any living being at will was as natural as breathing.

In that moment, I saw through the eyes of the one approaching me. As he made his way through the thick jungle, I saw myself come into his view. Between the trees and the soft twinkling light of the fireflies, he saw me. Through his eyes, I could see I was floating on my back, just a few feet above the jungle floor. Surrounded by dust and the light of the fireflies, he watched as they slowly wove an outline of my being into existence. Suspended in midair, my vision returned to seeing through my own eyes. I looked up as the brightness of the stars drew my attention to the heavens above.

At his guidance, the fireflies increased their speed and began forming a whirlwind of light and dust around me. Their collective movement projected light that caused shadows to dance from behind the ancient trees as they sped around and through me. On my back, I moved effortlessly upward with the flight and direction of these wondrous creatures. As they flew higher, the gravity of Earth had no effect over my weightless and forming body. Untethered, I began to float farther off the jungle floor, drifting slowly toward the shimmering constellations.

With my senses heightened, I could feel the compression of the earth under his now soft steps as he continued to walk toward me. He stood in all dimensions of time, the alpha and the omega, the beginning and the end. I felt him most intensely in the space between. His presence in all dimensions slowed my experience of time to a crawl. Even though he walked toward me in time and space, I felt all dimensions were contained within his being.

As they moved in a circular pattern around me, the bright, bulbous fireflies now smeared beams of incandescent golden light in the delicate air. Time continued to slow. With each one of his steps toward me, a sense of tranquility washed through my being. Stopping underneath me, he looked up; his eyes carried flecks of soft golden light that I also saw in the stars above.

With his proximity, his purpose became more clear, as did his anticipation. There was a curiosity toward me and a deep joy that radiated from his being, affecting everything around us in waves. The waves attracted many creatures of all kinds to draw closer to witness my creation. Inside every creature, I could feel a sense of love and awe as they watched their creator move toward me. As he had commanded the gravitational force of the entire universe, I felt the sea of stars draw nearer with every step he took toward me. It was as if they were leaning in for a closer look.

At the time of my creation, though I was a young boy, my mind was not that of a developing infant. I was never born from a woman. I was born from him. His essence was intertwined with mine. With a glance, we made eye contact, and I felt a warm love swell up within me as a series of awarenesses pulsated through my mind. In steady intervals, various understandings came into my consciousness. It started slowly, but it began to move at the speed of light. Understanding how the world was formed, his intentions for me, the DNA sequencing and design of thousands of creatures, music, mathematics, physics and the laws of the natural world he had created for us, the stories the stars would tell, language, even pieces of my future. My neurological connections felt like they were on fire, but the stream from him was not chaotic. It brought structure, peace, and clarity to my mind.

I gazed into his eyes. He shared with me everything I needed to know and nothing more. I was at peace. This was the first time we met, and I was fully known by him. Yet somehow, I could sense a curiosity within him. It was as if his omniscience began to flood behind the dam of his will, stopping so he could experience and discover this moment with me. As I saw a warm smile spread across his face, I knew he desired to see how close he and I could grow together. I knew that before he had formed the world, his desire was to have sons, to have daughters.

The stars released me from their embrace, and I could feel his gravity draw me back down toward him. As his hands touched the dust of the fireflies, the dust began to change into the material needed for the composition of my physical form. Hovering a few feet above the earth, his hands moved like that of a conductor shaping and forming my body. With swift and artful movements, his hands stretched, and muscles and flesh began wrapping themselves around my hardening bones. I felt blood rush through the tubes of my newly formed veins like water rushing down a river. I could feel the tingling of new skin as it raced across my open body. It covered me until I was fully enveloped in its protective cocoon.

He had spoken everything into existence: the world itself, every element, every animal, and all organic matter. Yet embedded deep within his heart was a desire to lovingly touch, to form me with his very own hands and to hold me within his arms. He desired a closeness and intimacy only touch could bring.

The chirping of the cicadas subsided. A gentle wind moved the tops of the trees. I saw the stars pulsate and start to harmoniously mirror the flickering of the fireflies. With the passage of time, both seemed to slightly dim as they awaited his next move. My attention shifted from the starlight back to him. I could feel an energy surge through his being. His eyes were soft, warm, and welcoming as he looked into mine. The bluish white starlight flickered like miniature flashes of lightning in the reflection of his golden-brown eyes.

I couldn't look away. I didn't want to. His eyes revealed a deep affection and abiding joy in his heart. I delighted him. Parts of his heart that were dormant were awakening. I saw something in his eyes, and I longed to know him even more.

As he held me, his chest swelled as he took a breath in. As he breathed in deep, thousands of fireflies surrounding us streaked by and seemed to chase the air he inhaled through his mouth and throat and then down into his lungs. Pulsating light seemed to now dance within his chest. He lowered his head and leaned toward me. With a gentle push, my lungs were instantly filled with his sweet and intoxicating breath. The rush of light and air went through my nostrils and into my lungs. As his breath coursed through me, it felt like a strange combination of lightning bathed in mint. A euphoria electrified every cell of my newly formed body. The intensity made my lungs feel like they were on the verge of rupturing.

With my second breath, I started to smell the fragrant scent of the tropical flowers. Ecstasy swept through my being. An overwhelming sense of peace came after. In an ancient tongue, he softly sang a quiet psalm of celebration. His voice was beautiful and carried a deep love within its cadence. The harmony began to calm every molecule within me as it was carried on the soft breeze that blew through the jungle. As I breathed in, I could sense the very breath and life of my father was now in me. A new life that knew of no beginning. A powerful life that knew no end. The breath that created the world was now moving through my very lungs. As I exhaled, it circulated through the jungle.

Inside of my connection with him, I was connected to all things. I celebrated all things and all things celebrated us. With my first breath came an understanding, which now moved with the rhythmic beating of my new heart: I belonged.

I belonged to this time. I belonged to this moment. I belonged to this jungle, to the heavens above and the Earth below. I belonged to the stars, to all the unknown inhabitants of this strange place. And more than anything, I belonged to him.

NOT ALONE

II

3994 B.C. ~ 10 Years Later

ADAM RACED THROUGH THE JUNGLE. AS HE RAN, the intensity of the moonlight pierced the canopy of the jungle above him, lighting his path. His fifteen-year-old heart pumped rapidly as he pushed himself to run faster. The Milky Way and twinkling stardust hung above the Earth like a breathing mural. Enormous silverback gorillas ran with him, flanking him on each side. Their massive muscles swelled just underneath the surface of their coats, their breathing was loud, and their graceful and swift movements defied their immense size. Often, they would accompany Adam as he explored the vast reaches of Eden's territory. Over the years, he had grown accustomed to their presence and welcomed their steady companionship.

Ten years had passed since his creation. He now knew this area of the jungle well. It was home. Each time he ran past familiar landmarks, he pushed himself. He wanted to know how fast he could really go. Did he have limits? What were they? Each time he pushed himself, it seemed like he only grew faster. As they raced through the jungle, up and down the terrain, the silverbacks followed alongside Adam with lightning speed. As he jumped over a creek, they jumped with him. The gorillas' landing brought a thundering crash that caused the earth to shake. As the earth quaked, it seemed to send an unequivocal message. A message that conveyed that Adam was under their watchful eye.

In the distance, a large body of water came into view. Adam had been here many times. Between the brightness of the moon and the sweetness of the air, it was particularly beautiful tonight. This was the sea his father called Galilee. Galilee was not an ocean but rather a freshwater lake of unusually large size. Its cool waters refreshed in the day. In the night, its smooth surface provided a perfect reflection of the glittery stars above. Sometimes, the banks of the sea provided time for contemplation; other times, arriving here meant discovery.

The silverbacks receded into the thickness of the jungle. Adam slowed his pace and scanned the shore from behind towering kapok trees. Oftentimes when the gorillas departed, it was a sign his father was close by. A gentle, warm breeze lightly touched Adam's skin. Looking around, Adam finally spotted him.

Elohim had created everything Adam had ever laid eyes on, every sound and creature, the plants and the animals, the contour of the hills, the depths of the seas, even the coolness of the waters and warmth of the sun. While he was many things, Adam knew him most as an artist and as his father. To see

Elohim was to see Adam's best and only friend. Together, they were explorers destined to have new adventures into uncharted territories. While Elohim appeared to be in his early forties, his true age was a mystery to Adam. What he did know was that his father's age had never been governed by the cycles or rotations of the Earth. This much Adam knew.

Elohim's skin was deeply tanned. The muscles in his back, chest, and arms looked like they stored a hidden and potentially explosive strength. Around his father's waist, a light gray material resembling loosely fit linens with white and gold embroidery provided covering. Adam's own clothing, which hung around his waist, looked like it was cut from the same cloth with a similar material but with silver embroidery. The clothing provided warmth during the cool nights and breathed well on hotter days.

Elohim reached down. Picking up a smooth stone, he glanced over his shoulder, looking back toward his son. A huge grin swept across his face. With a flick of his wrist, the stone skipped half a dozen times over the glassy water. Following his father's lead, Adam picked up a stone of his own and sent it skimming across the surface. The reflection of the stars warped with the ripples of the water. Adam walked up next to him.

"You found me," Elohim said as he tousled his son's brown hair. As Adam looked up at him, he saw a familiar affection in his eyes. Adam quickly brushed his father's large hand off the top of his head.

"Always do," Adam replied with his signature toothy grin.

"Watch …" Elohim picked up another smooth stone from the ground. As he reached for the stone, Adam saw the massive muscles in his back stretch as he bent down. Rising back up, he lowered his right hand, and with a flick of his wrist, he sent the stone skipping. This stone skipped a few times more than the one before.

With an appreciation of the challenge, Adam picked up his second stone, and mimicking the technique, he skimmed it across the water. This time, the stone traveled further with half a dozen more skips. Adam's chest swelled with a sense of satisfaction. This was good. Often, Elohim beat him, but this time, Adam's stone had skipped three more times than his! A huge grin, which Adam made no attempt to hide, spread on his face as he looked up at Elohim. Adam could see in his eyes his competitive side had been counting as well.

"That's it!" Elohim roared. A huge smile was plastered across his face. His eyes seemed to be laughing as he looked proudly at his son. He gave Adam a side hug and squeezed him in his massive arm. Elohim's emotion was on the surface. Adam was his son. Inside his joy, Adam saw him clearly. In seeing him, Adam knew him.

"Where are we going tonight?" Adam asked. They both looked across the water. As the concentric circles from the stones faded, Adam could see the perfect reflection of the stars twinkling on its cool surface come back into focus.

"You'll see." Elohim's voice was certain, and Adam could sense tonight was somehow different. "Come, follow me."

Elohim ran through the jungle; his speed surprised Adam.

Usually Adam would lead them to a new place of discovery with Elohim following behind. Tonight, Adam was pushing as hard as he could to keep up. Elohim loved the feeling of oxygen rushing his lungs and the pounding of his heart in his chest. He loved breathing in the fragrant air. He loved the companionship of the gorillas who escorted them. He loved seeing his son follow close behind with anticipation painted on his face. This night in particular was special. Its importance would forever mark Adam's life. His son would never be the same.

Elohim's heart was full as he thought about his son. Adam was a quick student, his curiosity was insatiable, his mind was sharp, and his humor and imagination would often leave them both rolling with laughter. Elohim loved him, and as he grew older, he only felt their connection strengthen. He experienced deep satisfaction as Adam had walked with him, making many discoveries in the world he had created for them.

They raced together alongside the riverbanks that fed Galilee. Parts of the river that snaked through the jungle were calm, other parts had strong currents, and some had powerful whitewater. After a few miles, Elohim slowed his pace as the roar of a distant waterfall came within earshot. Adam glanced at Elohim. A huge grin swept across Elohim's face. "This way!"

After a few more minutes of sprinting, two towering waterfalls that ran parallel to each other came into view. Elohim and Adam slowed down and walked toward the edge of the water. Adam stopped to catch his breath. Looking up, he saw millions of gallons of fresh water dropping from a few hundred feet above. Adam had never explored this far up the river, and the sheer volume of water surprised him. He had never seen anything quite like it. The highly oxygenated air from the crashing water was invigorating. This place was a gift hidden within the deep, emerald-green brush of the jungle. Pure white birds flew in an intricate pattern around the falls, their flight patterns strangely hypnotic.

"What do you think?" Elohim asked. As his father spoke, Adam felt a spark of creativity. Peace moved through his being.

"They're beautiful," Adam replied. A few moments passed. He looked on with a sense of awe as he focused on birds he had never seen before. "Their movements are elegant ... it's as if they're dancing between the falls."

"*And their name ...?*" Elohim joined his son in looking at the birds. Elohim chose in this moment, as he had many times in Adam's life, to pull back his awareness of the future like a curtain. When he did so, he was neither present to the past nor the future. Like rushing water that stops and pools at a dam, his stream of consciousness came fully into the present. He watched Adam's chest rise and fall as his son breathed in deep, still catching his breath from their run. Adam couldn't help but smile as his soft green eyes looked fondly on these graceful creatures. Elohim enjoyed the creativity and wonder that animated Adam's spirit. He wanted nothing to distract from the moment.

Adam continued to study the birds. Over many years, he had seen such a variety. Each species always brought something unique: their movements, shape, color, speed, songs, and altitude of flight; the way they expressed themselves with their own kind and other creatures; how and what they ate; and their larger role within Eden helping other plants and trees spread. All these things fascinated Adam. Adam noticed their elongated necks as they flew and glanced back at Elohim, who was still taking it all in himself. They were beautiful.

"I know …" Adam said. "I know this one …" His voice trailed off.

"And …?" Elohim asked. Adam glanced over at his father and paused. His father looked at him with anticipation.

"Well …" Adam slowly nodded as his body came into agreement with the decision made in his heart. "An egret," Adam declared as he looked back on the birds triumphantly. "Egrets!"

Elohim breathed in deep. "An egret …" He looked back up at the birds, seeing something new in the creatures he had never seen before. "I like it. It's a good name." Elohim paused and smiled. "A great name."

The egrets flew above with graceful movements. With Elohim's next breath, his exhale traveled instantaneously throughout Eden. It communicated the message to every creature that the egrets were now known by name. They were now part of the family of creatures that were named and known, that belonged. Adam looked over at Elohim and heard the jungle come alive with the sounds of thousands of animals, birds, and other creatures. All in their own language expressed their welcome to the egrets. Adam looked back up at the waterfall. Adam's ear easily distinguished the crashing of the waterfall from the reverberations of all creatures and their celebration of the egrets into the family.

Elohim hiked up the riverbank and walked toward the foot of the waterfalls. Mist from the rushing water blew at his and Adam's faces. Raising his head, he wiped the beads of water from his face and eyes and looked up. He flashed a knowing smile toward Adam. The top of the falls looked to be roughly a hundred feet above the bottom where they stood. Off to the side, Adam watched Elohim tug on some vines to test their strength. He pulled himself a few feet up; then, looking at Adam, he gave a nod.

Adam sprinted toward his father, and with a leap, he jumped on Elohim's back, wrapping his arms around his neck and riding piggyback as Elohim climbed higher. The boy's young legs pulled tight around his waist. Elohim's climb was certain and quick, his strong arms easily pulling the two of them higher at a steady clip. Looking down from the great height, Adam continued to marvel at the jungle below and the water that came pouring down from the top. Many egrets flew close by.

As they climbed higher, the roar of the waterfall crashing into the pool beneath them softened. Looking up a few dozen feet from the top, Adam reached out and gripped a pair of vines that ran parallel to the vines Elohim was using to climb. Adam pulled himself up with a slightly faster speed and reached the top before Elohim. Spinning around with an accomplished look on his face, Adam extended his hand to his father. Elohim placed his hand in Adam's, letting his son assist him to the top. He couldn't help but grin.

Adam looked toward the stars. His pupils grew larger as he drank in their light. The light from the stars gave Adam new strength and energy. Though he wasn't quite conscious of how it happened, he could feel the light somehow deepening his heart and his understanding of the world around him.

"There's so many ..." Adam's voice was barely an audible whisper as he looked at the stars.

"There were more," Elohim softly replied. Adam glanced at his father inquisitively.

Elohim peered over the edge of the cliff and gazed at the water falling. The jungle was alive tonight with a particular energy, a celebration that brought Elohim a sense of peace. His creation was beautiful. His creation was good. He turned back around and walked toward one of the many towering kapok trees that littered the top of the mesa. As he neared one of the trees, he looked back at Adam, whose large eyes had gone back to drinking in the starlight. Past the kapok trees, his eyes followed the river upstream. Unexplored mountains of great heights towered in the moonlit distance.

A lone egret that had made it to the top of the falls landed on a nearby stone. The jagged stone it landed on was near the edge of the waterfalls. Adam took in the sight of the white egret. Turning around, he walked toward his father. Elohim looked small in relation to the massive kapok tree. He sat down and leaned his back up against its huge trunk. Through the canopy of leaves, Elohim looked up at the stars, seemingly lost in his own thoughts. The moonlight was so intense it seemed to bounce off the leaves high in the canopy. A gentle breeze swayed the massive tops of the trees. Adam walked over and sat between his father's legs. He leaned back, resting his head on Elohim's chest. Adam could feel the strength of his father's heart as it beat steadily.

Adam looked back up at the stars. "There were more?" Adam inquired.

"Yes. Many fell," Elohim paused as he recollected the time. "Far too many."

The lone egret squawked and shook its wings. A gentle breeze continued to sway the top of the canopy.

"Before your time, a sound was heard in the heavens. It penetrated their spirits. To the gravity of this world they fell," Elohim said as he entered into the pain of the distant memory.

The boy looked up at his father. Elohim continued to gaze at the stars above them. It seemed there was a vulnerable sorrow in his eyes Adam had never seen, as if his father was visiting a tender memory that deeply affected him. From the edge of the waterfalls, a few dozen scattered fireflies brought their own light and moved toward the boy and his father. Adam looked back again at his father's face, and the sorrow had been displaced by a familiar, warm smile as Elohim looked on toward the bright lights of the twinkling creatures approaching.

"They do not create." Elohim breathed in and exhaled slowly. Adam listened closely to his father. "They seek to take the created kingdoms and make them their own."

"Are they with us here, in the garden?" Adam asked.

Elohim looked down on his son as Adam rested in his arms. He could see his boy growing tired. Returning his gaze back up to the stars, Elohim spoke in a voice that was steady but barely over a whisper. "There's no fear inside you, son. Nor should there be ... but know this: we are not alone."

Elohim's words opened his son's heart to a new mystery. His voice brought peace to his son's spirit. It confirmed an intuition Adam had always felt but never had put words to. With the rest of his spirit, Adam closed his eyes. The rhythmic beat of his father's heart invited him into sleep.

The fireflies flew through the thin air toward the boy and his father. Elohim looked down on his son and lovingly stroked his hair. His precious boy. There was knowledge and understanding Adam was prepared to hear and other things his heart needed to grow into. Elohim felt a powerful but unspoken longing inside of Adam. Elohim knew it wasn't good for Adam to be alone. And he wouldn't be.

Elohim moved his hand over his son's chest. As it rose and fell with each breath, his father waited patiently for his son to enter a deep sleep. Elohim saw him go deeper and deeper into rest until the time had finally arrived.

Elohim's intention and desire burned brighter, and with each passing breath, Adam's rib cage and the bones beneath his chest began to glow. At first, the amber glow was so soft it barely matched the brightness of the surrounding fireflies, but with time, the bones grew brighter and brighter until they resembled burning hot embers under Adam's chest. As the light within Adam's rib cage grew, the bones in Elohim's right hand matched the intensity of the light emitting from Adam's bones. Still, Adam slept. Elohim carefully moved his fingers and hand into his son's chest. Elohim's hand vibrated right beneath his son's heart. Slowly, he removed a rib from Adam's left-hand side. Elohim raised the rib up to his eyes and observed a slowly pulsating, amber-colored glow.

The grass and nearby foliage moved with a soft breeze as Elohim watched the fireflies move upward into the canopy. The roar of the waterfall came back into focus. Elohim watched the lone egret leap off its rock and fly into the air. The egret circled above them a few times. It then quickly flew down past the edge of the falls beyond Elohim's line of sight.

Flying downward, parallel to the waterfalls, the egret dove with increasing speed. Before hitting the pool of water below, it snapped its wings back and instantly transformed into a raven. The dark bird darted off into the deep blackness of the jungle.

BLOOD & BONE

III

ALARGE AND POWERFUL SILVERBACK MOVED FROM the depths of a cave and approached the entrance. Its muscles tensed. Its alert, dark brown, almost black eyes stared into the jungle. With a sudden leap, it dashed out of the cave and began moving with a fierce speed. The evening air came alive with expectancy. Every living thing within Eden could feel the shift. The moment had come. All living things pulsated with a new hope, a hope that seemed to eclipse the evening when Adam himself was born from the dust of the Earth and the breath of Elohim.

At first, one gorilla followed, then half a dozen others joined. The huge muscles that animated their massive frames blew by trees and broke through smaller ones they'd normally go around. Their mission was clear, and speed was required tonight. From behind thick foliage, the lead gorilla leapt from the top of the hill, flew through the air, and landed on the valley floor in front of Elohim. The ground shook violently. Elohim paused his walk and looked up. Elohim stood his ground as the momentum of the gorilla caused it to lean inches away from his face. Elohim leaned into the gorilla, his eyes piercing the soul of the creature. For a few moments, the two stared at each other. Elohim felt the massive animal's hot breath on his face. The gorilla looked into Elohim's eyes, then down at his hand. Elohim's right hand held a bone; Adam's rib still had a soft amber glow. The glow's intensity pulsated and seemed to match the beating of Elohim's heart. The two were synchronized. The gorilla looked back up at Elohim.

"The lawless one is not to go near him," Elohim commanded the creature. "Go. Now. Keep watch over my son."

The gorilla snarled and grunted. Elohim instantly understood its language. "We will go," it replied and looked back at the other gorillas behind it. "We will protect." The lead silverback dashed around Elohim, heading in the direction of Adam. The other gorillas sped past him in the same direction.

Elohim looked behind him and saw the huge creatures dash through the jungle toward Adam. He looked down at the bone in his right hand as it pulsated with a soft light. He started to march through the thick jungle. As he moved, all of creation seemed to bend and distort as if he had created a time warp in his wake. As he continued to walk, he pushed himself toward the edge of Eden's jungle. At the jungle's edge was the desolation, a vast barren desert that dwarfed the size of the gardens and the jungles that characterized the majority of Eden's territory. Adam had never explored this part of the Earth. His heart was not prepared to see the devastation and lifelessness inflicted by the lawless one on the rest of his world.

As Elohim stepped into the desolation, the ground under his bare feet was composed mainly of dry clay mixed with sand. Nothing grew here. Nothing could. There was no water, no plants, no animals, no life to speak of. No creature walked upon the soil; no bird graced the air with its flight. The air grew heavier with what appeared to be pale ash and soot.

As Elohim walked through the barren wasteland between the soot and ash, the dark sky above him took on a molasses-like quality. Slowly, it choked the light of the moon and stars above until no celestial light was visible. Elohim continued walking. The only visible light was now the light emitted from the pulsating bone in his right hand. The ash and soot seemed to only grow thicker. The bone lit Elohim's path as he continued his march across the dark, foreboding landscape. The air grew cold. As he walked, Elohim began to see his breath in the frigid air. Nothing beyond a few dozen feet was now visible from the light of the bone.

Dark spirits like ghosts flew above Elohim. Their eerie whispers bored through the darkness. "From dust to man ..." whispered one.

"From man to bone ...?" another whispered.

The voices of the spirits were nearly inaudible except to each other. Their voices were discerned more like vibrations than audible sound by the mind of Elohim.

Time passed. As Elohim walked, the brightness of the bone began to illuminate large, onyx black stones on the path in front of him. These massive rocks seemed to shoot up from the earth. As he walked, the light revealed the orientation of the stones, which were laid out in a circular pattern that Elohim was stepping into the center of. The sanctuary created by the pattern of stones seemed to hide a portal into another world. The large stones were slanted slightly and rose anywhere from forty to fifty feet in the cold air. Walking over huge roots, Elohim made his way to the center of the stones. At the very center, a lone stump from a previously massive tree proudly stood. The wood was ancient and petrified. The stump rose to Elohim's waist. The surface of the tree's roots wove in and out of the surrounding stones.

The musings of dark spirits were shared among each other. "Only death is here …" Elohim looked at the massive stones that encircled him and then back down to the stump.

Elohim gently placed the pulsating bone on the top of the stump of the once mighty tree. Slowly, the light from the bone faded. Its light and life vanished, and it appeared dead and dry. Elohim looked down at the bone.

"He goes to such a dry place. Barren. Without water. Without life," another spirit murmured.

Elohim paused and breathed in deep. Starlight within his eyes began to dance like unpredictable lightning on a stormy night.

"We are their life. We are their breath, their blood, their bone," Elohim spoke with a commanding authority. He looked up at the black sky above him. His low and steady voice bounced off the massive stones, and at his words, Elohim saw the dark spirits dissipate like smoke in the wind. Closing his eyes, he lowered his hands with palms facing down over the bone.

Defying gravity, the bone began to shake and rise a few

inches off the stump. Elohim opened his eyes. Light from the center of the bone began to break out in small but bright streaks. The frosty air was warmed by its energy. The light from the stars above began to pierce the ashen sky. What looked like millions of fireflies hovering hundreds of yards in the air overhead began to descend. Their light matched the intensity of the stars above. The pitch blackness that had blocked the stars faded completely. The stars began to burn brighter with anticipation. As the light from the fireflies got closer, a huge smile swept over Elohim. His servants and friends had come. He had readied himself for this moment. A joy he couldn't contain began to rise from the center of his being. A soft laughter bubbled up from within.

The desire in Elohim's heart began to beat like a drum and burst forth. More streaks of light broke out from the center of the once lifeless bone, blazing in all directions. Elohim reached out and held one of the streaks of light, then another. He began to bend each one and weave them together. His heart pounded with excitement. The fireflies slowly circled Elohim as they witnessed the works of his hands. As a composer, he began to fashion and shape the light until he saw her.

Playfully, Elohim pulled out more strands of light, weaving an outline of his daughter's form into being. In the reflection of his eyes, a glimpse of a young girl's face appeared. She opened her soft but bright blue eyes; light radiated from the center of her being. She twirled around with a smile on her face. Her hair, like her body, was composed of thin strands of light, which softly hit her father's face as she spun with delight.

Elohim was overcome with joy and laughter as he

fashioned his daughter. As she twirled, her form threw off different colored light. The light that blazed from her being seemed to wrap itself around the stones, chasing away all shadows. She possessed a magnetic allure, which the stars above responded to in waves. It drew them nearer to the Earth so they could take a closer look.

Eve breathed in and looked around. With her breath in, she seemed to pull the stars closer still. The fireflies moved in a slow, circular fashion around her and Elohim as they witnessed her creation. Taking a step back, she redirected her attention toward Elohim. As their eyes met, a love rose from deep within her. With a graceful movement, she moved toward her father.

As if awakened from a cosmic sleep, Eve began to remember things created before her time. She looked at the light swirling around her; she looked at the stars above. Her heart beat faster; the intensity of her father's joy drew her closer. As she looked at him, she saw both her father and the fondness of an old friend.

The starlight seemed to be pulsating even brighter than before. She lifted her right arm, and light flowed like water from her wrist. The light found definition and extended itself to form her hand and perfectly shaped fingers. She moved them around and looked at them for the first time. She lifted her left arm, and light flowed from both the tips of her right hand's fingers and her left wrist, beginning to form her left hand. Eve squeezed her left hand into a fist.

As she opened her left hand, Elohim approached her. He softly touched the center of her palm with his index finger as he locked eyes with his daughter. Eve looked down at her palm, and skin appeared like a small circle and rapidly spread until her whole body was covered by its radiant and beautiful tone. Eve looked back up into Elohim's eyes. She felt an unbounded affection as the rhythmic beating of his heart now beat inside her own chest.

They embraced. Her father softly kissed her cheek and forehead. He held her head with his large and powerful hands. As Elohim held her, a deep peace moved from his hands into her mind and flowed down deep into her heart. She felt his love. Eve felt her father's strength. She belonged to this time. She belonged to Eden and to the Earth. More than anything, she belonged to him. Eve was home.

THE SHAPESHIFTER

IV

T HE BLAZING SUN SAT HIGH ABOVE THE DESERT. The desolation was a brutal and unforgiving place. The smoldering hot sun scorched the sands below. The ash and soot in the air had dissipated, replaced with an unbreathable heat. Dunes surrounded the gray stones with the ancient tree in the center. There was no sign of Elohim or Eve.

A fleeting breeze blew a thin layer of sand slowly off the top of the dunes. A black snake slithered up and down the dunes as it headed in the direction of the petrified tree stump. As it got closer, the snake darted out its forked tongue, assisting its yellow and black eyes in discerning the direction it should go.

As it moved from behind the stones, it shifted its form into that of a black panther. It looked around at the massive stones with its yellow eyes. The sand under its paws crunched softly as it cautiously moved toward the tree at the center. Stopping to sniff the air, the black panther looked up. A pitch-black portal tore a hole in the sky above. Through the darkness, a cloaked figure hurtled down from the sky. The figure had large onyx black wings that had a dull matte, metal-like sheen. His wings towered above his body as he flew through the air. Ba'hal landed in front of the panther. His feet landed with a muted thud as they hit the hard ground beneath him. Seconds later, the portal vanished. Ba'hal's face was pure darkness; a wispy smoke rose from his shoulders.

The previous night, Ba'hal had taken possession of an egret. He had watched through its eyes as the Creator, Elohim, had put his son into a deep sleep. He had watched transfixed as Elohim had taken a rib from Adam's side. He had never witnessed such a thing. What did it mean? Ba'hal had been looking for weaknesses and vulnerabilities since Adam's creation. Was this it? Perhaps a unique opportunity was missed, he thought to himself. Should he have followed Elohim, stayed with Adam, or gone back to seek counsel? He could not be in all places at once. Time was short. As the hot sun beat down, he was infuriated that he may have made the wrong decision.

Ba'hal quickly turned toward the remains of the tree. He began walking toward it in a cautious manner.

"Where is she?" he growled.

With each word Ba'hal spoke, the sand on the desert floor seemed to vibrate. He looked around cautiously.

The panther followed him. Ba'hal walked toward the formerly alive tree and put his hand over its stump. Dark black smoke rose from Ba'hal's hand as he hovered it over the center of the stump. Ba'hal felt a violent energy left by Elohim and quickly pulled his hand back. The residual energy seemed to pierce his hand like a flow of arrows. The panther got on its hind legs and sniffed the top of the stump. Ba'hal was disgusted. He could not help but see the hand of the Creator in all his creatures.

"Fashioned from bone and light," Ba'hal murmured as he looked around. The panther took a step back from the stump. "In our territory, he formed her." Ba'hal paused and looked with an eye of accusation at the pathetic creature in front of him. The panther's eyes shifted from curiosity to fear. A fear he had come to somehow both enjoy and despise.

"Did he make an equal to Adam ... for what purpose ..." Ba'hal's mind mechanically pondered the possible ramifications. He looked again at the panther. "You will not fail our master again," Ba'hal opened his jaws and snarled at the four-legged creature.

Within the darkness, the creature could see his white, glistening teeth. The terrified panther looked to escape, but it was too late.

Like a shadow cast, Ba'hal leapt and dove into the creature, absorbing its life force. The panther writhed violently in pain as Ba'hal moved through the creature's nervous system. In an instant, Ba'hal's possession of the demonic shapeshifter was complete. Its mouth frothed white from the transition. Its black coat absorbed the heat from the sun as its head twitched unnaturally. Ba'hal now looked through the panther's new stone-gray eyes.

Through the possessed creature, Ba'hal left the sanctuary and headed back into the desolation of the desert. He would see if he could find anything else regarding the girl in Eden. Eventually he would head back to their caverns in the mountains. His master must know of the failure. Elohim had created in their territory. There must be consequences, he thought to himself.

QUESTIONS

V

3994 B.C. ~ 6 Months Later

EVE LOVED THIS TIME OF DAY. DUSK HAD ALWAYS been enchanting to her. It was a time for reflection, a time for rest. As she looked across the horizon, the white garments that covered her chest and upper thighs blew with the breeze coming from the ocean. Her brown hair had golden blonde streaks in it. Eve's radiant blue eyes looked down from the bluff to the whitecaps in the sea below. The regal silver embroidery on her clothing glimmered as the last rays of sunlight streaked across the sky.

Elohim walked from behind to join her. As he sat next to her on the sand, the steady wind continued to blow the long wild grass. The green grass was scattered in patches on the dunes that overlooked the sweeping ocean below the bluff where they sat.

Eve looked across the expansive horizon. Elohim cupped sand and watched it flow through the opening between the

41

bottom of his hands. The golden flecks of light from the sun seemed to dance within his brown eyes as he looked up from the sand to take in the beauty before them. He glanced at Eve, smiled fondly, and looked out to the horizon in front of them. He dug his hands deep into the sand, raised them again, and watched the sand move through them. Faint, barely discernible scars marked the palms of his hands. Eve watched the sand flow through his cupped hands and saw his scar-marked skin. A question she was unsure how to ask rose in her heart.

She had walked with her father for quite some time. With him, she had explored Eden with its dense jungles, mighty rivers, tall mountains, and rugged and serene coastline. They had made discoveries and shared laughs. Memories filled her heart with love.

While they usually explored Eden together, there were times she was alone and had made discoveries in solitude. When she was by herself, there was a mix of joy and sometimes sadness upon seeing a sight she wished to share. Throughout her life, her father had revealed much to her. She also knew there were things he had hidden that had yet to be discovered. Eden's beauty captivated her heart.

Mimicking her father, Eve cupped some of the soft white sand and watched a tiny stream flow between her palms. Above them, long white birds called egrets graced the sky. Eve looked up and watched their patterns of flight against an ever-changing backdrop of various colors. The orange, pink, and purple sky looked like it was on fire against its soft blue canvas. She marveled at the artistry. This was her favorite place. Her heart found peace as she looked across the seemingly infinite horizon.

"They're beautiful," Eve softly whispered.

Elohim's gaze joined hers and tracked the egrets flying overhead. Her soft voice sounded like music to her father's ears.

Elohim slowly got up, and he offered his hand to his daughter. She put her hand in his. They walked toward where the ocean met the sand. A soft breeze blew as they journeyed along the beach together.

"I've seen him." Eve recalled a handful of memories fondly.

"Oh ... you mean Adam?" Elohim grinned with a mischievous look in his eyes. He made no attempt to hide his joy as deep questions within Eve's heart began to surface.

"Yes, Adam," Eve responded. She elbowed Elohim playfully.

"Ouch! What was that for?" Elohim feigned indignation.

"You know what it was for!" Eve smiled teasingly, looking into her father's eyes.

"I do," Elohim responded with a sly grin.

The first time she had seen Adam was burned into her mind. It was near Galilee. That evening she had gone to pick fruit from trees that grew along its shores. From a distance, she initially thought the figure was Elohim, but as she got closer, she saw him for the first time. Eve had watched Adam in solitude skipping stones across the cool waters. It was as if he had been waiting for someone or something. Maybe he was waiting for her? She had held her breath, hoping that he would sense her presence and look back. But he hadn't seen her, and she had chosen to remain hidden.

From that moment, she desired to know him, yet her intuition said to keep herself hidden. The time wasn't right. It wasn't that she was afraid. Seeing him felt reassuring. She wondered if he had ever seen her. If he had, what had he felt in his heart toward her? Perhaps there was a time she had gone exploring near the sea: maybe he was behind her some distance, hoping she'd look around. She didn't think it was possible that he could see her without her somehow knowing, but the possibility ran through her mind nonetheless. The thought of them being united brought excitement and anticipation. She knew the timing was important. She knew it would happen but was uncertain when.

"Father ..." her voice tentatively trailed off. Her heart burned until the question resurfaced. "When will he know about me?" Eve asked. She looked up at Elohim.

Her father stopped. He met Eve's curious eyes with his own.

"He senses your presence. It brings him courage, Eve." Her father's words soothed her emotions and brought a sense of peace to her soul. Elohim looked softly at Eve. He gently squeezed her hand. "He's not been ready for you. But soon, my love, he will be. Very soon."

EVE

VI

ADAM CLIMBED TO THE TOP OF THE DESERT RIDGE. Water from one of the many tributaries of the Tigris dropped just a dozen or so feet into an aqua blue pool below. Adam looked across the horizon and surveyed the land. The Tigris was one of a handful of mighty rivers that flowed from the heart of Eden. The routes of these rivers seemed to spider web in all directions. Some, like this tributary, pooled at the edge of the desert. Along the banks of the river, different types of plants and trees grew. But a few feet beyond the banks in all directions, the land was dry and without any kind of vegetation or life.

Adam looked down and saw Elohim in the pool below. Just a minute earlier, Elohim had been by his side before he decided to jump in the refreshing waters below. Now he was motioning Adam to make the leap. The sun above was hot and the pool inviting.

With a sudden jump, Adam sprang from the top, held his

knees, and plunged into the deep turquoise water a few feet from Elohim. Adam popped up for air just in time to see the wall of water from Elohim's splash hit him in the face. Adam shook the water from his eyes long enough to see Elohim dive deep, saving himself from immediate retaliation. Adam scanned the water for the instigator. Abruptly, Elohim rose from the water underneath Adam and launched him into the air. Adam laughed excitedly as he was hurled through the air, landing on the other side of the pool. Popping his head above water again, he saw Elohim with a comically wide grin plastered on his face. Before he could splash Elohim, Adam heard horses neighing by the shore.

Adam looked to see two brown horses with black manes trot toward the banks of the swimming hole. They stooped down and began to drink. Elohim swam by him and climbed out of the water.

Adam swam to the shore and followed Elohim out. His father hugged one of the horses around its neck and ran his large hands through its mane. Adam sat on the bank of the pool. Plunging one of his fingers into the sand, Adam dragged it, making a finger-sized canal. Water from the pool flooded the tiny, newly formed tributary. Adam watched it until the dry ground absorbed the life-giving water. Adam looked out at the desert before him. Elohim kissed the other horse, then sat beside his boy.

"What do you see?" Elohim asked.

The two looked out at the vast desert in front of them. Adam knew his father was asking him to see beyond what was and into what could be. He was honored by the invitation. The opportunity seized his heart. The desert looked nothing like the garden. While it had its own beauty, it lacked life. What if it wasn't meant to be barren?

From the water's edge, Elohim dug his own minicanal with his finger. Adam watched intently as once again water from the pool followed Elohim's finger before sinking into the earth. Adam looked beyond the oasis and into the parched desert before him.

"What if the desert was meant to bloom and bear fruit?" Adam shared the dreams of his heart out loud with his father. "What if creatures of all kinds were meant to inhabit this place … what if it wasn't meant to be barren … without life?"

"There's a lot of dry land out there." Elohim looked at his son's eyes as they scanned the horizon. Adam's eyes followed the river's path from the desert to its source in the jungle miles away. As the river moved from the desert into the jungle, its banks became wider apart.

"There's a lot of water." Adam spoke with resolve in his young voice. "Four rivers run through Eden. Could the desert not be revived under the life-giving waters of the mighty Euphrates—or more from the Tigris?!"

The things that resided deep within Elohim's heart were naturally valued by Adam. Some of these were expressed through words, but most weren't. Without demand, without obligation, but rather out of love and unity of vision, Adam began to see through his father's eyes what could be.

Elohim knew the challenge would be bigger than what his son could accomplish on his own. Now that his son's heart was clear on what must be done, the time had come for him to understand he would not have to do it alone. Elohim sprang up and walked toward the horses. "Come, there's something I want to show you ..."

Adam glanced at his father and saw a special light in his eyes. His curiosity took over, and he walked over to Elohim and the horses. He put his foot into Elohim's hands and sprang up on the back of one of the brown horses. Elohim hopped on the other. Feeling a slight kick to the ribs, each horse jolted into a gallop. Father and son began their ride back to the heart of Eden.

Elohim rode hard with Adam close behind, following a tributary of the Tigris back to Eden, where the four main rivers flowed. They approached some tall kapok trees, where Elohim dismounted. Adam followed suit.

The jungle was alive with the sounds of animals and various birds. The afternoon air had the sweet scent of flowers. As they walked through the tall trees, Elohim stopped and looked up. Adam followed his gaze and saw something high within the canopy. Was it a monkey, a gorilla, or some other creature? Curiously, Adam looked up. However, his view was obfuscated by the sheer volume of branches, vines, and leaves between him and whatever was a few hundred yards up in the canopy.

"What is it?" Adam inquired.

"*What is it?*" Elohim laughed. "It's a wild creature with an untamable disposition."

Intrigued, Adam looked back at Elohim. As their eyes met,

he knew his father had some sort of good surprise for him. He gazed back up into the canopy, hoping to discern the nature of the wild creature.

"Along with you, my greatest treasure." Elohim fondly glanced above them. From the dense brush, half a dozen gorillas emerged. They surrounded Adam and Elohim. Two of the gorillas had distinct markings. Adam hadn't seen either before, but the others he knew well. They had often followed him and his father as protectors in Eden and the surrounding areas. The gorillas all looked at Adam.

Adam's excitement grew. What did Elohim mean ... *his greatest treasure*? His father had created so many beautiful creatures. Never before had he heard his father use that word to describe any of the beasts or creatures he had named. Untamable disposition? The creatures he knew were wild and free, but untamable was an unfamiliar category. His heart hung on every word from his father.

A small brown monkey leaped onto a branch a few feet above Adam's head. For a split second, Adam saw a strange grin spread on the creature's face.

"What are you waiting for?" Elohim asked with laughter in his voice. "Follow the monkey!"

Adam started to climb. His arms easily pulled him up, branch by branch. After a few minutes of climbing, he looked back down on the ground. His father and the gorillas were nowhere to be found. As dusk was just beginning to settle over Eden, he figured maybe they were finding some nuts or berries for dinner. Looking back up, he heard the monkey squawk again, and he began to chase it up the tree.

As his arms pulled and his legs pushed him higher, he felt something new stir in his heart. A burning he had never felt. He didn't know what this creature was, but he could feel in his heart it was different from anything else he had encountered. Adam saw the brown monkey stop climbing a branch above him. Realizing how high he was, he took a breath. Looking around, Adam saw Eve for the first time.

Adam gazed at Eve, and time seemed to slow to a crawl. His eyes grew wide with wonder. All the noise of the jungle faded as Adam could only hear her soft breaths as she dreamed. Eve slept within a hammock made of vines and covered with large leaves for support. This creature looked nothing like any animal Adam had ever seen. If anything, he could see himself in her; he saw Elohim in her as well. The similarities were there, but the differences were striking as well. His heart beat fast inside his chest as he walked away from the trunk of the massive tree toward Eve. He took short, deliberate steps toward the end of two strong branches. The two branches acted like two poles for the hammock that cradled Eve as she slept.

Adam's eyes took in her features: her light brown beautiful skin, full lips, and long eyelashes. She lay on her back, and her chest rose and fell gently under her white garments. Every breath mesmerized Adam. Her white garments resembled his and covered her chest and showed the bottom of her stomach. She was mostly inside the hammock, but her left leg was draped outside the makeshift bed. Adam slowly crouched down to maintain his balance and leaned in closer to her.

"Hello ... can you hear me?" Adam softly whispered. A soft breeze blew her hair. Who was this creature? She was more beautiful than anything he had ever seen. Above Adam, the small brown monkey squawked. It hung upside down by its tail and looked at Adam with oversized brown eyes that had a hint of amusement in them.

"Shhhh! Get out of here, monkey!" Adam, irritated, swiped his hand in the air to get the monkey to move on. The monkey twisted its tail slightly, dodged Adam's hand, and blankly stared at him. Adam thought he saw yet another slightly mischievous smile spread on the monkey's face. Its crooked grin was both goofy and slightly obnoxious. Adam decided to ignore the creature and looked back down at Eve.

"Who are you ...?" Adam asked, his voice trailed off to barely a whisper. Adam's eyes drank in the beauty of Eve. A soft breeze blew again, stirring Eve. She began to slowly stretch and open her eyes. Her sleepy and slightly blurred vision came into focus as she opened her eyes and saw Adam looking into them.

Startled by her beauty, Adam almost lost his balance. Quickly, Eve sprang up and offered her hand to him so he didn't fall from such a great height. Her bright blue eyes were astonishing; looking into them, he felt immediately inebriated. Surprised by his own reaction, Adam slowly walked a few steps back. He couldn't believe how striking she was as he looked at her in awe. A million thoughts began racing through his mind.

"You okay?" asked Eve.

"... Who are you ...?" Adam's response barely registered

as a whisper, but Eve heard and understood him. He felt light-headed and tried to maintain his balance on the limb. His heart and mind were intoxicated by Eve's beauty. He looked up again into her alluring eyes. Eve's heart beat faster, and she saw Adam unconsciously take a few more steps backward until his back was up against the trunk.

"Hello," Eve offered. Her mind raced for other words, but nothing else came. "I didn't mean to surprise you ..."

It occurred to Adam that he was now hearing the language of Elohim spoken by another creature for the first time.

"Who are you ... where do you come from?" Adam asked.

Eve walked toward him, getting permission from his eyes to come closer. She softly laid her hand on his chest and the scar across the left side of his ribcage, directly below his heart. At the warm touch of her hand, memories cascaded into Adam's mind. He remembered the night Elohim had taken him to the twin waterfalls. He remembered the climb to the top and resting within his father's arms. He remembered being in great pain the following days and weeks. While it gradually eased up over time, he had felt a pressure in his chest. Sometimes when he ran, it was hard to breathe.

When he had asked his father about the slight scarring beneath his heart, his father had looked almost amused. Elohim then shared with Adam that, at times, the most profound beauty would be experienced only after the deepest of pain. With those words, Adam felt as if he had been initiated into a higher order, a greater level of intimacy with his father without quite understanding everything that meant.

Eve could feel Adam's emotions surge through his being as

he sought to understand the pieces. Adam, unsure of his own thoughts, asked again, "Where do you come from?"

"I come from you ... I came from him," Eve offered quietly. She placed her hand over her heart. "I'm Eve."

"What are you doing up here?" Adam asked slowly.

"Well ... I was sleeping ..." Eve laughed softly.

Adam saw Eve smile for the first time. He didn't know how it had happened, but he wanted to somehow make her smile again. He had never felt compelled to speak before, but he couldn't keep the questions from bubbling up. With each question and answer, the little brown monkey looked back and forth, seemingly smiling to itself.

"What brings you to Eden ... why are you here?" Adam asked.

"I'm here to help," Eve responded. Eve saw the confusion in his eyes. "Help you ..."

"Help me ...?" Adam asked.

The brown monkey squawked from its upside-down position. Eve looked up at it, then back down at Adam. The monkey jumped down on the branch between Adam and Eve. Eve backed up a few feet.

"Is that your monku?" Eve asked. The brown monkey tilted its head slightly and looked directly at Eve.

"His monku?!" it replied in an amused tone. "My name is Tonka. And we're monkeys, not monkus! Do I look like someone's pet?!"

Eve didn't know what to say and looked back at Adam with curiosity in her eyes. Adam shrugged his shoulders. He looked equally curious and surprised. He began to walk toward

Tonka to get a slightly better look. Tonka relaxed a bit and grinned. He brushed a leaf from his shoulder.

"Understandable ..." Tonka said.

Adam looked up at Eve, still surprised by the creature's speech.

"They speak ...?" Eve asked incredulously. She looked at the small monkey, then back at Adam.

"They don't speak ..." Adam responded and looked down at Tonka, who had just put a nut in his mouth.

"Pretty sure we do," Tonka replied, shaking his head as he swallowed the nut. Did humans really believe they were the only ones with language? He looked at Adam, then at Eve before hopping onto a nearby branch that provided him eye-level contact with them. With Adam and Eve watching, he slowly and deliberately pulled out his tongue with his two hands until its full length was out of his mouth. Tonka released it, and it snapped back into his mouth. "Do you not see? Am I without a tongue? Without voice? All of creation speaks. Am I not part of creation?"

Adam looked up at the monkey. A big grin spread across Adam's face as he could see much of Tonka's disposition was simply a show. "Relax, monkey ..." Adam said.

"You can call me Tonka," Tonka replied with an equally big grin. "And you are Adam, Elohim's son." Tonka swung on another branch closer to Adam and put his hand on Adam's chest. It tickled, and Adam swiped it off.

"I'm Eve!" Eve offered. Tonka leapt to a branch closer to Eve and did a slight bow before her.

"Of course you are," Tonka replied and slowly raised his

head from the bow. "You know, Eve, I saw you … When Elohim brought you in from the desert. What a spectacular night that was! You had fallen asleep in his arms. I walked with your father, my creator, as he brought you through the jungle and into our garden so you could rest. I was there; I saw everything. Few creatures can say that."

"You saw her right after she was created?" Adam asked, amazed. He thought once again of the night he and Elohim had climbed up the vines to get to the top of the twin falls. It seemed like it was a few months before his lungs had been able to take in a full breath and he was able to run again. His breath had been taken away then and his breath was taken away now. Adam thought of the subtle and evolving nature of Elohim's humor.

"There's many mysteries and riddles born from this place." Tonka opened his eyes wide and looked around as if about to share a secret. He lowered his voice. "Few are hidden from these eyes." Tonka flashed a toothy smile.

Eve and Adam looked at each other before bursting into laughter. There was something about the smallness of Tonka and the seriousness of his declarations that caught them each off guard. Tonka jumped back down onto the main branch Adam and Eve were standing on.

"You see that?" Tonka motioned at two squirrels on an adjacent kapok tree playing together. "Or that?" Tonka pointed above him at two birds nestling each other.

"What about them?" Adam asked.

"Look!" Tonka motioned them to look down. A few

hundred feet down at the base of their tree, Tonka, Adam, and Eve saw two horses fawning over each other.

"Some have called me the broker of bliss, cupid's comrade, doctor of devotion ..." He used his monkey fingers to tick off the names. He jumped on Adam's back and climbed up on Adam's neck, taking him by surprise. He raised his tail to Adam's eye level, and inches away, Adam saw a ladybug and a butterfly seated on Tonka's tail facing each other. Eve came closer to see. Adam's and Eve's faces were now inches apart as they looked at the mismatched insects. "Infatuation intermediary." Tonka laughed to himself softly.

"Infatuation?" Adam asked. The butterfly flew away, and Tonka used his fingers to gently move the ladybug off his tail and onto a nearby leaf. "I don't understand," Adam said. He realized how close Eve was. His heart skipped a beat as they locked eyes. Tonka leapt onto a branch a few feet away.

"The birds and the bees," Tonka offered. Seeing no understanding within Adam's face, Tonka looked at Eve with delight. "Yes ... they help each other ... have you not seen this yet?" Tonka studied Adam's reaction, then softly laughed. "That's okay, young Adam ... In time, you will," Tonka said with a twinkle in his eyes. As he looked at the two future lovers, a ridiculously large smile spread across his face. He popped another nut into his mouth as if it was popcorn. His eyes grew large with love as he saw Adam and Eve, finally together.

"My work here is done." With that, Tonka swung from branch to branch beyond Adam and Eve's line of sight. Adam looked at Eve, and as their eyes met, she felt pure love.

THE TWO TREES

VII

ADAM EXTENDED HIS HAND TO EVE AS THEY HIKED down toward the valley. She chose her footing carefully as Adam gave her his assistance down through a narrow ravine. Surrounded by tall trees, huge rocks, and the large sun overhead, they had been walking for a few hours by themselves. It had been weeks since Tonka had introduced them. Though they had sporadically looked for him in the jungle and the gardens, they hadn't seen him again.

Eve had shared with Adam many memories of her time with Elohim. Certain things began to make more and more sense to Adam. It became clear to him that Elohim had been preparing him for her. Beyond that, he also had a sense that Elohim simply wanted to spend time with his daughter.

When Elohim had been gone and Adam had been on his own, the mystery had never really bothered Adam. His heart had been guarded by a deep sense of peace and confidence that no matter where Elohim was, he would return. And he always did. The pace of their relationship and intimacy felt natural, and no fears had arisen in his heart. Adam had known that wherever Elohim was, he must be thinking of him in the same way Adam was thinking of Elohim. They were never far from each other's thoughts.

Now that Adam knew Elohim had spent much of that time with Eve, he was grateful. Grateful that she had been with him. Grateful that she hadn't been alone. He would never want her to be alone. Now that they were together, it was increasingly difficult for him to remember a time before her.

As she took Adam's hand, he saw her bright eyes sparkle. Adam returned her smile. When she smiled, he felt like his heart wanted to jump out of his chest. It was amazing to him that he could somehow bring her joy and laughter. And that's really all he wanted to do.

"Why can't a leopard hide?" Adam asked as they continued to walk. A toucan squawked in the canopy above.

"Why's that?" she asked as she looked at him with a grin.

"Because they're always spotted …" Adam responded. Eve shook her head, laughed, and shoved him a bit. Her touch seemingly sent electricity through his body.

Above in the tree canopy, Adam noticed Tonka moving from branch to branch. His presence with them was a welcome surprise. In the distance, Adam saw Elohim picking blackberries. Eve ran to him and gave him a huge hug.

"Father!" Eve exclaimed with delight.

"Hey there!" Elohim threw her up in the air and caught her. Her hair tickled his face. He put her down softly and looked at Adam. Before Adam knew what was happening, Elohim grabbed him and gave him a bear hug.

"Exploring?" he asked with curiosity in his eyes.

They nodded. Elohim motioned for them to follow him.

"Come!" Elohim said. Eve and Adam looked at each other with anticipation in their eyes. They knew that they would see something special.

They followed their father through the jungle. As they walked, the terrain gradually changed from the unkept wild jungle to the serene garden of Eden. Every time they entered the garden, its boundaries seemed to expand. They had worked together with Elohim to cultivate it. Their garden was an ever-expanding oasis of beauty where their hearts always found a deep sense of belonging. There were hidden wonders and certain animals found only in the garden. Flowers bloomed everywhere, fruit trees were all around, and many animals moved within the garden, animating its beauty with their energy.

Adam glanced over at Eve and saw her eyes get big as they walked down a path with massive trees on each side. These were the largest trees they had ever seen. They were easily a dozen or more feet in diameter. On their left, a small, slow-moving river streamed by. Its waters were a mix of turquoise and dark green depending on the rays of light piercing the canopy above them. In front of Eve were a few monarch butterflies, which landed on some berry bushes on their right.

From behind some brush, they heard branches break. A massive silverback gorilla emerged from the trees. Tonka leapt down from a branch up in the canopy and landed on Adam's shoulder. Eve glanced over at Tonka. He slowly bowed and then winked at Eve.

"This is Azrael." Elohim looked proudly at the silverback. "There's more to him than meets the eye. He's one of the guardians over Eden. Over you."

Eve and Adam had seen many silverbacks before, but Azrael looked to be almost twice the size of the largest one they had seen. With his right fist, Azrael pounded his dark gray chest twice.

"That's a big monku." Tonka's eyes grew wide as he whispered in Adam's ear. Eve approached Azrael. Azrael bowed low, and Eve put her hand on his head.

"Stay," Elohim commanded the creature. Azrael nodded in acknowledgement.

Elohim led Adam and Eve down a new path neither of them had ever walked before. As they walked, they entered a grove of even more massive trees than those they had passed minutes ago. Though Adam didn't know their names, these trees had leaves the size of elephant ears. At the center of a cluster of leaves, various types of fruits grew from the same tree. Elohim reached up and grabbed a piece of fruit.

Adam placed his palm on the largest of the trees at the very center of the garden. As his palm touched its trunk, he felt time slow down. He could see rays from the sun hitting its leaves and the light traveling slowly from the leaves into the branches, down the trunk, and into his hand. The light gently coursed through his body as if he had taken a drink from a fountain. Adam looked over at Eve as a new love for her was imprinted on his soul.

"What is this place?" Eve asked as she looked at Adam and saw the difference in his eyes. Adam looked up at the tree again and back down at Eve. Eve saw Adam's eyes sparkle with a new intensity as the light from the tree seemed to now dance in his eyes. Adam offered Eve his hand. She took it, and he gently placed her palm on the tree. Time again seemed to slow down as light traveled from the tips of the tree's leaves, through its branches, into its trunk, and finally into Eve's own hand. A warmth and new love flooded Eve's being.

"The tree of life," Elohim answered.

"It's different … it's bigger," Eve whispered.

"It's life and strength, not knowledge and words, you get from it," Elohim responded. He put his hand on the tree, and a soft amber light flowed from his palm into the tree trunk and traveled into all its branches and finally into the leaves, which seemed to shimmer for a few seconds before returning to their regular color. Elohim reached up to its lowest branch. With surprising strength and a quick snap, Elohim broke the low-hanging branch off the tree. To the awe and surprise of Adam and Eve, a new branch grew in the same place with a speed neither had ever witnessed.

"Before the world itself was created, I had plans for this." Elohim smiled broadly. With his large, strong hands, he broke off most of the smaller twigs and leaves from the branch. He left a small cluster of twigs and leaves toward the narrower end of the branch intact.

"Etz Hayim," Elohim proudly declared. He looked at Eve, then at Adam. "It means 'tree of life.'"

Eve and Adam looked curiously at Elohim. While Elohim

walked, he put his hand on the broader end of the Etz Hayim. The narrower end hit the ground as Elohim used the branch from the tree of life as a walking stick.

They continued their walk, following Elohim. As they walked, Adam noticed a separate grove of trees of a much darker wood. Eve looked at Adam with wonder. Elohim stopped and looked toward the center of the grove. In the center, a tall tree with almost black-colored wood grew. This tree was similar in size to the tree of life. Eve and Adam followed Elohim as he walked toward it. Adam looked up and noticed its trunk and branches were an ashen gray color and it only bore one type of fruit. Its fruit was dark purple and roughly the size of a large pear.

"The tree of the knowledge of good and evil." Elohim looked up at it, then directly at Adam. "Its fruit is poisonous."

Adam jumped up on one of its low-hanging branches, pulled himself up, grabbed one of the dark purple fruits, and leapt back down. Eve looked at the fruit curiously as Adam showed it to her.

"You may eat from every seed-bearing tree in the garden. But fruit from this tree—and this tree alone—you must always keep from your lips," Elohim softly commanded.

Adam looked at the fruit in his hand. A question stirred inside of him. Why would his father allow something poisonous within the perfection of Eden and so close to the tree of life? Adam cracked open the fruit to see the inside and its center.

Eve stepped closer and looked over Adam's shoulder as he split it open with his hands. At its center, the dark purple seemed to glisten. As Adam looked into its center, he could see it possessed a dark, mirror-like quality. He searched diligently, but to his amazement, he saw the fruit contained no seeds. He glanced up at Elohim.

"No seeds?" Adam asked.

Adam looked closer to make sure he wasn't missing anything. As he searched the fruit, the purplish dark mirror at its center came to life. Adam moved his head to the left, and he saw his reflection within its center also move to the left. Without warning, his image stopped mirroring his movements and took on a life of its own; the boy returning his gaze seemed to sneer, then a panicked expression took over his face. Startled, Adam looked away and glanced at Eve. Her eyes searched Adam's. Elohim offered his hand, and Adam quickly gave the dark, seedless fruit to him. With one hand, Elohim held the Etz Hayim; with the other, he held the poisonous fruit.

He smiled at Adam, and as if waking from a dream, Adam once again felt his presence of mind return and his heart calm.

"Would you ever eat a stone?" Elohim asked, looking first at Adam, then at Eve.

Quickly shaking off the unsettling feeling they both had, Eve and Adam shook their heads.

"A piece of wood?" Elohim asked. His question was a mix of merriment and encouragement. A smile spread across Elohim's face as he watched the countenances of his children.

Once again, they shook their heads no.

"Not even a branch broken off the tree of life itself?" Elohim raised the Etz Hayim up to his teeth, pretending he was about to take a bite from the branch.

Adam and Eve laughed.

"Nah ... I think I like my teeth!" Adam offered a beaming smile that showed off his white teeth. Elohim laughed.

Elohim set the Etz Hayim on the ground. He looked down at the purple fruit in his hands and slowly put the two pieces back together. The fruit seemed to meld itself as if it were never split in the first place. Slowly, Elohim lifted it up, and rays from the sun began to pierce the fruit. It began to emit a soft hissing sound, as if it were begging to be returned to the shade and away from the light.

"The knowledge of good and evil has a place ... a place and a purpose in our garden," Elohim shared. Adam and Eve studied his eyes to determine the meaning as he spoke. "But your life comes not from your ability to discern on your own good from evil. True discernment, life itself ... this flows from our connection alone."

The fruit continued to hiss as it shriveled and shrunk until the once pear-sized fruit was now the size of an acorn. Elohim looked directly at Adam with love in his eyes.

"Our connection, Adam." He looked over at Eve. Eve drank in her father's love as they locked eyes. "Eve, our connection ... no knowledge, no fruit from any tree can replace that. Understand?"

Eve and Adam nodded with understanding. This was the first time Elohim had ever forbidden anything. Up until that point, they had had no boundaries, only complete freedom. While Adam could feel the weight of his father's command, paradoxically, he didn't feel as if any freedom had been taken away. If anything, Adam felt, in some sense, that Elohim had opened himself up to Eve and him in a new way. Inside of this opening, Adam felt that Elohim had made his heart somehow more vulnerable to them. Elohim trusted them, believed in them. Inside of that opening, Adam felt even more free. To do what Elohim told Adam not to do struck Adam as the deepest of betrayals. Adam swore to himself that he would never do such a thing. He would fiercely guard Elohim's heart and their connection. He knew of no other way.

Elohim released the acorn-sized fruit to fall. As it fell, it disintegrated like dust. Adam saw Eve put her hand out, and the dust flew through her fingers and was carried off by a soft breeze.

"Father ... why no seeds?" Adam asked again, his heart searching for the significance.

"To eat of that tree would open the world to death," Elohim responded.

"What is death?" Adam asked. Elohim saw the curiosity in his son's eyes.

"To no longer know me is death. He who animates death resides in our world. He desires to create a separation. A separation would give him the ability to reproduce himself. He has no seeds on this Earth to do so. Nor does he have authority here," Elohim responded flatly. He pointed to the Etz Hayim, and Adam picked it up and handed it to his father.

Adam couldn't imagine a world where he no longer knew his own father. The thought itself struck him as almost absurd. How could that ever come to pass?

"And what of the other trees?" Eve asked.

"Every seed-bearing tree gives life," Elohim softly responded. "Come ... this way."

Adam and Eve followed him down another path. As they walked, Elohim pulled down some vines and formed a sling. He slung it over his back and then put the Etz Hayim in the sling, freeing up his hands. Eden grew in its beauty, and the fragrant flowers were intoxicating. Hearing footsteps behind them, Adam turned around to see a massive black lion following. Elohim turned around to face it.

Adam walked up to the large black cat. Adam saw its muscles tightening under its coat. Its large black mane had streaks of gray. Its eyes were golden with flecks of bright yellow and green. It let out a huge roar that shook the very ground and reverberated throughout the garden. Eve laughed as the force of the roar pushed Adam's hair back. Adam stared into the creature's eyes, breathed in deep, and returned a roar of his own. It slightly moved its whiskers.

"Hey boy!" Adam said as he patted its head. It began to purr loudly.

The lion happened to be one of their father's favorite creatures. Eve saw Elohim's chest swell with pride as he looked on its massive form.

Elohim walked toward one of the large kapok trees and began to climb.

"This way!" Elohim said.

Eve jumped to grab onto a low-hanging branch and started climbing upward with Elohim. Adam hugged the lion's face, and when he kissed its forehead, Adam knew the name given to the lion by his father.

"I won't be long, Gabriel. We can play later," Adam

whispered in its ear. Its long tongue slurped the side of Adam's cheek, and he patted Gabriel's head.

Adam jumped to grab a branch to follow Eve and Elohim. As he ascended, it looked like they might have an hour before the sun fully went down. The tree was home to a variety of tropical birds and monkeys. Eve glanced down and grinned at Adam as he caught up to her and Elohim. Her eyes drew him in. Adam returned her smile. Elohim was a dozen feet above them, climbing with the Etz Hayim on his back.

"Your birthright is to be fruitful, to extend the beauty of our garden," Elohim bellowed from above.

The rays of the setting sun glimmered through the moving tree canopy that swayed with a gentle wind.

"Father … I love our garden …" Eve looked from the glorious view high up the kapok tree. At this time of day, the garden seemed to embrace and kiss them with her soft rays of sunlight and warm breeze. They continued to climb, following Elohim.

"Yes …" Adam added, looking into Eve's eyes again. "It's beautiful here."

She gave him a knowing smile. Adam felt peace. They were now at the end of the branches that could support their weight, near the top of the dense canopy. Elohim began to break off some large leaves and vines to construct a hammock for them to rest in.

"The heavens are my kingdom," Elohim said as he fastened vines between two branches. "The Earth, Eden … this is my gift to you …" He glanced up from his work at his children. He continued to work as they helped him rope vines back and forth between the two large branches. "As I father you, you are to father, to mother, and to love it. You are to extend the boundaries of her beauty." He looked fondly at his children. His eyes contained an intense mixture of excitement, joy, and curiosity.

They placed large leaves on top of the vines and climbed into the hammock. Eve laid down to Adam's left. Elohim was on Adam's right. Adam felt the softness of Eve's skin and the warmth of her body as they both laid down and looked up at the sky through the thick canopy. Bright rays of sun occasionally hit their eyes as the wind blew the branches of the tall tree. Near her side, Adam's hand found Eve's. He softly squeezed it, and she returned the affection.

Elohim retrieved some nuts from a pouch and shared them with his son and daughter. Adam reflected on how his life was full of adventure. It was full of discovery. He loved exploring with his father and now with Eve. He loved Eve—more than anything. He adored her. He understood that he only knew Eve in part. Perhaps inside this new adventure his father was calling them to he could more fully know Eve. His father's words were clear. They were to extend Eden's boundaries. The words seemed to echo deep in Adam's heart.

Adam remembered the finger-sized canal he had made at the desert oasis before Elohim had introduced him to Eve. At the time, bringing water to the desert had felt like it was more like an interesting idea or possibility. With his father's words, it took on an entirely different nature. It now felt like a mission, as if he now had clarity around his purpose. Adam began to see the desolation of the desert as an affront to his father's will. He could not accept it anymore, nor would he.

Adam was to take dominion of the desolation and any other uncharted territories beyond Eden's boundaries. These places were not meant to be barren. These places were meant to teem and overflow with life. This would require water, a lot of water, Adam thought to himself.

A slight breeze moved the leaves of the canopy above, and the piercing sunlight kissed their faces. Elohim raised the Etz Hayim with his arm and pointed it at the sun. The Etz Hayim began to vibrate in Elohim's hand. Adam and Eve gazed in amazement. Elohim lowered his arm, and as if there was an invisible string tying the tip of the Etz Hayim to the sun, it began to descend in real time. Eve and Adam looked at each other in wonder. Right before the sun hit the horizon, Adam looked at Elohim. Sensing the curiosity in his son's heart, Elohim handed the Etz Hayim to Adam.

As Adam took the branch from the tree of life, it felt surprisingly light for its size. Adam pointed the tip of the Etz Hayim directly at the sun. Immediately, he could feel the Etz Hayim begin to vibrate in his hand as it surged with an invisible energy. A huge smile spread on Adam's face. It was as if the sun itself was a magnet drawn to the movements of the tip of the Etz Hayim. Adam slowly began to point it higher, and the sun popped back up over the horizon. Adam pointed directly above, and the sun moved above the three as if it were the middle of the day.

Eve looked at Adam with a mixture of surprise and excitement. Wonder swept across her face at the success of Adam's experiment. Her soft blue eyes looked like they were emitting a beautiful light. Adam looked back at Elohim.

"Having fun?" he laughed as he looked sideways at Adam.

Adam smiled back and turned to look at Eve. She wrapped her hand around the Etz Hayim. Eve and Adam both felt Elohim's soft touch. He tenderly pushed down on their hands until the tip of the Etz Hayim crossed below the horizon and the sun fell behind the mountains. Like a soft pop on the tip of the Etz Hayim, Eve and Adam felt the gravitational connection to the sun stop.

In that moment, the vastness of the desert faded from Adam's mind. He was with Eve. He was with his father. This was family. With his family, nothing was impossible. But how exactly does one conquer the desert and bring life to such a barren wasteland? The questions stampeded through his mind like a thousand elephants in search of a new watering hole. As night fell over the garden, Adam was determined to make a way and find out.

THE DREAMS BEGIN

VIII

EVE WOKE UP WITH A STIRRING IN HER HEART. SHE looked up to the blackness of the jungle night above them. The stars were out in all their glory and accompanied by a sliver of the moon. Scattered clouds above seemed to absorb the moon's soft light. She felt Adam's sweet breath softly on her face as he drank deeply from a much-needed rest. She peeked her head and saw that Elohim had left.

"Hey, wake up!" Eve softly whispered. Adam continued to quietly snore. "Pssst ... let's go!" She gently patted his face with her hands. Eve saw the movement of Adam's eyes behind his closed eyelids. She was taken aback by how handsome he was. But as she watched him, it became clear to her he was dead to the waking world and alive only to his dreams. Dreams of the desert becoming a new Eden.

Sleep was important. Dreams were important. She wondered what he saw in the desert. What kind of plants were to grow and what kind of animals were to wander within its vast boundaries? Eve had never visited the desert, but from Adam's descriptions, it had taken on a life of its own in her imagination. She had witnessed that what hearts conceived in dreams could spring to reality inside of Eden. Her relationship with Adam had been such a dream in her heart. She now lived her life with him.

Above, a monkey squawked. Eve looked up, recognizing Tonka.

"Shhhh …" Eve playfully shushed Tonka as she looked fondly down at Adam. Tonka looked down with her. "He's dreaming of what will be," she said as she softly caressed his cheek. Tonka again squeaked a few feet above. Eve got up and pressed her finger against her lips, motioning for him to quiet down. He blankly stared at her before a look of amusement spread across his face.

"What is it?" Eve asked.

"Follow the monku …" Tonka whispered, smiling at Eve.

With a leap, he started descending branch by branch down the tall kapok tree. Eve followed suit. Tonka then jumped off the last branch onto the jungle floor. Eve leapt down, and her feet landed softly on the ground. To her surprise, her father's prized black lion was asleep at the foot of their tree. Eve got close to Gabriel.

"Get up, follow me …" she said. But Gabriel, too, was fast asleep. She petted his mane. Besides the soft buzzing of insects and Tonka, all the garden seemed fast asleep.

"This way!" Tonka said from a few feet ahead of her before running off into the garden.

"Wait!" Eve chased Tonka. Leaping over rocks and brush,

she ran through the jungle terrain in pursuit. After a few minutes, it was clear she'd lost him, and she slowed her pace. Eve caught her breath and raised her gaze to the moon above. Her heart was full of anticipation and a joy that moved through her entire being. She thought of the honor and love of her father. His instruction to expand the garden was clear. Her heart felt alive with excitement and anticipation.

But to extend it into the desert, the desolation, to the wastelands outside of Eden's boundaries was a new thought. It was something entirely different. All her life had been spent exploring the gardens and the jungle all the way west to where Eden's territory met the vast oceans. She had listened closely to Adam describing his journeys with Elohim east of Eden. She found it hard to believe that a place without animals, without water or any life could even exist. She had heard excitement and anticipation of what could be within Adam's voice as he described its landscapes, its lack of creatures, its waterless terrain.

After Elohim's words, she had felt a shift in Adam. She had felt it the moment her father's words traveled through the air and hit Adam's ears. The future Elohim was calling them into electrified Adam, and she could feel it too.

Earlier that evening, she had met her love, Adam, inside his dream. She had followed his spirit and seen through his eyes the beauty that could be. Through his eyes, she had witnessed the barren, lifeless wasteland being transformed. She knew this was anything but an impossible task. Once she saw its beauty through Adam, it was more of an inevitable outcome. Perhaps its future beauty, what she and Adam could create together, could surpass even Eden's beauty. Her heart came alive at the thought.

Her mind wondered in awe what the desert could one day be. What could they create together? When she had stepped into his dreams, she could feel the excitement burning deep within her husband's heart. His excitement caused her to long to set foot on the desert's sands, survey its boundaries, and explore its lonely dunes.

As she had done many times in the past, Eve's heart, spirit, and mind began to converse with Elohim's spirit as she walked. While he wasn't there in the flesh with her, she began to share her excitement with him. He in turn shared his joy over the things within her imagination that she showed him. She began to laugh.

"Hey you!" Elohim said. From behind a tree, Elohim surprised Eve and grabbed her. His powerful arms tossed her lightly up in the air. A huge grin covered Eve's face as she landed in her father's arms. His voice carried a deep peace that captivated her focus and made every challenge seem not just doable but inevitable. "Couldn't sleep?" Elohim asked.

"I met him in his dreams!" Eve shared excitedly. "I saw the desert bloom!"

A huge smile swept across Elohim's face. Elohim gently lowered Eve and kissed her forehead.

"Come." Elohim put his hand out, and Eve eagerly took it.

They walked through the garden and a gentle, warm breeze began to blow. They stopped near some berry bushes. Elohim and Eve began to pick raspberries. The berries had a faint red glow to them. Eve and Elohim both reached for the last berry.

"Good, aren't they?" Elohim asked his daughter with a bright smile. Eve nodded. As their eyes met, it filled Elohim's heart with love. "I thought you might be hungry." Eve nodded. He picked the last berry and handed it to her. She looked at the depleted bush.

"Grow …" Eve whispered gently as she looked at the now barren vines. With the sound of her voice, the raspberry bush began to pull up the nutrients from its root system at an accelerated rate. The nutrients moved through its stems, and at first one, then two, then whole clusters of raspberries began to grow within a few seconds. Eve picked a newly formed berry and tossed it directly into Elohim's mouth. "One berry, two berries, three berries." Eve laughed as she continued to fill her father's mouth with berries until Elohim's cheeks were stuffed like a chipmunk.

"I think that's enough!" Elohim gurgled out in a muffled voice. Eve just laughed louder as Elohim's eyes lit up with laughter.

"Just a few more!" Eve howled with merriment as she tried to put in one more berry that just wouldn't fit. With wide eyes, Elohim squeezed his cheeks and shot berries from his mouth directly at Eve, who tried to swat them away. The sound of their laughter was carried through the garden.

Across the river, about fifty yards away and behind thick

vegetation, a black panther slowly approached. Ba'hal peered past the foliage at Eve and Elohim laughing. Hiding behind some bushes, he crouched. His coal-black eyes held intense hatred. Crouching low, he followed the path on the other side of the river to get closer.

Menakiel, heaven's chief angel and highest ambassador to Earth, flew sure and steady above the garden. Menakiel's wings were twice the height of his body. The outside of his wings had an intricate and beautiful pattern of silver and ivory. The inside was solid gold. His body came in and out of material being as he flew above the garden. He shifted from translucent to solid and back to translucent as he flew above and then through some of the taller kapok trees. A large silver sword nearly the length of his body was strapped to his back. In the moonlight, the edges of the sword had a menacing sheen that almost seemed to be glowing.

Gabriel had alerted him to Ba'hal's departure from the desolation and entrance into Eden. Gabriel was now awake and stood on guard beneath the tree Adam was sleeping in. Menakiel flew mostly above the trees and followed the river upstream. He spotted Ba'hal and began his descent as his wings moved through the trees and various foliage like a ghost. Menakiel hovered a dozen feet above the panther. Ba'hal was oblivious to the emissary.

Menakiel knew that when Ba'hal took illegal possession of an animal, such as a panther, Ba'hal's senses were divided between spirit and the flesh of the creature. Menakiel knew his singularity of being during combat would give him the advantage over Ba'hal's duality. With a swoosh, Menakiel landed behind the creature. The panther jerked his head around to see behind him but saw nothing.

Eve and Elohim ate their fill of berries. Finding a hole through the thick jungle canopy, they laid down on their backs and gazed at the shimmering stars above them.

"Father, why would there be a tree planted in our garden whose fruit we are not to eat?" Eve's question bubbled to the surface. Elohim loved Eve's inquisitive heart. He looked over at his daughter. Eve returned his gaze and saw starlight dance in her father's golden-brown eyes.

"Gifts are freely given ..." Elohim tilted his head to look back up at the stars. At this age, Eve understood her father at times would explain other concepts before answering questions. Eve loved learning in this way. She listened intently.

"Gifts demand nothing of you. They flow from generosity. You can do nothing and still receive a gift." Elohim paused for a moment. "Did you and Adam work for Eden or did I create and give Eden freely to you?" Eve looked up at the constellations. She saw the beauty all around her.

"This place is a gift," Eve said quietly with gratitude in her voice. Her hand found her father's hand and squeezed it. "A beautiful gift ... in a way, Adam is also a gift to me, is he not?"

Eve's heart was satisfied with love as she thought of Adam and engaged with Elohim's line of thinking.

"He is a gift. As you are a gift to him. This is true, " Elohim shared, "but rewards are different."

"How so?"

"Rewards are earned when you freely choose love when you could easily choose another option. I want to give you and Adam gifts, but I also will reward you for decisions you freely make." Elohim spoke softly while looking up at the stars.

"But why the two trees?" Eve asked. Elohim once again turned his head and looked warmly into Eve's eyes. Her eyes seemed to dance with the same starlight that was within his own eyes.

"The two trees are an invitation. An invitation for you to know me more and for you to be more fully known. When you are fully known, Eve, is when you will open your heart to being fully loved. Only a free heart can ever truly receive or give love. This is why the two trees must be with us, why the options must be there. There's no end to my love for you and Adam. The presence of options is an invitation for you to experience how deep my love is. Without the two trees, I could give you my love, but you would never be able to accurately perceive its depth, accept it fully into your heart, or enter into the vastness of its joy."

"But what if we were ever to choose the wrong thing? What if I made a bad choice?" Eve paused as her heart stirred with more questions. "What if Adam were ever to choose the wrong tree?"

Elohim breathed in deep.

"On the other side of that choice would be a fuller understanding of who I am as your father. The limits you have are governed only from the depth in which you've experienced my love. On the other side of that choice, you'd understand there's no limits."

Eve's young mind listened intently to the wisdom of Elohim. The very tone and tenor of her father's voice ushered a deep peace into her spirit. His perceptions brought a clarity to her mind and enabled her to see further than what she could see with her own eyes.

Menakiel manifested in the physical dimension and folded his wings back. He looked at Ba'hal. He had known Ba'hal from the third heaven before one-third of the heavenly host had fallen from their place as servants of Elohim. Menakiel had seen him many times around Elohim's throne, though not in this form. He had watched him bow his knee reluctantly to the King of Heaven many times even though his allegiance was now to the first one who fell. A fire rose in Menakiel's heart. Ba'hal's duplicitous nature made him a threat. He was a danger Menakiel had been sent to stop. Ba'hal crept closer until he was about twenty-five yards away from Eve and Elohim. Ba'hal's eyes focused on Eve, waiting for an opportunity. Menakiel drew his sword from his back.

With a newfound alertness, the panther stopped abruptly in his tracks and waited. Ba'hal could now sense the angelic presence and the immediate danger. Knowing if he took the time to look back, he might forfeit his life, Ba'hal leapt in the opposite direction of Eve and Elohim. With all the strength his self-preservation could muster, he ran back into the blackness of the jungle, leaving the presence of Elohim and the threat of Menakiel's sword.

Menakiel watched the fallen one disappear into the thickness of the jungle. He glanced over at his Lord, Elohim, then at his daughter, Eve. She had seen neither Ba'hal nor him. A faint smile touched his otherwise stoic face. Eve was stunningly beautiful. Her eyes seemed to carry within them a mystery that even Menakiel didn't know the full meaning of. To be such a close witness to Elohim with his daughter stirred a deep love inside Menakiel. He knew it was an honor only a few of his kind had been given. When he saw Elohim with Adam and Eve, it was as if he understood the Creator at a deeper level that had been previously inaccessible to his mind. He followed Eve's and Elohim's gazes to the stars above. Maybe one day she would know the stars the way he did. He wasn't sure. As he looked up at his brotherhood, the mesmerizing pattern of stars above, he certainly thought it was possible.

His task, however, was incomplete. Ba'hal was gone and, with him, the threat on Eve's life. But the one who had sent him was yet to be confronted. This was Menakiel's main task. He knelt and wrapped his wings around himself. The gold on the inside began to glow like fire and overtake the silver and ivory that was previously on the outside. Then, like a rocket, he launched off the jungle floor and shot up high into the heavens. In his wake, he left streaks of golden light in the night sky.

Eve wanted to go back to Adam before the sun rose. She wanted him to awaken with her by his side. She kissed Elohim on the cheek. Elohim saw her desire and nodded approvingly. She got up and found the path back to Adam.

Elohim continued to rest on his back. He saw Eve stop from her journey back to Adam as she looked above curiously to see the streaks of golden light above her. As she saw the light display against the backdrop of the dark, pre-dawn sky, she felt protected.

PAINT THE EARTH RED

IX

B A'HAL SPRINTED AS HE MADE HIS WAY TOWARD the mountains. He had sensed his impending death, and it propelled the panther to move with a fierce and enhanced speed through rocks and tall trees. The pale moonlight reflected on his dark coat. He breathed heavily as he ascended the mountain.

On the side of the great mountain, two fallen angels kept guard. Wordless, he made his way past the dark angels and moved toward the entrance of the cave. Torch light smattered the walls of the large tunnel with yellow and orange light. The passageway led Ba'hal into a huge, dimly lit cavern.

The eyes of creatures followed Ba'hal as he approached a cloaked figure with pale gray wings. The figure stood in the center of the cavern on a raised platform. The platform resembled an altar. Two large bronze dishes were at its center on a raised stone counter. One contained fire. The other contained water. Twelve columns with an indiscernible height were spaced evenly around the perfect circle. The Prince of the Earth took a sharp, ceremonial stone and made a small incision on his left wrist. With his right hand, he squeezed his left forearm, forcing black liquid that appeared to be blood into one bronze basin. As the blood dropped into the water, the Prince slowly moved his finger through it, mixing the two. He lowered the basin from the stone counter and put it on the floor.

Sensing the invitation, Ba'hal made his way onto the platform. He dipped his snout into the water and began to drink the mixture. As the new blood coursed through the possessed panther's veins, it energized Ba'hal's spirit. He roared in anguish and split the body of the panther in half. Ba'hal emerged from the carcass. He looked on with pride at his towering onyx black wings. Ba'hal then kneeled in submission to the Prince.

From the passageway Ba'hal had entered, another dark angel emerged from the shadows. Thousands of open eyes looked on with anticipation at their brother Kobiel. Kobiel looked at the vast army. His silver and yellow eyes carried defeat within them. His wings were mangled from the battle that had waged just hours before. The air in the cavern was thick with anticipation for Kobiel's witness.

"Abraxas and his forces were routed by Michael. He was stopped on his way to the thrones of heaven," Kobiel offered, his voice weak and tired. The Prince stared down at the floor, eyes hidden beneath his cloak. "Only a few made it back."

"And your efforts?" The Prince's words struck Kobiel as dry and procedural.

"Azrael stands guard over Adam and the girl. Gabriel is there as well. His divisions mainly take on the form of the creatures known as gorillas. Taking the life of man by force is not like that of the other animals. It's not been possible," Kobiel dutifully reported.

"What does he call her?" asked the Prince.

"The one fashioned from both bone and light?" Kobiel responded.

"Yes—the girl."

Kobiel lowered his voice. "She is called Eve ..." Kobiel could see a glint of light reflect in the eyes of the fallen as they absorbed her name in their minds. He could feel their thoughts travel from the tips of his wings into the center of his being. They questioned what her name meant. He sensed a mixture of fear and curiosity animating their thoughts.

"It means to breathe; it is one who gives life. Within her womb, she can bring new life made in his image into our world ... it's very clever." The Prince softly laughed to himself before finally looking up and into Kobiel's eyes. "Their blood ... it's their secret; it is a mixture of the dirt found only on this planet and Elohim's very breath ... their life is found in their blood."

Two archangels of translucent white light descended and landed face to face with the two dark angels at the entrance of the cave. As their feet hit the ground, they transformed from light into solid figures. The two fallen angels braced themselves, but neither the angels of the light nor of the dark made a move.

A golden orb of blinding light filled the center of the cavern, revealing its massive size. The orb illuminated all the fallen angels, who covered their eyes with their wings until the intensity subsided. As the harshness of the light diminished, a lone figure stood. At the Prince's side, Ba'hal channeled his previous possession and growled. Menakiel, heaven's emissary to Earth, looked around. A putrid combination of rage and shame filled the fallen. They tried to forget, but the sight of Menakiel conjured up the memory to their collective minds of their banishment by the King of Heaven himself.

Menakiel's powerful wings looked like massive shields adorned with silver and white like ivory on the outside. The inside color shimmered like liquid gold. All the fallen bowed immediately. The Prince of the Earth, Lucifer, remained standing and looked on at the spectacle with a slight smile turning the corner of his mouth. His blue eyes had a hint of purple as he took in the sight of Menakiel's arrival.

As their heads looked up, hate and contempt filled their eyes.

"I've been expecting you," Lucifer stated flatly.

From the far side of the cave, a huge fallen angel twice the size of Menakiel broke into a run. Filled with rage, it used its feet and wings to rush toward Menakiel. On the edges of its wings were what appeared to be sharp razors. Lucifer raised his hand, and as if on a string, the fallen one jumped toward Menakiel. Swiftly, Menakiel reached for the sword on his back, and with two hands, he drove the tip of his blade deep into the stone of the cavern floor. In a flash, a white force field expanded like a bubble around Menakiel. As the creature flew through the air, it tried to stop its momentum toward Menakiel, but it was too late. As it passed through the field, it shrieked in pain as its body burned up.

Menakiel grabbed the sword out of the ground, and the force field vanished. He looked at the large pile of ash from the fallen angel, then directly at Lucifer.

"Enough," Menakiel said using his heavenly language. Lucifer stared at Menakiel as a slight jealousy surged through his being. The jealousy was swiftly followed by contempt. All eyes within the cavern fixed themselves on Menakiel as he approached the unkneeling Prince they had sworn their loyalty to. Thousands of eyes emerged from the edges of Menakiel's wings. Quickly, they assessed all threats as they took in the sight of Menakiel's surroundings.

"If you had only joined me ... none would have remained by his side." Lucifer tilted his head and looked to see the response in Menakiel's eyes. "You know ... it's not too late to change your allegiance." A smirk spread across the Prince's face.

"What has become of you?" Menakiel asked. Lucifer looked surprised at Menakiel's response.

"You think this is where it ends? Is that it? You think we were banished from heaven to be ruled by them?" Hate dripped with each word as it traveled through the air. "Earth is nothing but a beachhead back into eternity. To rule and reign over the weak. To the thrones that are rightfully ours. To the worship that is rightfully mine."

Ba'hal growled again. With a quick glance, Menakiel's eyes lit up like torches and Ba'hal stepped back. Menakiel slowly walked up the platform, getting just a few feet from Lucifer. The eyes on the edges of his wings focused on Lucifer. As the emissary from heaven stepped closer, Lucifer's veins began to turn black beneath his pale gray skin. His blue eyes began to twitch. Lucifer collapsed to his knees. With everything in him, Lucifer fought the movement of his body, which seemed to now follow an unspoken law.

"Leave … you MUST LEAVE!" Lucifer heaved as his desperation grew. Menakiel came closer until he was only a few inches from Lucifer, who now knelt before him.

"You know why I've come," Menakiel responded, his eyes burning brighter.

"Yes—she's my favorite." Lucifer's voice dripped with contempt.

Menakiel looked around the cavern. The fallen angels that surrounded him now had previously served the King of Heaven. They fully understood what he was capable of. Dread filled their eyes. Menakiel placed a hand on Lucifer's cloak; he pulled it back, revealing Lucifer's now contorted face.

"Get back!" Lucifer violently shrieked.

"You are under the rule of the sun and moon, of space and time," Menakiel whispered into his ear. Leaning back upright, he surveyed the cavern. Thousands of dark angels started moving from the walls and began to lean in as if their destinies hung in the balance of Menakiel's spoken word. "And time—that is the prison from which none of you will escape."

Lucifer seethed at Menakiel's proclamation.

"One day, the protection will lift. They will be given the option of the two trees—without heaven's influence. I know him too well. He will have it no other way." Lucifer's words were defiant. "It's inevitable. At that time, there will be nothing you or Azrael can do to protect them." Menakiel listened closely as the Prince continued, "Tell me, are you willing to sacrifice yourself for them?"

"This world was created for their delight. Your punishment is subjugation. Not just to the King, but to the reign of his sons and daughters." At Menakiel's words, Lucifer's eyes lit up like torches, but the light was quickly extinguished. Slowly, his eyes turned into black pools and tar began to stream down his face like faux tears.

Lucifer's voice shook with rage. "Tell Elohim I'm coming for them. VERY SOON. I will hunt them down. I will pick them off. One by one. Their blood is a portal; it is a gate into eternity. Be sure of this: I WILL DRINK MY FILL."

Menakiel turned around and began to walk away. His enormous wings, previously tucked behind him, began to expand. They went in and out between a state of light and solid form.

"You had a choice. They will have theirs. That time will come. But you are to wait," Menakiel declared. As he walked away, he wrapped his wings around his body. The outside ivory and silver transformed to a shimmering gold that began to glow like burning hot steel. Within a couple of steps, his wings had created a portal of light. He walked through the portal and vanished from their sight.

Lucifer got up from his bowed position. He walked into the place where his sacrificial angel had run into Menakiel's force field. Covering his head with his cloak, he bent down to the pile of ash. He ran his finger through the ash of his previously loyal brother in arms. What a pathetic creature, he thought to himself. Bringing his finger up to his lips, his hand transformed into a feminine hand with deep red fingernail polish. Lucifer laughed with a high-pitched laugh, having shifted into a she.

"Elohim will pay a price. A very great price." Her soft voice now echoed within the cavern. "We will paint the Earth red with their blood."

THE ETZ HAYIM

X

~ 6 Months Later

A DOZEN HORSES RAN HARD THROUGH THE jungle. Adam led the pack on a brown horse with Eve close behind. He looked back at her. Eve was radiant. Adam saw her long flowing hair, and he couldn't help but notice what a remarkably skilled rider she was. It was strange to find a piece of himself in her. Now that they had been together for some time, Adam began to forget what it had been like before they met. She was wild and unpredictable. When he was with her, he became more aware of his own strength. He had never felt so alive.

Everything wasn't perfect in the garden, but the fallen ones had no access to their hearts. Unbeknownst to Adam and Eve, their connection intimidated the darkness. Their presence meant the end of the desert, but its dry sands wouldn't be quenched without a fight.

Arabella, a black and white horse near the back of the

herd, ran hard. As she raced down a ravine, she clipped her front right leg on a rock half a dozen inches above her hoof. She howled in pain as she stumbled and fell. Adam forcefully grabbed the mane of his horse and turned her around. Eve followed. They both circled back to the fallen horse, who now writhed in pain.

Elohim rode on a white horse heading their way. Eve knelt; feeling Arabella's pain, a tear streamed down Eve's cheek as she looked up at Adam. Elohim dismounted and knelt to join Eve. He examined the gash and motioned for Adam to come closer. Elohim took Adam's hand and placed it on the wound. Within a few seconds, Adam's hand became warm.

"What is that?" asked Adam. Elohim looked lovingly at Arabella.

"She's brave and strong." Elohim looked into the horse's eyes and directed Adam's hand up and down the gash. Adam felt a warm energy pass through his hand as he looked down at Arabella with love. Within moments, the fissure in the horse's wounded leg began to heal and her breathing became less labored. Adam looked up in wonder into the eyes of his father. "Son, it is love that releases healing through your hands. It is what brings wholeness to the creatures around you." Elohim's golden eyes seemed to dance as he glanced at Eve." It's released through your touch as well."

Eve's eyes sparkled with amazement as she looked at the leg, which had no signs of a wound. Neighing, Arabella rolled back up on her hind legs to stand. From his satchel, Elohim took out a pear and fed Arabella. Before she took a bite, she licked Adam's cheek lovingly. Eve laughed as Adam wiped off the horse's saliva and kissed her cheek.

"You're okay, girl, you're okay …" Adam softly whispered.

"Where are you riding to?" Elohim asked.

"To the edge of Eden." A big grin swept over Adam's face as he glanced over at Eve, catching her inquisitive eyes. "I'm going to show her where the water is to flow."

Eve felt a tangible love enter her lungs as she breathed in. Adam's words connected to her heart. Elohim studied Adam for a second. A fleeting concern faded from Elohim's face and was replaced with a look of determination.

"There's an unfamiliar spirit in the desert. The journey is not one to be made alone," Elohim said. Eve and Adam wondered for a moment. Was this the same spirit Elohim had warned them about, the one that desired to replicate itself? The spirit that could enter their world through the tree of the knowledge of good and evil? Understanding their thoughts, Elohim nodded. "It is the same."

They jumped back on their horses. Elohim climbed up on his and looked at his beautiful boy and his lovely daughter.

"You lead the way," he said.

Adam nodded and gave his horse a slight kick with his heel. It took off with great speed. Filled with excitement, Adam looked behind him as Eve and Elohim followed his lead.

With a few hours of daylight left, they began riding fast through trees and up and down hills. The horses ran hard. Finally they slowed down as they reached the edge of Eden.

The trees got less dense, and Adam could see the desert. Eve caught up, and they rode side by side until they got to one of the last groves of tall trees. Above, a hawk squawked.

Adam stopped his horse. He looked intently at the hawk. He breathed in deep and sent his spirit into the bird flying above. Looking through the eyes of the hawk, he surveyed the surrounding area. With a second deep breath, Adam's spirit returned to his body. When he opened his eyes, his irises and pupils slowly re-formed. He looked over at Eve as she took in the vast expanse. The mixture of dirt under their horses had eventually given way to clay and sand.

"This is where it begins," Adam said in a steady and sure voice. He looked into Eve's sparkling eyes and saw a soft glimmer of hope. "Can you see it?" Adam asked. Eve closed her eyes. Her imagination came alive with dazzling pictures of the future.

"I see the rivers flowing here, an abundance of animals, and various trees and plants that will begin their march across the desert from the banks of the river. I can see its beauty," Eve shared as her vivid imagination exploded with images of new life. She was mesmerized by the desert's beauty and the potential for it to be a second Eden. Adam nodded in agreement as Elohim rode up from behind.

"Do you see it?" Eve asked Elohim.

Elohim looked up at the expanse. He closed his eyes and entered into his daughter's imagination. As his vision came to life with the desires of her heart, delight spread across his face. He saw the beauty and life spring up in every direction. Eventually, Elohim opened his eyes.

"I do," Elohim shared lovingly with Eve. He looked proudly at Adam. "It's getting late. Let's set up camp here."

The sun had set, and the desert air began to cool quickly. Eve rolled out some mats made out of mullein leaves. Adam collected wood with Elohim. They sat under two trees with trunks that had unusually large circumferences. It was as if they had sucked up all the water in the area as they were significantly larger than any of the other trees near the edge of Eden.

Adam rubbed two sticks together and, with a handful of dry brush, started a small fire in the palm of his hands. He blew on it softly and placed the tinder beneath the large pieces of wood. Eve sat across the growing fire.

Elohim placed a large log over the growing flame and sat down between them. He pulled out the Etz Hayim from the sling on his back. Adam noticed it was the same branch he had broken off from the tree of life months ago. With a sharp stone, Elohim began to refine the branch he had taken from the tree of life and named. As he carved into the wood, he took off most of the remaining loose twigs. Elohim glided the sharp stone over the Etz Hayim until its protective bark was fully removed.

Elohim refined the top into a handle. He continued to work with the wood and carved a map of Eden and its surrounding areas into the side of the Etz Hayim. Slowly he carved on its other side a set of symbols. Adam looked on in fascination. The Etz Hayim was being transformed from a simple branch from the tree of life into an ornate staff with various symbols containing hidden meanings. The Etz Hayim was roughly five feet long, and the diameter varied from two inches to three and a half inches. Adam and Eve were mesmerized as they watched their father. With the final carving finished, Elohim blew the remaining dust away and inspected it closely. He looked up from his work. A timeless light shone in Elohim's eyes as his son and daughter looked on at him with wonder.

"Son, this is for you ..." Elohim showed him one side first. "Here's a map of Eden." Elohim gradually turned it over. Adam and his father looked at the symbols carved into the other side. "One of my names... when your heart is ready, the meaning of that name will be revealed." Elohim's eyes met Adam's as he gently handed the Etz Hayim he had formed from the tree of life to his son. "If we're ever separated, this gift is my way back to you."

Adam reached out, took the ornate staff, and pondered the words of his father in his heart. On the staff, he saw his father's depiction of the garden of Eden etched into its hard blonde wood. He peered closer and saw etchings of the four rivers that flowed out of the heart of Eden. As he turned it over, his eyes gazed at the symbols. He wondered what they meant. The Etz Hayim was hard and dense but surprisingly light. The very top of it, near the carved-out handle, had two twigs that stood out on each end. Each twig had two small, green leaves. The veins of the leaves had a soft, pulsating green light that seemed to emanate from within. Despite it being separated from the tree of life, it somehow seemed to contain life within itself.

While Adam continued to marvel at his gift, Elohim reached out and put his palms near the fire, warming them from the cool night air. As he reached out, Eve noticed what appeared to be scars in the palms of his hands. She had seen these before. Slowly she reached out and turned his left palm up with her hand. She began to trace her finger along the ridges of the scar. Her eyes followed the pattern of the scar before she finally looked into his eyes.

"Father ... what's this?" Eve asked.

Elohim softly smiled. She noticed the light from the fire that reflected in his large golden-brown eyes as he returned her gaze.

"This is Adam's name," Elohim said softly.

Eve turned over the palm of his right hand and saw a similar scar pattern.

"And this ...?" Eve asked.

"This one ... this is your name, my love," Elohim responded, his smile growing broader.

Adam set the Etz Hayim down by his side. He looked at his own palms and saw no scars. Eve examined her own hands and saw no scars. Eve looked back up at Elohim. A curiosity burned inside her.

"Our names?" Eve asked.

"Before I formed Adam from the dust and fashioned you from the bone in his side, your names were written on my hands. They were here before this world. They will remain after it is gone." Elohim looked with a deep joy into Eve's eyes.

Adam picked up the Etz Hayim and hovered the end of it with the handle and the two twigs above the fire. The green leaves at the end of the twigs burned in the flames. Adam took the Etz Hayim out of the flame to examine where the leaves had burned. He saw that the wood itself had neither burned nor even charred. It was as if Elohim's gift to him was impervious to fire. When Adam brought the handle close to his eyes, the four leaves on the two twigs re-grew in moments. The light pulsed once again from within the veins of the four green leaves.

"Our names were on your hands before the world was created … They'll be there when it is gone?" Eve asked. Elohim returned Eve's gaze.

"They will be. Understand … time is like a droplet of water. When you look only through time, it curves light, it bends space. It distorts all you perceive. Eternity is in your heart, Eve. It purifies your vision. It enables you to see clearly without distortion, without illusion," Elohim shared softly. He looked at Adam.

Adam had once again put the Etz Hayim into the fire to watch the four leaves from the two twigs regrow. Elohim returned his gaze to his daughter. "It's the only way to see any-thing as it actually is," he said.

The fire had grown bigger. Elohim looked over his shoulder and saw the shadow his body cast on a tree directly behind him. A sly, playful grin spread across his face.

"Watch!" Elohim said excitedly, catching Adam's

attention. He raised his hands in front of the light emanating from the fire and created a shadow of a bird on the trunk behind them. The children watched as the shadow seemed to fly around the backdrop of the incredibly large trunk. "Look! What is it you see?"

"Owl!" Adam hollered.

As soon as the words from Adam's mouth hit the air, a large white owl popped out from the shadow Elohim had created. Adam and Eve laughed with glee. The owl flapped its large, powerful wings and flew high into the tree above them until it found a branch to perch on.

The children looked again. Excitement and anticipation were plastered on their faces. Elohim raised his hands once more; this time, he formed the shadow of a butterfly.

"... Butterfly?" Eve nearly whispered.

Once her words traveled through the air, a real butterfly emerged from the shadow. As the shadow cast from Elohim's hands moved around, a steady stream of live butterflies flew out from the shadows until hundreds of multicolored butterflies with translucent wings flew all around them. Their wings emitted a soft glow. The butterflies encircled them and then began to fly higher into the night sky.

Eve stole a glance at Elohim as the three of them looked up at the ascending butterflies. Elohim smiled softly as he watched the wonder on his children's faces grow.

"Father ..." Eve caught Elohim's attention. "What was it like before Adam, before me?"

"It wasn't as fun," Elohim responded.

"Was it lonely?" asked Adam.

"There are others here. Some in the garden with us," Elohim said. "Some are above." He glanced up toward the stars.

"What do they look like?" Eve asked.

"Kind of like you." Elohim grinned.

Adam grew tired. He laid his head on the Etz Hayim as if it were a pillow. Fighting off sleep, Adam tried to keep his eyes open as he listened intently to the conversation. As the fire continued to dance, embers softly popped in the air.

"Adam and I ... are we different from you?" Eve asked.

"We both are artists. You and I create. You and I take joy in what we make." Elohim moved his hands closer to the flame.

"But we are different ... aren't we?" Eve's question lingered for a few moments before Elohim responded.

"We've always been. While you'll have no end ... you and Adam had a beginning. We know of no such thing." Elohim's words were soft and caring as he looked into his daughter's eyes.

"You've always been ..." Eve pondered his words before asking quietly, "And you've had no beginning?"

He could feel in her emotions that she was unsettled. He longed to bring her to a place of peace, a place where her heart could find rest.

"Breathe with me ..." Elohim inhaled deeply. Eve joined him before they both exhaled. "As important as oxygen is to our lungs, mystery is the lifeblood of our relationship. Where your knowledge ends, mystery begins. Mystery itself is a sacred and beautiful place. Within mystery lives trust. Where there is trust, love can abound. Do you trust me, Eve?"

"I do," Eve responded. "But I also want to know."

"I understand. And it's okay, Eve, to want to know ... but understand that while knowledge is important, it has both a beginning and an end. Love knows no such boundaries. Love is generative; it is limitless, and within its boundaries is perfect vision. Perfect clarity. Perfect freedom," Elohim said. He took a final deep breath and Eve joined him. "You breathe in love, and it moves through your entire being. You exhale love, and you give it to every living creature. You don't simply know it in your mind. It is a life and language unto itself. It brings a freedom too sacred to be comprehended by the mind alone or to be solely captured by words. It brings nourishment and life to who I've created you to be."

Elohim glanced over at Adam sleeping. A few moments passed. Elohim motioned for Eve to join him, and she put her head on his chest. A few more embers softly popped as the stars above them streamed overhead. Elohim held his daughter and caressed her cheek with his hand. Sleep was beginning to enter Eve's large blue eyes. She looked up at Elohim.

"Can we meet in my dreams?"

"Always ..." Elohim softly whispered.

Eve fell into a deep sleep. It could have been minutes, perhaps hours later—she didn't know—but her spirit awakened though her body remained asleep. Slowly, her spirit rose out of her body and began to float above Adam, Elohim, and the smoldering campfire. Somehow, she could still feel the cool, crisp air. Hovering above the trees, she looked toward the jungle; she knew within it lay their beautiful garden, her home.

Eve turned around and looked out toward the expanse of the desert. It seemed to be calling to her. Its siren song reached out and began to pull on her with desire. Her heart began to want to explore its barren but beautiful landscapes. Millions of stars above her watched as a combination of desire and curiosity fueled her flight over the desert expanse, leaving the encampment behind.

As she flew through the sky, she thought about her father and their conversation. She thought about Adam. She wondered and marveled at what they could do with the desert below her. What might grow? What animals might make their home in this new habitat? What type of birds might grace these lonely skies? What might it look like in the future?

As she flew, the landscape beneath her began to change from flat ground predominantly composed of cracked clay that would splinter beneath her to sand and small dunes. She looked ahead, and as far as the eye could see were rolling dunes that moved like gentle waves above the great depths. As she flew, the dunes grew in size until they appeared more like mountains than hills. She wondered if the sands were soft like the ones near the ocean or more coarse like the sand and gravel near many riverbeds. The sand seemed to invite her. Slowly, she descended.

Eve's feet landed on the dunes of the desolation for the first time. The fine grains of sand were soft and cool to the touch. A gentle, inviting breeze kissed her skin and moved through the white garments she was adorned in. As she looked around near the top of the dune, she saw in the distance a lone figure walking. Immediately, Eve was gripped by curiosity. Who was this man? Why was he here? The figure must have been a few hundred feet away. He wore a white robe and had a cloak draped over his head. His steps were silent, and had she not seen him, she would not have known he was there.

As she looked at him, her heart began to ache. Her intuition became alive. She could feel a terrible sense of loneliness. As if he was a man of deep sorrows. As if he had been walking for a long time and needed a friend but had none. Her heart was reminded of the many times she had seen Adam alone while journeying through the jungle. She recalled following Adam at a distance and hoping that his heart could feel her love, though his mind may not have been aware of her presence.

As the figure continued to walk ahead of her, Eve's impulse was to provide him with her companionship. She wanted to know him and what brought him to this isolated place. Eve continued to follow the man in the white robe as they both walked on the top of the dune.

Toward the end of the dune, the figure stopped walking. His robe rippled with the gentle breeze. Eve continued to walk and began to close the gap between them. As she got closer, a series of revelations coursed through Eve's being.

Visions of the figure's past cascaded into her mind. She saw he was at the end of a forty-day journey. But it had been more than simply a journey. For this man, it had been a crucible. His body ached with hunger and from a fight with only celestial witnesses. Though his body was at the end of its strength, his spirit was strong.

Suddenly, the man fell to his knees, and as she strained her ear, Eve heard him weep softly. As she moved toward him, the stars above her began to stream against the pitch-black sky, as if fast forwarding through time itself. She felt strangely out of breath.

Eve continued to walk toward him. With every step she took, the light of the stars quickened. They were now like streaks of light, as if every single one was a shooting star. Eve felt lightheaded but pushed past the fog that seemed to be engulfing her.

A few feet away, she stopped. Eve was completely transfixed as a mystery unveiled itself to her heart. The man's forty days had been mostly lonely, but as she stood behind him, her visions came into greater focus. He had appeared weak. But the appearance was intentional. He had used his appearance of weakness to slowly and deliberately draw out his opponent. He had lured and vanquished a powerful adversary. She somehow knew the man in front of her was dangerous. He was a threat to the spirit of the desert. Despite his victory, he wept as if a deep and uncontrollable anguish had overtaken his troubled soul. Eventually, the fog lifted. Eve felt time stand still. She knew that while his foe was no longer present, the fight was far from over. Her heart began to break as she realized a complete victory would demand his life.

Inexplicably, she had an urge to pull down his cloak and look into his eyes. His presence felt both familiar and foreign at the same time. She felt comfort but also imminent peril. Eve's heart broke. As she heard him weep, she burned with a desire to ameliorate his pain. Slowly, she reached out her hand and pulled his cloak down, revealing the back of his head. His dark brown hair was slightly wavy. She put her other hand on his shoulder. The moment her hand touched his shoulder, the desert disappeared.

Eve looked at her hand, still on the warm shoulder covered by the white robe. Eve glanced around to see three men in the distance running toward her. The man she had touched continued to weep. Eve looked around and saw familiar olive trees. These olive trees were much older and much more mature than the ones she remembered in the garden of Eden. The moon above was no longer a sliver; it was full. Eve knew she had been transported to a different place and time.

She moved around and knelt in front of the man. She placed a gentle hand on his shoulder. His face was now touching the ground as he wept in an anguish Eve had never witnessed. Her heart began to throb. She wanted to escape. She wanted to soar back into the sky and return to Adam and Elohim, but she couldn't. The man's tears and pain were like the gravity of the Earth, pulling her into his world. She heard him whisper, his voice quaking in pain.

"If it is possible ... please," his body shook, "please, Father ... take this cup from me ..." His body continued to tremble.

This was her father's voice. This was Elohim. His heart was broken.

Eve's mind raced with questions. What was her father doing here? What made him weep? Who were these men approaching? What was happening? Her heart ached in pain as she inexplicably watched her father weep. The men drew nearer as they ran toward Eve and Elohim.

"Yeshua!" a tall man with a full beard cried out. Two other men gazed on and were speechless behind him. "Master, are you okay?!" Distress plagued the man's strained voice.

Eve looked around as the men gathered around her father. She felt invisible as they looked right past her to attend to their friend. While she did not know them, she knew they somehow had a deep connection to him. Despite their fear, she could feel the love in their hearts for him. Yeshua? Why did they call him Yeshua? She placed her hand on her father's shoulder a second time. When she touched him, the men vanished like ghosts and the garden of Gethsemane disappeared.

Eve felt the soft sand from the dunes under her knees as she knelt and looked up at Elohim. Slowly, Elohim lifted his face from the sand. His face no longer touched the ground. For a moment, she felt lost and disoriented. As their eyes met, the anguish faded from his face. A tear streamed down her cheek. Elohim softly met her tear with his hand, wiping it softly from her face. Her heart seemed to vibrate with a stream of questions she didn't know how to ask.

"It's okay ... I'm okay ..." Elohim wiped another tear from Eve's face as she tried to discern the meaning of what she had seen. Love flowed through Elohim as he gazed into his daughter's eyes. "Eve, you must know something ... I too have a father." Elohim's voice carried an unexpected weight as she took in each word. "The prince of this world is coming; he has no hold on me. He comes only to reveal the true nature of my father's love. There will be a time when you'll see that it's as strong as my love for you."

The stars overhead slowed down. With the decrease of speed, a wind seemed to steal the tempo of the movement of the stars. It began to blow sand from the dunes. The strength of the wind increased until Eve and Elohim were hidden within a cloud and tornado of sand and dust. As it blew, the very sand underneath Eve and Elohim was blown into the distance until she found her knees on dry clay. The wind felt like it lasted for an eternity. Slowly Eve opened her eyes. She looked around and saw no dunes. A flat landscape of dry and cracked clay was under her feet.

In the distance, she saw the bright eyes of dark creatures surrounding them from all directions. As they ran toward Eve and Elohim, she could make out that the creatures were hundreds of black panthers. She had never seen so many in her life. Elohim held her in his arms as they came running toward them from every direction.

Leading the charge was Ba'hal, who she saw for the first time. Though she knew him not by name, she saw his dark metallic wings and a broad sword raised above his head. A rage emanated from the center of his being. Ba'hal hated her. He hated the Creator she represented. As he dashed toward her, Eve froze. She wanted to escape. She wanted the safety of the encampment. She wished this was only a dream. A desire for cruelty resided deep within the eyes of the approaching panthers. She knew Ba'hal had come to take her life. She gripped her father.

A dozen feet away, the first wave of panthers closed in. Ba'hal leapt into the air. Eve held her breath as she saw the dark angel move his sword higher in midair, preparing to strike. The panthers followed and sprung toward Eve and Elohim. Their teeth glistened, and their razor-sharp claws came into focus. Eve screamed and raised her arms to protect herself.

With a swift movement, Elohim pulled his cloak over Eve as she cried out. The panthers came crashing down. Ba'hal's sword pierced the empty white cloak as he drove it into the ground, shrieking with an ear-piercing rage.

ACT TWO

THE GREAT DRAGON

LEVIATHAN

XI

3979 B.C. ~ 15 Years Later

BRIGHT STREAKS OF WHITE LIGHTNING RACED across dark, foreboding skies. An angry torrent of rain assaulted the ocean below. Leviathan moved swiftly under the surface as the seas and wind violently roared above. The encroachment of the children of light over the years into the desolation had hit a tipping point. They had begun to transform the desert. While their progress had been small, it was there, nonetheless. The Lord of the Desert, the Prince of the Earth demanded their presence. Their incursion and their progress would be stopped. Ba'hal had commanded Leviathan to break through the angelic protection. His mission was simple. He was to retrieve the children of Elohim and bring them back to the Prince of the Earth for questioning.

Ba'hal knew, however, it was more than just questioning. He had seen and admired how the Prince had persuaded a third of all of heaven's armies to switch allegiances. Why would his children be any different? They were the new prize for his master. If more of heaven's angelic presence could be turned to swear a new allegiance, so be it. If their loyalty was found unwavering, Leviathan now had permission to take them in battle and then take the children by force.

As Leviathan approached the shore, he could sense the angelic. The guardians were present. His eyes scanned the thickness of the jungle brush.

Azrael and five of his brothers took on the forms of gorillas and raced toward the beach. From underneath the depths of the salt water, Leviathan rose. Ocean water glided off his black armored wings as they beat the air. Gradually he gained altitude. Leviathan's head was adorned with three massive bone-white horns that each stretched out six feet from his skull. The dragon scanned the shoreline for threats.

Emerging from the jungle brush, the gorillas looked above them. Beads of water from the torrent of rain ran down the gorillas' massive frames. Their tense muscles hid an explosive strength. Leviathan peered down at the angelic force. From deep within Azrael's chest, a shaft of bright white light hit Leviathan's dark gaze like a spotlight, temporarily blinding the dragon. As the light diminished, Leviathan saw Azrael's bronze armor as Azrael shifted from gorilla to his native angelic form.

"Bring his children to me!" Leviathan's roar pierced through the wind and waves. "My master demands it!"

Azrael stood defiantly. With a swift movement, he retrieved two swords from the sheaths on his back.

"Return to the sea or die." Azrael's voice was lower but matched the power of the dragon's.

Leviathan beat his wings and flew down to where Azrael stood on the shore. In a few short seconds, the distance between Leviathan and Azrael collapsed to less than a few feet. Leviathan eyed Azrael. His hot breath produced a rancid vapor.

"A third have defected; your chances of victory diminish daily. Surrender Adam ... and I may let you live." Leviathan's voice dripped with arrogance.

"Return to the depths, foul creature. If you heed not my words, you'll heed my blades," Azrael replied calmly. Bolts of white lightning splintered across the dark sky. One of the bolts zigzagged, splintered, and hit the tips of Azrael's raised swords. The swords gleamed white with electric power.

Incensed with rage, Leviathan beat his wings to rise again. Then with a sudden movement, Leviathan darted down and, with his center horn, pinned Azrael to the sandy shore. With a second thrust of his dark wings, Leviathan pierced the bronze metal, leaving Azrael with no escape.

"ARRRR!" Azrael grunted in pain. Instantly, Azrael's body vanished. Surprised, Leviathan thrust his wings back to get his horn out of the sandy ground. Before he gained altitude, one of the other gorillas, who had been stoically watching, leapt and landed on Leviathan's scale-covered head. Leviathan tried to shake the massive gorilla off, but the gorilla hung onto his left horn.

With a thunderous crack, the gorilla reached out and with a violent motion tore the center horn off Leviathan's skull. Black armored scales and blood burst from the center of Leviathan's head. Flesh from the roots of the horn hung onto the bone itself. Shrieking in pain, Leviathan frantically beat his wings to gain altitude. With one hand, the gorilla swung onto his right horn and grabbed it firmly. With the other hand, he held the broken horn and thrust it into Leviathan's right eye. Enraged, Leviathan lost his sense of direction. With a second surge in strength, the gorilla thrust the horn in deeper. Leviathan's eyelid spasmed as he shrieked in rage.

The other gorillas watched intently as Leviathan's large body seemed to convulse as he howled in pain hundreds of feet in the air. With a sudden flash, Azrael reappeared, hovering just a few feet above Leviathan's long neck. With a sudden movement, Azrael's sword cut through the air and moved swiftly through Leviathan's neck until his head was completely separated from his body.

Leviathan's body crashed into the sea. Moments later, his head hit the sandy beach. Leviathan's eye twitched and the lid tried to shut, but it was stopped again by the horn in the center of it. Azrael landed on the beach. The rain came down harder as rolling thunder boomed in the distance. He tilted his head and looked at the creature. Leviathan's eyes were vacant as the waves slowly tugged the dragon's head back into the ocean.

Like a ghost rising from a body, Leviathan's spirit rose above the physical body of the great dragon. Leviathan looked down on Azrael. He knew he must now return to Ba'hal. Ba'hal and the Prince of the Earth would have to find another way. Leviathan had chosen one of the strongest creatures on Earth to possess. It was clear the angelic forces were too strong. Neither they nor the children of Elohim could be taken by physical force. There had to be another way.

Azrael returned his gaze to his brothers in arms.

"This battle has not won us the war. The fallen will try a new tactic once Lucifer understands he cannot take Elohim's children by force. Keep watch. I'll warn the others." Azrael's deep voice spoke in an unemotional tone. The other gorillas gazed into the stormy abyss, ready to address any additional dangers from the dark sea. Azrael beat his bronze-colored wings, gained altitude, and flew in the direction of the jungle.

Eve's piercing scream traveled through Eden. Dozens of gorillas swiftly sprinted toward the sound of her cries. They halted abruptly.

"You'd better stop!" Eve howled with laughter. Adam pinned Eve on her back to the grass of the meadow. He stopped tickling her ribs. He brushed his hair aside as a sly smile spread across his face. Adam was no longer a young boy; he was a young man. Eve had grown into a beautiful young woman.

"… or what?" Adam grinned.

"Or you'll have to get your own berries." Eve's eyes sparkled as she held up a satchel filled with blackberries. Without breaking eye contact, she took one in her hand and lifted it to Adam's lips. Before he could take it in his mouth, she popped the berry into her own mouth. Eve wrestled Adam until she was on top of him. He leaned up until their mouths met with a slow kiss.

Behind the trees and the brush, the gorillas had formed an unseen circle of protection. Hearing the rustling of the creatures, Adam looked around, and Eve's eyes followed his gaze.

"Shhhh …" Adam put his fingers to his lips. "They're here!" he said in an excited but hushed tone. Eve nodded. Adam helped Eve get up from the ground.

"I think they're in this direction." Adam motioned, and they began to walk north.

"Why do you think we've seen more of them?" Eve asked with a hushed tone.

"They're here for our protection," Adam answered.

"Protection from what?" Eve asked.

"The shadow creatures, the same ones you saw in the desert … years ago with Elohim. They wish to stop our expansion," Adam said quietly. A look of concern showed on Eve's face. "The desert will flourish. It must." Adam's eyes possessed a confident determination.

In the distance, Adam and Eve heard a horse trotting toward them. They looked and saw Elohim on a black and white horse. They saw the joy on his face spread as he approached them.

Elohim dismounted. Eve leapt into his arms. Elohim hugged his daughter and kissed her on the cheek.

"My beautiful girl." Elohim's eyes seemed to dance as he looked at his daughter with joy. He smiled and looked toward Adam. "Ahhh! My handsome son!" Elohim embraced Adam.

"It's been a while—good to see you again!" Adam said excitedly.

"I felt you might need some time together," Elohim responded coyly.

"Where have you been?!" Eve asked.

Elohim looked at his daughter and paused for a moment.

While still youthful, Eve was no longer a little girl. Elohim's heart swelled with affection and pride.

"I've been training someone!" Elohim lovingly stroked Arabella's black and white mane.

Eve looked over at Adam with an inquisitive look in her eye.

"Are you going to show him, or do you want me to?" A sly smile spread across Eve's face.

"Show me what?" Elohim asked. Adam's eyes had a wild look to them, and his grin grew ridiculously large. "What is it?" Elohim said.

"This way—you'll see," Adam responded with pride in his voice.

The tent's poles were made of bamboo. Vines secured the top, which reached about fourteen feet high. As Adam entered, the light from the flickering torches illuminated his face. Eve and Elohim followed. Adam set to the side the Etz Hayim staff that hung in a sling on his back. In the center of the tent was a rug where they sat down. Adam reached underneath the rug and pulled out a thick sheet of parchment that was wrapped with twine. He slowly unwrapped the twine and spread out the map for Elohim to see for the first time. Elohim studied the map, then looked back up at Adam. The map cited geographical landmarks of Eden, water sources, and the land's topographical information.

"See …" Adam pointed down at the map. "We've already

redirected waters from the Euphrates to flow east into the valley here. Pishon to flow here." Adam motioned his finger southeast.

"This is good." Elohim spoke in a hushed tone as he grinned at Eve.

"Based on the current flow of this tributary from the Euphrates, it will take thirty-four days for this basin to fill," Eve said as she did the calculation in her mind. "With the water, we expect figs and almond trees to grow along these banks here and here." Eve pointed her finger to the newly formed riverbanks.

"The land could be very fertile there," Elohim replied.

"There will be additional water we can then use to irrigate these areas south. We think we can grow an abundance of new plants and trees. As they grow, they'll invite animals here as well. This should further enhance the soil, and one day, it may be a place where the trees grow as tall as they do here in our garden," Adam offered.

"It will take time, but I can see it," Elohim said. Eve and Adam looked at each other and grinned. "May I?"

Adam nodded. Elohim flipped over the parchment. The backside of the brown parchment was blank. Elohim spread it out so it was completely flat.

"I know you've seen the shadow creatures in the desert and the arid plains." Elohim spoke softly and looked over at Eve. "The same ones we encountered years ago in the desert."

Eve nodded as she recollected the time. Elohim waved his hand over the parchment, and as he did, new ink began to detail out a sketch of the world Adam and Eve hadn't seen. He centered his hand over the middle of the new map and slowly raised it. As he did, the parchment rose from the ground and began to shift its form into a sphere.

"This is our Earth, isn't it?" Eve asked softly. Elohim's eyes met with Eve's as he nodded.

"It's time to bring the shadows you've seen into the light of understanding," Elohim shared with a resolute voice. To the amazement of Eve and Adam, Elohim spun the floating sphere, whose parchment had disappeared entirely and was replaced by a true to life representation of their planet. Elohim moved the sphere until Eve and Adam were looking at a mountain range that sat on the other side of the planet from Eden. Elohim looked toward the northernmost tip of the mountain range. Eve and Adam looked closer.

"Hold my hand." Elohim put his left hand out, and both Adam and Eve placed their hands in his. He wrapped his fingers over their hands. With his right hand, he touched the mountain range on the other side of their world. Instantly, a wormhole opened up and the three were transported to another time and place. They traveled to the same range of mountains Elohim had touched with his finger but to an earlier age prior to their creation.

THE REBELLION

XII

ADAM OPENED HIS EYES. HE FELT HIS FATHER'S hand release him and Eve. As they looked around, they found themselves toward the top of a mountain of great height. Dark clouds with rain in their bellies were scattered among a backdrop of blue sky and a setting sun. Tall trees were everywhere. The air smelled fresh from a recent rain. Adam and Eve moved their eyes from the valley below them to the top of the mountain behind them. Directly behind them was a very large, open-architecture-style home with multiple rooms and balconies.

The floors were made of smooth, light gray stone, and its walls were made of warm woods. The ceilings were more than thirty feet high, and hung between the large beams were beautiful black pots with a variety of flowers in them. The home was unlike any structure Adam and Eve had ever laid eyes on. It was beautiful in form and seemed to blend in with the mountainous environment. Large granite boulders from the foundation below provided breaks between rooms. In the center of the home, a small waterfall between two of the largest boulders provided a sheet of water that had a mirror-like quality to it. The water fell into a basin, which then overflowed back into the stream, which ushered it out of the home. Elohim motioned, and Eve and Adam followed him into the home. As they walked, they got closer to the water fixture. Adam and Eve looked at each other, then at their own reflections in the water.

"He was here, before your time," Elohim said.

From another room, an incredibly tall angel with light gray robes walked in. His beauty took Adam's breath away. Eve, slightly intimidated, took a few steps back.

"Calm, child, you are invisible to him," Elohim responded. "We have traveled to a time prior to your creation. You are in his future. He cannot see you nor does he know you are here."

The angel's wings were pure gold on both sides; a soft amber light seemed to dance between his shoulder blades and the tips of his wings as he walked closer to the basin. His eyes were a pinwheel mix of sharp cobalt blue with a golden amber color. His jaw was squared with slightly round corners.

"He was my light bringer, my morning star, a servant, and a friend … Lucifer is his name." Elohim looked at his children, then back at the angel. "I had covered him in every precious stone. He was blameless in all his ways from the day I created him."

As Elohim spoke, Adam's eyes focused on the angel's chest, which was adorned with a silver mirror-like plate that had a grid of gems of various kinds. Adam recognized many of the stones. There was sardius, topaz, emerald, carbuncle, sapphire, diamond, opal, agate, amethyst, beryl, onyx, and jasper. Though he didn't quite understand the meaning, Adam sensed that the stones had meaning beyond the physical minerals; they represented gifts, power, revelation, and wisdom Lucifer had been given by his father.

Lucifer walked over to get closer to the basin. Adam felt as if through the water Lucifer could see him. He shook off the feeling. Eve walked to the other side of the falling water to where Lucifer took a closer look at himself. She put her hand on his chest and moved it over the stones as Lucifer leaned into the water. As she moved her hand over the various colored stones, light from the stones traveled through her hand as she touched them. Eve looked up toward Lucifer's transfixed gaze. She followed his gaze to the water and noticed on the opposite side the water was no longer transparent but had taken on a mirror-like quality. Lucifer looked into the mirror and smiled broadly.

They heard a soft whistling sound as if an arrow was flying through the air. Elohim, Eve, and Adam looked up as a figure cloaked in an emerald-green robe landed a dozen yards away on one of the outside decks. Its dark robe clashed with the brightness of its wings, which seemed to have silver tips at the very end. Govati, the messenger angel, folded his wings behind him and moved through the open terrace and into the room with Lucifer. Lucifer's eyes used the water as a mirror and glanced over at Govati and then back again at himself.

"His beauty and position entangled him; his heart began to swell under the dark spell of his own pride," Elohim shared.

A sadness permeated his voice. Eve and Adam looked toward Elohim and could see a deep regret in his eyes.

Govati took a couple of steps closer to Lucifer so he was just a few feet behind him.

"You have been summoned." Govati's voice appeared flat and unemotional. The angel reached under his robe and stretched out his dark brown hand to offer Lucifer a scroll.

Lucifer paused before turning around. As he turned around to face Govati, the amber gold in his eyes was replaced fully by a dark blue.

"Thank you, Govati," Lucifer said.

Govati nodded, bowed, and took a few steps back. Lucifer unrolled the scroll and began to read the message. About halfway through, he looked up at Govati.

"Have you ever imagined a world beyond the scrolls?" Lucifer asked in a deep voice that seemed to carry through the house. Govati shook his head. "Without the arbitrary protocol ... without the hierarchy?" Lucifer continued the train of thought.

"I have not." Govati peered into Lucifer's eyes but sensed Lucifer, while in front of him, was currently in a different world as he uttered the words.

"And why not, Govati? You serve the King of Heaven well ... but what about what you want? What about what I want? Imagine what could be ..." Lucifer shared with a deep pleasure in his voice. As he looked now directly at Govati, the color of the stones on his breastplate faded and turned to gray. The air turned frigid, and as he spoke, Eve backed away. She turned toward Elohim.

"Father, what's happening?" Eve asked. Elohim put his hand out, and Eve took it. Adam, Elohim, and Eve looked to see Govati's response.

"Do you see it?" Lucifer asked with anticipation on his face.

"I focus on my tasks," Govati responded.

The gold faded from Lucifer's wings and turned to pitch black. An orb of light appeared between Govati and Lucifer. The orb flashed, and from the center of the light, two archangels, Michael and Gabriel, stepped out. They were the same size as Lucifer but with bright white wings that had a reflective sheen. In unison, they looked at Govati, who bowed, then toward Lucifer. Gabriel motioned with his hand, and within moments, a portal appeared. Adam and Eve looked through the portal and saw an ocean of stars in the blackness of space. Michael motioned with his hand, and Lucifer nodded.

"Why not?" Lucifer asked in a flat, rhetorical tone. His cobalt blue eyes turned back to a golden amber color as he looked at Gabriel.

"Now." Gabriel's voice was low and authoritative. Lucifer stepped through the portal, followed by Govati, Michael, and Gabriel.

The portal closed. The angels disappeared. Adam and Eve looked at each other, then at Elohim.

"Where was he taken?" Adam asked.

"To a place and time before I breathed my spirit into you

… come, look." Elohim approached the basin of water and motioned for Adam and Eve to look with him. "His heart was filled with violence." As Elohim spoke, the water flowing into the basin turned black, and within the blackness, Adam and Eve saw an image of the Earth from space. In an instant, an equally large portal appeared above the atmosphere of the Earth. As if stones were shot from a sling, the four angels—Govati, Michael, Gabriel, and Lucifer—flew from the portal above the Earth and began to race through space as streaks of bright light. As they flew, their speed increased.

Eve, Adam, and Elohim continued to peer into the basin and watched as the four angels flew past the Milky Way. Slowly, stars moved from their positions and began to follow them. Eve's and Adam's eyes were transfixed as they saw all the stars from every position and direction in space begin to chase after the orbs of streaking light. It looked almost as if the heavens were collapsing and chasing the angels through space and time.

Adam and Eve glanced over at Elohim, who watched the scene unfold. As they looked at him, his countenance changed, and his eyes lit with a fire they had never witnessed.

"He wished to enslave all who came into his orbit." Elohim's voice sounded like rumbling thunder. "Take Eve's hand," Elohim declared. Adam reached out to Eve's already outstretched hand. He looked on her with anticipation in his eyes. He knew deep in his heart his father was about to reveal the origins of the shadow creatures. He took Eve's hand, then firmly gripped Elohim's open hand. Elohim put his left hand into the water basin.

As soon as Elohim touched the dark water, the three vanished from the face of the Earth.

The last thing Adam felt was Elohim's hand locking around his. He looked back and saw fire in Eve's eyes for the first time. He felt a power and authority burn within her that he had not experienced before. As she wrapped her hand around Adam's, he could feel the intensity increase. She wanted to follow Elohim and see the threat this creature posed destroyed.

Within seconds, they ascended through what looked like a ball of fire and light. They flew past layers of clouds and out of the atmosphere. Eve looked around and no longer saw Elohim but only the fire and light that surrounded her and Adam. After a few minutes of travel, they saw the four streaks of light from Govati, Michael, Gabriel, and Lucifer in front of them. They raced past planets, the sun, asteroid belts, and stars of various vivid colors. Eventually, they raced past the angels, and in the distance, Adam saw a black hole that all light from the universe appeared to be traveling toward. Eve and Adam raced toward its entrance with tremendous speed. Everything went dark except the orb of light around Adam and Eve. All the light from the stars in space suddenly vanished. Adam felt weightless. The orb faintly lit Eve's face. She glanced over at Adam; a look of curiosity and intense anticipation was on her face.

"Where are we going?" Eve asked. Adam looked around. All he could see was the orb casting yellow and orange light on their bodies. When Adam peered beyond its bubble, he couldn't perceive a single star or planet. They looked behind them and saw the four streaks of light from the angels coming straight toward them.

Adam and Eve felt a jolt of energy, and as if the night sky was turned back on, they emerged on the other side of the wormhole surrounded by millions of stars. Their colors were purple, red, orange, blue, and yellow. Their light seemed to bend, blend, and connect at various points in the dark atmosphere surrounding them.

In the backdrop stood a giant planet, which was mostly turquoise and emerald green. The light from the various stars seemed to dance and weave around its orbit. This planet was clearly different from Earth or any of the planets they had just witnessed. It was the first time they'd seen ribbons of golden amber light seeming to emanate from a planet itself.

The four streaks of light zoomed past Adam and Eve. The streaks of light went in the direction of the planet. Adam glanced over at Eve to see a slight smile on her face as she looked at the planet with wonder in her eyes. Adam did not know the name of this place, nor did it look like anything he had ever seen, yet it somehow felt familiar. It felt like Eden. Adam knew it was their second home.

As they both looked on, they saw a purple and golden light approach them. Within seconds, from within the light, a large golden angel appeared in front of them. Deep purple ribbons of light seemed to be orbiting his body. Adam could see the outside of his wings were bright white; the insides were completely golden. The angel smiled broadly.

"I'm Menakiel, heaven's ambassador. You are invited as

witnesses of the judgment. The judgment of what has been. The judgment of what is to come." With his words, ribbons of purple light formed a new orb around Adam and Eve. "This way," Menakiel commanded.

Adam opened his eyes. He felt an iron scepter in the grip of his right hand. Looking to his left, he saw Eve sitting on a throne. She was adorned in a white robe with purple embroidery. Eve wore a crown of ivory with silver and gold lacing. To Adam's right was their father, Elohim. Elohim looked at Adam and smiled warmly, then he directed his gaze in front of them.

As Adam and Eve looked around, they saw about thirty yards away were twenty-four thrones arranged in a semicircle facing them. On the thrones were men and women of different ethnicities and royal robes who were all seated and looking up. They were surrounded by large pillars made of translucent crystal.

As Eve looked above her, she saw no ceiling but rather thousands of angels flying above them in different patterns. Every angel had a different combination of ribbons of light emanating from their bodies. The ribbons trailed the movement of the angels and at times seemed to be dancing around them. Unlike on Earth, neither Adam nor Eve could discern a single source of light in the skies above. As Eve looked on, it was difficult to discern the time of day as certain parts of the sky looked like dawn, other parts looked like dusk, and still others looked like noon and night.

Suddenly, the angels above formed a circle, and the four flashes of light that carried Govati, Michael, Gabriel, and Lucifer traveled through the circle before landing between where Adam and Eve were seated and the twenty-four thrones. Adam glanced over to see Elohim engulfed by orange and bright white flames.

The archangel Michael approached the throne. He folded his large wings behind him as he approached. Menakiel, who had been hovering above Elohim, flew down and met Michael. As Michael came near, the very tips of his wings lit up with fire. Menakiel faced Michael and the twenty-four thrones. The two archangels exchanged words in a heavenly tongue Adam did not understand. Both turned and gradually knelt before Elohim. Gabriel and Govati stood on both sides of Lucifer. All three bowed.

Adam glanced at the twenty-four who sat on their thrones. The back of each of their thrones had ornate carvings. Some carvings resembled animals Eve and Adam had seen on Earth. Other carvings had creatures they had never laid eyes on. Each member of the royalty held a silver scepter. On top of each of their armrests were statues of snakes carved out of the thrones with mouths open showing their fangs. Each king and queen had an air of authority that Adam somehow knew all the angels in heaven yielded to. In unison, the royalty raised their scepters and hit the ground. With a single motion, they stood before their thrones, then knelt before Elohim. All of heaven was silent. Elohim looked at the elders, then at Lucifer.

"Stand," Gabriel commanded Lucifer.

Resolutely, Lucifer stood. He glanced behind himself at

the royalty who had taken a knee. A look of contempt flashed in his eyes before he turned back around and met Elohim's eyes. Menakiel flew and hovered above Elohim's throne before turning back around and facing Lucifer. Adam looked up to see hundreds and then thousands of eyes emerge at the edges of Menakiel's broad wings. Many of the eyes looked at Lucifer, some at the twenty-four, and others looked directly at Elohim, Adam, and Eve.

With a scepter of molten iron and fire, Elohim raised and with force pounded his scepter onto the ground. The royalty rose up from their bowed position and sat once again on their thrones. Elohim stood. As he stood, Adam and Eve sat transfixed by the being of fire that remained seated on his throne. The one had become two.

Adam's gaze followed Elohim as he walked down a dozen ivory steps past Michael toward Lucifer. Encircling Elohim were white and golden ribbons of light. As he approached Lucifer, the fire from his body dissipated completely. Lucifer looked bewildered and lost as Elohim came within just a few feet of where he stood. Lucifer tilted his head.

"Who are you?" Lucifer's voice was low and uncertain. He looked back up at the King of Heaven seated on the throne. "Who is this, Lord?"

Then with a voice that sounded like a thousand rivers, Elohim spoke.

"He is my father. We are one," Elohim declared.

Lucifer took a few steps back. Adam locked eyes with Lucifer for a moment before he saw Lucifer's eyes go completely black. His face grimaced with a mixture of hatred and contempt as if he had just been betrayed. Lucifer looked toward the throne and momentarily shielded his eyes with his left wing. As his eyes darkened, the light brought Lucifer great pain. He lowered it enough to look again at Adam and Eve. He then glanced back at Elohim.

"They look like you," Lucifer said in a low tone. Elohim glanced back at Adam and Eve with joy on his face. Adam, seated upon his throne, smiled back at his father. Eve watched inquisitively.

"They are like me," Elohim stated proudly. Elohim walked toward Lucifer and whispered in his ear. "Your time has come. Make your case."

Elohim turned around, but the white and golden ribbons of light streamed off his body and slowly began to orbit around Lucifer. The moment Elohim set foot on the ivory steps leading back to his throne, his body lit up again with fire. As he sat down, his body merged with the being of fire already seated on his throne. In a spark of revelation, Adam and Eve knew the light that encircled Lucifer was the Spirit of God. The same Spirit who was present at the creation of their world. The fire, the light, and Elohim were one.

Lucifer started to frantically look around. He began to pace, but the ribbons of gold and white light seemed to confine him. Then with a rushed but broken voice, Lucifer spoke and for the first time verbalized the accusation that laid deep in his heart.

"There are things he keeps from us!" Lucifer looked up at the angels flying above. "He withholds! He forces us to eat from his own hand, from these scrolls ... from his words ..."

With each accusation, heaven remained silent. "He wants to keep us in an unseen bondage." Lucifer looked back at the royalty seated on their thrones. They stoically returned his gaze before Lucifer looked above, addressing the tens of thousands of angels who now hovered in the skies.

"WHO ARE THEY THAT WE SHOULD BE SUBJECT TO THEM?!" His voice carried a deep hatred. Lucifer pointed to Elohim while staring at the royalty. "WHO IS HE THAT YOU SHOULD BE SUBJECT TO HIM? TELL ME IF YOU KNOW!"

Heaven stood still. His voice seemed to fill the atmosphere, and Lucifer's black wings began to grow. Lucifer breathed in deeply. He glanced all around before addressing the heavenly host with a whisper, "There's life beyond his world, beyond his dreams, beyond his will." He then roared loudly, "WHAT OF MY WILL?! WHAT OF YOUR WILL!" Cracks began to form in the crystal pillars at the vibration of Lucifer's voice.

Eve and Adam looked above them. The color in some of the angels drained from their bodies, and they turned a pale gray. As they turned gray, their wings began to disintegrate, and a multitude dropped from the sky and landed all around them. The true allegiance within their hearts was revealed.

"I WILL!" Lucifer roared into the atmosphere. All of heaven was filled with his voice alone. As he shrieked, more angels fell from the sky.

A sea of angels, one-third, had fallen all around. Adam could only look into their eyes momentarily as he was repulsed by the darkness that had replaced the light in their eyes. The eyes on Menakiel's wings seemed to track and follow each angel who fell. Lucifer felt exhausted and accomplished. Slowly, he uttered an encouragement to the fallen ones.

"We will ..." Lucifer whispered defiantly as he looked back toward the throne of Elohim. Both Adam and Eve saw scenes of war and violence in Lucifer's eyes. With Lucifer's words, pitch black wings began to grow on the backs of the fallen.

"Our rebellion is one you have brought on. But it doesn't end here," Lucifer addressed Elohim insolently.

The fallen angels began to amass behind Lucifer. Menakiel darted down from his position hovering above the throne. The eyes at the tips of his wings each focused on one of the fallen. He landed in front of Elohim's throne and spread out his wings like a shield as if to protect Adam and Eve. At his movements, the fallen angels stepped back in sheer terror and looked back at Lucifer. Slowly, Menakiel bowed before Elohim.

Elohim rose from his father and walked down the ivory steps toward Lucifer and the fallen. With a deep sadness, he declared, "In perfect freedom, those in heaven have made a choice ..."

Lucifer took a step back and looked around at the royalty. An unwavering determination resided deep within their gaze as they raised their scepters. Menakiel stood. As the scepters were raised, the statues of the snakes alongside their armrests broke from their stony forms and came to life. The royalty tilted their scepters toward Lucifer and the fallen angels. The snakes slithered toward the fallen.

"The choice they have made will be honored." Elohim's

voice thundered in heaven. The wings of all the angels above, the two-thirds that had not fallen, were set ablaze. With that, Elohim's father rose from his throne and walked toward Elohim as a pillar of fire. Elohim's father walked into and merged with Elohim, his son. Elohim was now one with the fire of his father. With one voice like a thousand rivers, they spoke. "TO THE DUST OF THE EARTH WILL YOU BE BOUND."

Lucifer looked at Elohim. Behind Lucifer, the snakes approached and encircled him. He then looked at his fallen brothers. "We WILL resist!"

From among the royalty, a queen of African ethnicity spoke.

"With the passing of time, your self-indulgence will rise," she declared. Snakes crawled onto Lucifer's feet and up his calves. He tried to pull them off, but he wasn't strong enough. "But your newly found kingdom will wane in power," she continued.

Elohim waved his scepter and instantly a portal opened beneath Lucifer. By now, Lucifer was covered in snakes; they bound him as if they were living chains. Through a gap in the snakes covering his eyes, Lucifer looked beneath him through the portal and saw the Earth.

"The dust," Lucifer gasped. "It cannot contain me!"

From among the royalty, a king of Asian ethnicity rose. "Division will be found only in the lower realms."

Another king of Caucasian descent stood. "Your war will not be fought here. You will be judged and subdued on the Earth."

The rest of the royalty immediately stood. After what

seemed to be a few moments of silence, each member of the royalty hit their scepters into the ground. As they did, thousands of portals appeared, one beneath each of the fallen.

Elohim hit the ground with his scepter, and the ground began to shake. One by one, each fallen angel was pulled into the portals and vanished from the realm of heaven. Lucifer gripped the edge of the portal, but the gravity of Earth was too powerful. He lost his grip and fell through, hurtling toward the Earth. The royalty looked on as all portals except the one Lucifer was pulled through closed. Elohim faced Menakiel.

"See to it my children are fully awake," Elohim commanded. The eyes on the edges of Menakiel's wings focused on Eve and Adam. In a split second, he flew up into the sky and then down through the portal. As soon as he went through the portal, it closed. A bright light emanating from Elohim filled all of heaven. The luminosity was so intense Adam and Eve shielded their eyes with their hands.

Adam opened his eyes. His vision was blurry, and he felt light-headed. As his vision came into focus, he saw Elohim kissing Eve's forehead. He felt dizzy. He looked around and saw they were back within their tent. The same one where Adam and Eve had been sharing with Elohim their plans and progress on terraforming the desert. Adam's mind felt scattered, and he felt sick to his stomach. As he slowly regained consciousness, Adam overheard Eve speak.

"What are we to do?" Eve asked, looking into Elohim's

eyes. She looked back at Adam. Adam immediately stood as he felt rage course through his being.

"INSOLENT CREATURES!" Adam seethed, barely able to control his rage. "THEY BETRAY YOU?!"

Adam looked at Eve and then glanced over at Elohim. "EARTH is OUR kingdom. They CHOOSE REBELLION?! THEY SHALL SUBMIT."

Elohim was calm as he looked up at his son. Adam saw a mixture of pride and warning in his father's eyes.

"Son, come, look …" Elohim said softly as he spun the holographic Earth with his hand, the same one he had used to take them to see Lucifer's dwelling. Eve and Adam looked closer and saw the Earth was composed of a single landmass surrounded by vast oceans. To the west on the land mass, they saw Eden. Eden was small in comparison to most of the land, which was dry and lifeless. Elohim spoke again. "The Earth was scorched when he fell."

At the sound of his father's voice, Adam began to see clearly again as the rage washed through his emotions. There was a certain sadness in Elohim's voice as he surveyed the destruction of the Earth Lucifer had caused.

"Father"—Adam's eyes met Elohim's—"he will not stop us. We will take dominion; we will bring life and water to the dry places. The places Lucifer thinks belong to his kingdom. The whole Earth will reflect the splendor of Eden." With his words, Adam made a promise to Elohim, one that he would dedicate all his strength to fulfilling.

Adam's mind immediately returned to his plans: the rivers and springs they'd redirect; the aqueducts he planned to build to the north, south, and east of Eden. Eve listened to her husband's thoughts. She pondered her father's words in her heart.

"And what of Lucifer?" Eve asked.

Her question somehow brought a new light to Elohim's eyes. All of Adam's plans seemed to fall out of his mind and were completely forgotten as he earnestly awaited Elohim's answer.

"The darkness fears you." Elohim looked at Eve, then at Adam. "As it should."

EXPANSION

XIII

3976 B.C. ~ 3 Years Later

THE SUMMER SUN BLAZED BRIGHT IN THE SKY ABOVE. Two massive, dark gray hawks scanned the arid plains below. In three years, dozens of oxen had been lost to the venom of desert cobras and vipers. The hawks had been trained by Adam for a specific mission: to protect the team of more than two hundred oxen below. Elohim had taught Adam how to utilize the strength of the oxen to great effect. Their labor had been used to dig a network of canals that carried water from the heart of Eden into the desert.

While it had taken time, Eve and Adam began to see a variety of plants and trees begin to take root along the banks of the canals. An abundance of wild grasses grew and provided food for the oxen. A variety of animals began to migrate and move from Eden into the new territory. The work was hard, but the strength of the ox expedited the dredging of the canals.

Eve stood near an empty pool at the eastern end of the

canal system and waved a tan flag. Adam was a few hundred yards away to the west. Adam raised the Etz Hayim above his head as a signal to a team of eighteen oxen. Strength from years of work showed in the larger muscles they had acquired over the years. The oxen began to move in unison to remove a three-foot-high pile of stones mixed with clay that was acting as a dam. A net that Adam had made of thick jungle vines strained as inch by inch the oxen made progress, dragging the mixture of stones and clay up onto the shore. As they moved the stone and earth, water began to stream into the newly dug canal. The life-giving water began to flow east toward Eve a quarter of a mile away before stopping in the pool. She felt accomplished as the water rushed by and flooded the basin.

Above the hawks, a dark portal opened, and two fallen angels entered the atmosphere. Adam and Eve looked above as the two angels flew east toward Eve. In a sudden flash, Azrael appeared by Adam's side. His bronze armor reflected the hot sun. He glanced over at Adam. They both watched the two fallen angels descend and land a few dozen feet from Eve.

"Son of God, I am your servant." Azrael's voice carried an invisible electricity that seemed to cut through the hot atmosphere. Adam put the Etz Hayim into the sling on his back. He glanced over at Azrael and saw two silver swords strapped across his back like an X. The swords burned bright with a white fire. Adam reached for one of Azrael's swords.

"This way," Adam commanded.

As Adam carried the sword from Azrael above his head, they began to walk toward Eve and the two fallen angels in the distance.

Eve felt the hot air on her face from the pumping of their enormous wings as Abraxas and Amon landed. The outside of their wings was black like onyx. The inside was as white as ivory. As Eve looked closely, she saw various designs that looked like they were carved into the inside of their wings. When Eve focused, they seemed to come alive and depict scenes from various battles they had been in. The massive size of the angels' wings temporarily covered the sun as they got closer.

As the water flowed, it rose to the edge of the canal. Eve's eyes were drawn to various wild grasses and red flowers that grew along the banks. She marveled at their beauty and reached down to pull up a flower with vibrant red petals. Eve inhaled its sweet fragrance. Abraxas's dark eyes looked at the flower, then at Eve.

"What are you doing here, child?" Abraxas's voice dripped with contempt. Amon's coal-black eyes darted from Eve to Adam and Azrael, who were fast approaching. Abraxas stared at the girl.

"See how these grow?" Eve took a second deep breath of the flower's fragrance and smiled. "Soon they'll cover this expanse as far as the eye can see." She looked up at the fallen angels with a steely determination in her eyes. She knew they sought to intimidate her. She knew they wished to discourage them from their work. She would have none of it.

"This is a fool's errand. The water you bring will be evaporated by the hot sun above you. It will sink into the unquenchable sands of the desert beneath you," Abraxas said.

"You are not safe here," Amon seethed.

Adam and Azrael were now just a few feet away. They approached the two fallen angels.

"You are the one not safe here," Adam said as he approached Amon, putting the glowing blade of his borrowed sword toward the fallen angel's throat.

"Relax, child. The Prince of this Earth desires to have an audience with you. See if there are terms that everyone can agree to. You continue to deny him an audience at your own peril." Amon took a few steps back. He looked at Azrael, then back at Adam. "Try putting a blade to my throat without your friend here." His tar-black eyes focused on Adam. Azrael closely watched Amon's movements.

"We will not negotiate with him. The Earth was given to us by our father. It is ours. He has given us a vision; tell your master we will carry it out," Adam commanded the fallen angels.

Abraxas turned toward Amon.

"Don't worry; they're in our territory," Abraxas said to Amon.

"Perhaps we can help you with your expansion of Eden …" Amon said. He looked toward Adam, then smiled wickedly at Eve.

Azrael spoke, "You heard the son of God. The Earth has been given to them. Leave now or forfeit your lives." As he spoke, he reached for the remaining sword on his back. The length of his blade grew within his hands.

"Very well," Amon stated flatly. He flashed a fleeting smile at Azrael. He then stared at the children of Elohim. "Stay as long as you like …"

Amon beat his wings a handful of times and gained altitude. Abraxas followed. Azrael's eyes were fixated on them as they departed. He looked back at Adam and Eve.

"This will be the last time that you call on me and I will come. Your father has told me that it is time. He has chosen you to face the fallen with his spirit that he has given you," Azrael stated. Adam looked at Azrael and nodded. Adam returned the other blade to him.

"The time has come. I understand. I will need your weapons no longer. Elohim has given us everything for the work that must be done." Adam tapped the Etz Hayim that was slung across his back. He motioned toward Eve. "I have everything," Adam reiterated with steely resolve.

Adam approached and gave Azrael a long, strong hug. He then took a step back.

"Thank you. We are indebted to you for your service, for the years we saw you and for the many years when we were younger and knew nothing of your protective hand." Adam spoke with affection in his voice.

"It will be up to Elohim, but I may return," Azrael replied. Eve thought she saw a small smile on his lips. "Are you okay?" Azrael asked Eve.

"I'm fine. They don't bother me anymore," Eve responded, smiling firmly at Azrael.

"Good. But know, Eve, these creatures take many forms. Sometimes foul. Other times, they may cloak themselves in beauty. Be mindful," Azrael cautioned.

"We will," Eve replied. "Thank you again."

"It's time for us to go," Adam said, looking at Eve. He took out the Etz Hayim as a walking staff.

Adam offered his other hand to Eve. The sun began to set over the desolation as they walked back toward their encampment. Azrael looked on as they left. He knew they needed rest. Hopefully, the night would bring the refreshment both needed for the work ahead.

It had been a long day, Adam thought to himself. They had made progress, but the desert, at times, felt overwhelming. Adam held Eve as she slept under the moonless sky. Without her, none of this would be possible. His heart swelled with love for his wife. He looked up at the stars above. The work was hard. He hoped their progress would please Elohim. His mind began to wander as his body ached from the long day. Adam closed his eyes and felt the world of dreams slowly pull him in.

Adam awakened in his dream and found himself somewhere much farther into the desolation. He made his way through the sun-scorched earth and to the top of a small dune. He wondered where Elohim and Eve were. He wondered if he could even find them in the greatness of the expanse. He walked up to the top of a much larger dune to get a better vantage point. As he made his way to the top, the muscles in his legs burned with exhaustion.

Arriving at the top, Adam looked around. As far as he could see were rolling dunes in every direction. His heart sank. There was no sight of his encampment. This was a desolate place with no trees, no animals, and no life. He could not tell in which direction Eden lay. He longed for her cool waters. He was too far, and he could no longer see her rivers. Adam felt disoriented and unsure of the direction he'd have to go to find his way back home. A hot wind blew. His dry tongue stuck to the roof of his mouth. He thirsted for some spring to quench his thirst and bring vitality back to his body.

While unafraid, he was wary that, in his weakened condition, Amon and Abraxas might find him and take advantage of the situation. He despised the fallen. They always plotted and connived, looking constantly for weaknesses. Their betrayal of his father, the King of Heaven, grated on him. He did not understand why they inhabited this planet nor was he clear on why they seemed to resist him and Eve. What was clear was that they hated the work he and Eve did to cultivate and expand the beauty of Eden. The fallen perceived the desert as their territory.

No springs were here. No clouds graced the skies, but in the distance, a great wind stirred. As Adam peered into the distance, he saw a giant wall of sand race toward him. Was this another spirit sent by the Prince of the Earth? Perhaps it was the Prince himself. Adam wasn't certain.

Behind the wall of sand, the spirit of the desert advanced. Adam felt the weight of despair it brought. The wall of dust fast approached where Adam stood. Its enormous size blocked out the sun. Adam quickly covered his eyes. He felt a brooding rage behind the spirit. It was angry at the work being done. Adam could sense it was resentful. Somehow it knew of Adam's plans and despised him for them. Adam sensed the spirit itself had plans as well.

As the dust and sand blew past him, Adam looked up and saw he was surrounded by a sand so thick he could no longer see more than a few feet in any direction. Adam clenched his fists.

"Enough," Adam commanded.

Dust and sand began to fall from the sky like snow. Adam shielded his eyes again. After a few minutes, the sand had collapsed all around him. Adam could once again see the sky. The volume of sand that had fallen smoothed out the otherwise steep peaks and valleys between dunes. The dunes themselves were now barely visible. It was more as if Adam were standing on a beach without an ocean.

Adam felt an unsettling presence. He glanced to his left. Slowly a pillar of brown sand arose. As it emerged from the ground, it took Adam's exact shape and mirrored his form. To Adam's right, yet another pillar rose, followed by another directly in front of him. The three pillars were made of fine sand. All three of their forms took on Adam's exact resemblance. The sand creatures encircled Adam.

"Son of God ... do you count your days?" The left figure leaned toward Adam. "Why do you toil against me ...?"

"It is my father's will. It is my will." Adam's dry tongue barely formed the words.

"Is it? Are you sure there's not another purpose to all this?" The figure in front of Adam now spoke. The voice emanating from each sounded like his own voice. Adam felt his head begin to hurt.

"Is there not a compromise to be made?" The figure on Adam's right came closer. It touched Adam, softly caressing his cheek with its rough hand. "Are you unaware of the danger?" Its sand-laden eyes were somehow alive. Adam saw a rough reflection of himself in them.

Adam grabbed its hand to remove it from his cheek, but his grip simply went through the sand. Unfazed, the spirit continued to speak.

"Your task was never possible. To complete it is only a dream. An isolated thought in your head—is it not?" It spoke in a soft and almost friendly tone.

Adam could see the contempt in the corners of its smile fade as the creature of sand collapsed in front of him. Its words pierced Adam's heart like a million daggers as its form dissolved within seconds.

"Never possible." The left figure echoed the words. Then with one voice, the two remaining figures spoke. "The ancient tree. Go to it. If you plan to successfully invade our territory, you will need more wisdom than you currently possess. You must go. Don't delay."

"I can't ..." Before Adam's words left his mouth, the two figures moved closer. The center figure thumped his finger on Adam's chest with a surprising amount of force that knocked Adam down. Stunned, Adam looked up at the figures, who moved closer to him. The left figure of dust extended a hand. Cautiously, Adam took the hand and its form kept; with its strength, it helped Adam back on to his feet.

"We've been here since before you were formed. We are in you. You are a part of us …" Even though its mouth moved to articulate the words, it was as if the sound actually came from its chest. "But when you have passed, we will still be here."

"My father knows the path that gives life to the dead. That calls things that are not as though they were. While you see no water and no life, this place SHALL BE a second Eden," Adam replied defiantly.

"You think you're his only son …" the center figure scoffed. "You think he fathered only you … is this what you truly believe?"

The other figure of dust took on more of Adam's form, no longer looking like dust. It changed in front of Adam's eyes and took on his exact resemblance. From the tone of his skin and the clothes Adam wore to the color of Adam's eyes, they now appeared identical. It put its hand on Adam's shoulder, and Adam could feel its warmth. Adam was taken aback as the figure whispered into his ear, "You're no more his son than I am. He knows not your struggle, the dangers you face, nor the answers you seek. He has left you here alone, to do this on your own … what kind of father does that?"

Startled, Adam took a few steps back. The figure mirrored Adam's movements, taking an equal number of steps back. A sadness spread across its face. "It's a lonely path you must walk," it said.

The two figures turned and began walking away. As Adam watched them go, a slight breeze blew. The dust from their figures blew with the wind, and each figure's form vanished into the dry dunes.

Adam woke from his dream. Troubled, he looked up at the dark night sky. He searched the constellations. The shimmering patterns brought him assurance at times. Tonight, they provided him with nothing. The once large fire a few feet away had turned into some faint embers. Turning back to Eve, he saw her eyes frantically move behind her eyelids. Adam knew she too might be encountering at night the spirit they had encountered in the day. Perhaps the same spirit he had just encountered in his dream.

He knew the world of dreams was as real as the physical world. The world of dreams was a gateway where spirits clashed, visions were given, and revelation from the night would pierce the world of the day. The colors, sounds, and seemingly chance encounters within dreams revealed a prophetic dance that Adam was just beginning to learn. He knew that with enough time, the fights, victories, and defeats would eventually play themselves out in the physical world.

Adam heard a distant cry. While faint, it sounded to Adam's ears as if it were another person. Careful not to disturb Eve's sleep, he slowly got up, put an extra cloak around himself, and started walking in the direction of the cries. He glanced around to see where the sound was coming from.

He walked along the canals, reminding himself of the progress they had made. It took a small army of a few hundred trained oxen with specially made plows approximately a month to dredge a mile of canal. The task was hard, but not impossible. They had worked a little more than three years and had extended a system of waterways to increase Eden's borders about forty miles east into the desert. Though vegetation and animal life were sparse, they were no longer nonexistent. He had seen an increasing number of birds. With their help, Adam knew eventually more plants and trees would spread as the birds dropped their seeds from the sky. Each seed had exponential potential to spread its kind through the newly minted stretch of Eden.

The cries turned to a whimpering. Adam walked past some desert brush and saw the form of a girl. Who was this? What was she doing out here by herself? Adam's mind began to race. He saw she had dark black hair that was matted on her back, and it looked wet, as if she had been swimming in the canal. From the back, she appeared to be Eve's height. She sat at the canal's edge with her feet in and her head between her hands, softly crying. As she wept, Adam could see she was naked from the back. With caution, Adam approached. As he got closer, he began to hear her speaking to herself in a barely audible voice.

"Why … why would he let this happen?" she cried as tears streamed down her cheek. "I'm not enough … maybe I was never enough …"

"Hey …" Adam began, and the girl turned her head around. She quickly moved her forearms against her chest to cover herself. She was Eve's age. The desert grew cool at night, and he could see her shivering. Adam took his cloak off and gently offered it to her. "For warmth …"

She tentatively took the tunic and wrapped it around herself; the length covered down to her mid-thighs. Her light complexion seemed to almost glow in the light of the moon.

"Thank you ..." She wiped the remaining tears off her cheeks and stood, turning toward him.

"Who are you?" Adam asked.

"I don't know ..." She let out a soft sob at the answer. She tried to collect herself. She looked around nervously, then back at Adam. They locked eyes. Adam drank in her striking beauty. "I'm Lilly ... that's what he had called me, but I don't know anymore ... where am I?"

Adam looked at Lilly, clearly still shivering under his coat.

"I'm Adam ... these are the arid plains, the very edge of Eden," Adam offered. He had never seen a woman besides Eve. Surprised by her presence, a series of questions dashed through his mind with dizzying speed. Who was this girl? What was she doing out here near the canal? Was she alone? What happened to her clothes? Were there others?

"I must go!" Lilly interrupted his train of thought. "I can't stay here; this is an evil place. If you knew what was good for you, you'd leave too."

"What do you mean? It's okay. You're safe here." Adam looked to reassure the scared girl. He looked up at the starry night sky, then back down, locking eyes with Lilly. She looked anxious, afraid. "This is the edge of Elohim's garden, our garden. I have dominion here. Nothing here will harm you."

Lilly let out a nervous laugh and took a few steps back from Adam.

"You don't know, do you?" She gazed incredulously into Adam's eyes.

Looking into her steady gaze, Adam felt almost intoxicated. Her light brown, almond-shaped eyes had small flecks of silver light. Her features were soft and alluring. Adam saw the top of her chest, uncovered by his cloak, rise with her breath. Adam's spirit was unnerved by her question.

"Safe? We're not safe. We're orphans. Look around you. He has left me. He has left you and Eve by yourselves … he's abandoned you."

Adam's confusion grew. More questions rushed into his mind. It was true that it had been a few years since he and Eve had seen Elohim, but "abandoned"? No—it was impossible. Elohim had simply left them to their work. While he disregarded the notion quickly, the word "orphan" seemed to thrust a thousand daggers into his mind. He knew not the meaning, but it felt ominous, as if the protection of Elohim was more illusory than real.

Her presence caused a flood of impulses. For the first time in his life, he felt as if he lacked the ability to decide. Abandoned? Not safe? He felt rage enough to rebuke her and the inference that his father couldn't be trusted. Yet she seemed nervous and afraid, so he also desired to comfort her and calm her fears. He wished to share with her that Elohim would never abandon her. Adam felt a strange attraction and yet he also wanted to run from her presence too. He felt a danger around her but could not describe why, and he knew not how to vanquish it.

Lilly saw Adam's confusion. She discerned his attraction and walked toward him slowly. As she approached, Adam felt as if his feet and mind were quickly sinking into quicksand. His father loved him and would never abandon him. None of what she shared could be true, he looked to reassure himself.

She gazed into his frozen eyes, and a smile dashed across her face as she leaned in.

"Loved you?" Lilly shook her head in dismay. It was as if she could read his thoughts. "He said the same to me once …" she shared, pity ringing in her voice. "I must go."

"Go where?" Adam found himself reaching out and grabbing her hand.

"Away from here …" Lilly responded. "To the only place that is safe."

She squeezed his hand inside of hers before letting him go. A soft light of empathy passed through her eyes as she looked at Adam before turning and walking away.

Adam stood still as Lilly headed back in the direction of Eden. As she left, the stars above seemed to grow brighter. Though his mind buzzed with questions, the heaviness he had felt seemed to lift off his shoulders. He turned around and started heading back toward the encampment.

With each step he took back toward Eve, a familiar peace seemed to displace the burden of the interaction. Perhaps Lilly was lost; maybe she was just confused. Perhaps it was something more: maybe she was a danger. He decided he would do the only thing that seemed to make any sense. If there was a genuine threat, he would seek Elohim's strength to protect Eve. He needed the wisdom of his father now more than ever.

Lilly's walk turned into a run. She wanted to have Adam see the direction she was going. Once she was out of sight, she increased her pace toward Eden. Her feet hit the soil of the arid plains with an abnormally fast speed. As Lilly ran, she saw in her peripheral vision tens, then hundreds of holes opening in the ground all around her, following the wake of her steps. Hundreds, then thousands of snakes emerged from the holes and began to chase her.

Her heart beat rapidly as she ran toward Eden. The snakes seemed unnaturally fast. Magnetized by her being, they quickly caught up to her. They began to wrap themselves around her ankles and up her calves. As she ran, more began to inch higher and higher, wrapping themselves around her thighs, torso, chest, and neck. She fast approached a final canal between the dense beauty of Eden and the arid plains behind her. Leaping over the canal, she shapeshifted midair into the form of a panther and charged into the darkness.

As Adam approached the encampment, he saw Eve was up from her dreams and was preparing for the day. He felt dazed, shocked, and uncertain about what he had witnessed or how to share what he had seen with Eve. The dawn was upon them, and the light from the sun began to cast its gentle rays upon the landscape all around.

Adam passed by dozens of oxen. An ox bellowed as Adam walked by. Adam welcomed anything that would help distract him from his interaction with Lilly. He stopped and caressed its cheek with his hand and kissed the top of its head.

He loved these animals. When Elohim had introduced

him to them, he knew they were made for work, but at the time he had named them, he did not know the type of work. The canals would have been impossible without their strength. He moved past the animals and walked toward Eve.

"Good morning, love!" Eve said as Adam approached her. "Beautiful morning, isn't it?"

Adam gazed into Eve's sparkling eyes. They were flooded with love for him. He felt an unshakeable peace with her.

"It always is." He smiled. She was stunningly beautiful. Whenever he looked at her, it was always hard for him to look away.

"Where were you?" she asked. Adam felt a tight pain in his chest. His mind raced, then wandered. Not knowing what to say, he took in a deep breath. Eve looked into Adam's eyes and could see he was deeply troubled. "Are you okay?" Eve finally asked.

"I saw someone." Adam motioned in the direction of the bend in the canal. Eve paused from her work.

"Saw someone—what do you mean?"

"I don't know. She was not from here. I have never seen her before."

"She?"

"Yes, she said her name was Lilly. She was distraught, lost ... confused. She said Elohim had abandoned her."

"She's a daughter?" Eve asked, perplexed.

"I'm not sure. She was disoriented, as if she didn't know where she was," Adam said. Suddenly, his mind began to make some connections between events he had previously thought were unrelated. "Last night, I dreamt again about the spirit of the desert. He took on my form. He touched my hand. He said this task was too great for you and me. I think it's time to return to Eden and find Elohim. It's been too long since we've seen him, and I have many questions. We need to ask him about her."

Eve searched Adam's eyes. Adam walked toward her and softly kissed her on the lips. Looking at her, he felt love flow through his being toward his wife.

"What do you make of her?" Eve asked.

"She was beautiful like you. But something was off. She said this was a dangerous place," Adam responded.

"Was she speaking about the fallen? Did they hurt her?" Eve asked.

Adam searched his memory. He tried to recollect if he had seen any wounds on Lilly.

"She looked unharmed," Adam said with a deep sense of relief. "I gave her one of my cloaks."

Eve paused and gave thought to Adam's encounter.

"Everything will be okay. The purpose behind this will not remain hidden," Eve said. "Come, let's go back into Eden, and we'll find Elohim. He'll know who she is and how to help her. I'm sure of it."

FORKED TONGUES

XIV

ADAM WALKED WITH THE ETZ HAYIM FIRMLY IN his hand. He and Eve went past the canals and near the source rivers. As they approached the jungle, they began to see hundreds of holes in the ground. Littered across the ground were thousands of dried snakeskins.

Adam picked one up and held it up toward the sky. The sun's light streamed through it, illuminating all its detail. It glimmered in the sunlight, and he slowly handed it to Eve. She examined it closely and looked around.

A gust of breeze from the heart of Eden blew toward the desert. Eve released the snakeskin, and it floated away in the wind.

"I've never seen so many," Eve stated. Adam watched the snakeskin as it flew in the air and shrugged his shoulders.

"The hawks take care of them so the oxen are unharmed." Adam responded. He looked down at the tracks that seemed to indicate the snakes had traveled in the direction of Eden.

"I've never seen this many either ... this would be too many for the hawks."

Adam started walking again, and Eve followed him deeper into the jungle.

"Look ..." Eve stopped. She knelt down and pointed to the tracks of what appeared to be a large cat of some sort. "Panther tracks." Eve looked up at Adam. The air was still as Eve tuned her ear to distant noises in the jungle. Adam gripped the Etz Hayim tighter.

"Stay close," Adam cautioned.

They hiked up a plateau. In the distance, about a day's hike away, was the heart of Eden. The sun began to set. They looked at the various rivers that flowed from the heart of Eden to the south, north, and toward them in the east. The water this time of day looked like a translucent turquoise that shimmered and almost appeared to glow. It was as if the rivers were made of both water and light. Certain sections of the rivers weaved gently through Eden. Other sections contained intervals of intense white-water rapids.

"We should set up camp soon. Before the sun falls," Adam said. Eve nodded in agreement. "If you want to pitch the tent, I'll collect some wood for a fire."

Adam placed the Etz Hayim next to Eve, then headed down the plateau in search of fallen branches. After a few minutes, he heard a sound and began to follow it. Behind some trees, he saw Lilly sitting down in front of a small fire. She wore his cloak. In her hand was a stick. At the other end of it was a large frog she had speared. The frog's eyes were open but glazed over as it cooked above the fire.

"... Almost done," Lilly said.

Adam stepped closer. Underfoot, a twig snapped.

"Who's there?!" Lilly sprang to her feet and grabbed a larger stick nearby that she held up as if it were a weapon.

"It's me!" Adam whispered.

"Adam? What are you doing here!?" Lilly asked, startled.

"Eve and I are heading back to the heart of Eden. We've set up camp on the plateau up there." Adam pointed in the direction of their encampment. "I was collecting some wood for our fire, and I heard you."

Lilly took a few steps back from Adam.

"It's okay, Lilly; I'm not going to hurt you," Adam said as he looked into the eyes of the frightened girl.

"What do you want from me?" Lilly asked.

"I want nothing. I came here looking for wood. Eve and I are going to find our father," Adam stated. "You don't have to be alone. If you'd like, you can join Eve and me. We can find Elohim together." Adam slowly put out his hand.

Lust within Lilly displaced the fear as she took in the sight of Adam. She saw the strength in his chest and arms. She craved his flesh. Adam saw the change in her eyes but didn't understand the meaning.

"I am heading the same way, but you will not find Elohim," Lilly remarked.

"Why wouldn't we? We always do. Come with me. I will introduce you to Eve. I've already told her about how we met. Don't worry. We'll find him together; you'll see," Adam said.

Adam walked back with Lilly and an armful of dried branches. Eve had prepared their tent and collected some fruits and nuts. Eve looked up and saw Adam with Lilly. As she looked at Lilly, she saw her beautiful brown eyes and lightly tanned skin. She saw Adam's cloak draped over her shoulders, covering her long, shapely legs to about mid-thigh. Lilly was stunning in her beauty. Eve felt a little lightheaded.

"Is this her?" Eve asked Adam.

"Yes, this is the girl I spoke with you about," Adam responded. "Eve, meet our new friend Lilly."

Lilly bowed slightly. Eve smiled softly.

"I have many questions," Eve said. Eve felt a rush of emotions and impulsively reached out to Lilly and gave her a hug. As she hugged Lilly, she thought how Lilly's skin seemed unusually cool. Stepping back, she searched Lilly's eyes.

"I know this must be confusing for you, Eve. Elohim did not speak of me or the others. I'm not sure what answers I can give you," Lilly responded, then looked back at Adam. "I can only share what I know."

"It's been a long day. Let's eat first," Adam suggested.

Adam prepared the fire as Eve handed some nuts and berries to Lilly. The three of them sat around the fire. The flames grew as darkness fell over Eden. A silence hung in the air as all three ate quietly.

"It's a cool night. I'm going to gather a bit more wood. I'll be back shortly," Adam said. He looked at Eve, and she nodded. Adam got up and started looking around nearby for more firewood.

"What are you doing out here?" Eve asked. Lilly stared at the fire. Lilly waited until Adam was out of earshot.

"If I share with you, you must not tell Adam. I can see you two are in love. I do not want to make trouble," Lilly said.

Eve slowly nodded. "What are you speaking of?"

Lilly gazed into the fire. Eve's heart began to long for Lilly's next words. As time passed Eve saw shadows multiply and encircle her and Lilly. Maybe her eyes were only playing tricks she thought to herself.

"Alatar was his name. He was my companion." Lilly glanced over at Eve. "He was my own Adam ... my best friend. But he was taken from me." Lilly's words turned like gravel in Eve's stomach. "Elohim had told us we should make our home in the desert. We were to turn it into the garden we had both come to love."

"He said to make your home in the desert too?" Eve asked curiously. Lilly nodded. "What happened?"

"We were asleep. One of the shadow creatures took him while we dreamt. I awoke ... he was gone. I looked everywhere. I only saw tracks from a panther. I've not seen him since." A tear streamed down Lilly's cheek. She turned toward Eve. Eve's heart sank. She searched Lilly's eyes. "He is lost and therefore I am lost ..." Lilly shared softly. She wiped the tear quickly from her face before returning her gaze to the fire.

"I'm sorry, Lilly ..." Eve offered. "We'll go to Elohim. We'll find him." Lilly shook her head. Her face seemed to be trying to hide a strange combination of grief and contempt Eve had never seen. It was as if Eve's words fell like a bird from the sky. A few moments passed, and finally Lilly looked up from the fire.

"You know, Eve ... there is no difference," Lilly whispered.

"No difference ...?"

"Yes, no difference between him and the fallen. There's no difference between Elohim and the shadow creatures. You may not know this now, but he is everywhere, in everything. He is also the shadow inside those creatures." Her words were cold and slow. The heat of the crackling fire didn't seem to reach Eve.

"The shadow?" Eve asked.

"Don't you understand yet?" Lilly responded slowly. The fire's reflection in Lilly's eyes seemed to dance. "Elohim ... he is also the shadow. They are one and the same. Was it not he who created the panther? He cloaks our world in his shadow ... it envelops us, entraps us. He created all the creatures. Including the ones who take. So how would he not be the one who also took Alatar from me?" Lilly's question wrapped around Eve's heart like a cold, wet blanket.

"No ... no ... it can't be." Eve's mind felt like it was detached from all reason, from all love, from all connection. Her focus began to travel and search her memories. "That can't be so. I don't believe you."

"I don't need you to." Lilly looked vacantly into the fire. "Just protect yourself." Lilly paused before looking up at Eve. "There's another side to Elohim. A side that is very dark. It is that side of him that I am lost in."

"Elohim is nothing like you speak of. We will find Alatar. I promise you," Eve replied firmly.

"You have made a promise you can't possibly keep," Lilly answered. "And Elohim ... well ... He's not who you think he is. We all are lost in the light that we cannot see."

Adam stepped into the encampment carrying a bundle of wood in both arms. He put it down next to Eve and sat down beside her. He put some fresh wood into the fire, and it began to roar once again. The fire crackled, and the stars above shone brightly.

Adam kissed Eve on the cheek. He could tell something had shifted inside her.

"Everything okay?" Adam asked. Eve nodded. "It's been a long day. Let's get some rest. There will be plenty of time for us to talk tomorrow," Adam said. He looked at the tent Eve had set up. "I'll prepare another tent for Lilly."

"It's a cool night," Eve interjected. She looked at Lilly, then at Adam. "Can she join us? She shouldn't be alone."

"It is cold tonight. Would you want to join us?" Adam asked.

Lilly's brown eyes seemed to twinkle in the light of the fire as she looked at Eve, then at Adam, and slowly nodded.

Adam noticed her soft features; his eyes took in her form, and he felt an intrigue around this mysterious girl. He wondered what she and Eve had spoken about. When he and Eve were alone the next day, he would ask.

Adam and Eve walked into their tent. Lilly followed.

THE SUN THAT DOESN'T RISE

XV

"'Which of the trees of Eden can be compared with you in splendor and majesty? Yet you, too, will be brought down with the trees of Eden to the earth below.'"—Ezekiel 31:18 (NIV)

EARLY THE NEXT DAY, THE MORNING SUN POURED its rays into the deep jungle. Adam woke. In his arms, he held Eve. His mind was troubled. He sensed deep questions stirring in Eve's heart as she slept. Perhaps she was meeting with Elohim in her dreams as she had done many times before. A variety of birds began to chirp. The jungle started coming alive as the creatures within Eden began to wake. The sweet aroma of various flowers wafted through the air.

An arm was draped around Adam's chest. He slowly turned his head and saw Lilly sleeping. Her silky black hair stood in contrast to her lightly tanned skin. Her loose-fitting clothes revealed the swelling of her breasts as she breathed.

Adam's heart beat faster at the unusual sight of another woman so close to him.

"My love," Eve whispered. "It's time. Let's go." Adam turned over to see Eve facing him. "This girl needs help. We need to find Elohim."

"I know, my love," Adam whispered back. He got up and extended his hand toward Eve. Lilly woke up slowly, stretched, and looked at both of them standing.

"Another day in paradise," Lilly glibly offered. The corners of her mouth turned into a soft smile as she stood. Eve smiled back reassuringly.

"Let's go." Adam picked up the Etz Hayim and started heading west on the path toward the garden of Eden. Lilly followed a few dozen feet behind, and Eve waited for her.

"I know you're looking for Elohim. But you won't find him," Lilly whispered to Eve.

"Don't say that. We always find him. Trust me." Eve looked over at Lilly. She had a look in her eyes that left Eve feeling unsettled.

Adam began to sprint. Eve and Lilly started to run to keep pace. They traveled up and down hills, went between trees, and leapt off large boulders. Enormous gorillas flanked them beyond their line of sight, closely following the three as they made progress toward the center of the garden.

Adam approached a fast-moving river. He sprinted over a fallen, moss-covered tree, which provided a makeshift bridge across the water. As Eve ran across, her foot slipped. Eve screamed in panic as she fell into the cold waters. Adam turned around and saw Eve being taken by the current down the river. Lilly jumped into the water after Eve. Adam dove in after them.

The white water of the river was powerful. The current pulled Eve under. Popping above the surface, she gasped for breath and saw Lilly swimming closer; Adam was far behind. Eve grabbed a breath before another strong rapid pulled her underneath. Adam swam as quickly as he could toward her, but the waters were too fast.

Eve gasped for air, but instead of oxygen, she took in a mouthful of icy water. Eve started to panic as her lungs began to cry out for oxygen and fear gripped her chest. She entered into a blackness beyond the cool waters. Eve heard nothing; she saw nothing. Gradually, she stopped struggling. Her limp body drifted with the current before a cool hand grabbed Eve's upper arm and dragged her to shore.

"Eve!? You okay?!" Lilly had pulled Eve to the riverbank. Adam quickly swam and pulled himself to the shore. "Can you hear me?!" Lilly whispered into Eve's ear. Adam scrambled to Eve and lifted her head. Fear and confusion filled his eyes.

"EVE! Please!" Adam put his mouth to Eve's and pushed air into her lungs. Silence. "Please … Eve …" Adam breathed heavily; he pushed air again into her lungs. "I need you … I need you to come back to me …"

Lilly placed her hand on Adam's forearm and looked him in the eyes. "It's okay … Adam … maybe she's gone … she fell … it's not your fault …"

"NO!" Adam shouted. "DO NOT SPEAK. She is NOT GONE." Adam looked back down at Eve. "My love … come back to me; I don't care where you are … I will find you … I will always find you …" Adam lowered his lips toward Eve's and pushed another breath into her lungs. Adam caressed Eve's cheek; leaning down again, he kissed her forehead. Adam's heart sank as he held his wife. The world went quiet. The sound of birds and the river faded.

Suddenly, Eve coughed and river water came streaming out of her mouth. She opened her eyes and saw Adam above her. "You're okay … you're here. It's okay …"

Eve smiled weakly.

"I went somewhere. I don't know where it was …" Eve responded as she slowly took in her surroundings.

"Shhh … it's okay … you're here now …" Adam lovingly touched Eve's cheek and kissed her forehead again. "I would have found you. No matter where you went, I would have found you." Relief spread across his face as he looked into Eve's eyes. "Next time, don't go swimming without me …"

"I won't …" Eve cracked a smile.

Adam, Eve, and Lilly traveled for a few more hours until the sun began to hide itself behind the last range of mountains between them and the garden.

"Let's set up camp," Adam said. Looking back, he saw Lilly. There was a sadness in her eyes. He remembered his unkind words.

"I'm sorry, Lilly … I didn't mean to shout at you," Adam said softly. "I thought I had lost her."

"It's okay. I'm not upset." Lilly's bright eyes dampened. "I know how you felt." Lilly looked around. "I'll find some wood for our fire. We'll rest for the night, and tomorrow we'll find Elohim." Lilly offered a reassuring smile.

Eve looked inquisitively at Lilly.

"You want to find him as well …?" Eve softly asked.

Lilly nodded. "Yes … perhaps Elohim will help me find Alatar in the same way he helped Adam find you today."

"Alatar?" Adam asked. He looked at Lilly, then at Eve curiously.

"Yes. Someone I have lost," Lilly responded quietly. "I'll tell you more, but first let me find some firewood for the evening before it gets too cold."

Eve looked at Lilly before watching Adam begin the preparation for the night that was to come. A soft wind blew as Lilly walked away to find wood.

As Lilly left Adam and Eve to set up camp, she could smell the scent of the creatures from heaven. She had been aware of their presence from the moment she had lured Elohim's son and daughter closer to the forbidden tree and away from their task in the desert. As she walked, she could sense them close in on her. She looked behind her. She was out of sight and earshot of Adam and Eve.

"I know you're here." Lilly laughed out loud. "Show yourselves!"

She looked all around. Her dark eyes peered into the brush.

"You think I'm afraid of you?" Lilly began to laugh to herself, and she continued to walk. She approached a meadow with a giant tree in the center of it. She walked around the tree and softly traced the fingers on her right hand around the trunk. The sun was setting, and Lilly grew impatient. From the tips of her fingers, five snakes grew. They traveled from her fingertips and slowly encircled the tree. She paused her walk around it after the snakes had fully surrounded the tree.

"I know you're here," Lilly seemingly whispered to the center of the trunk. "You were planted in his garden, like an oak of righteousness," she said lightly, as if quoting a lyric.

From the jungle, a dozen gorillas appeared and formed a circle around the tree. Lilly looked at them with contempt. The once small snakes from her fingers had grown into pythons and were seemingly choking and squeezing the trunk with an unnatural strength.

From the center of the tree, the groaning of cracking timber was heard. Suddenly, the trunk got larger and the snakes broke like threads of rotten rope. Lilly stepped back and smiled. From the center of the tree, Menakiel stood. Slowly, the remains of the snakes started to slither and make their way back to Lilly.

"You don't hide yourself well," Lilly remarked, amused.

Menakiel's eyes burned with a flame that made Lilly step back.

"True power is not found in your form. It is found here," Lilly mocked and pointed to the side of her head. "I took a third of your kind. You really think I can't take two humans?"

Her bright eyes disappeared into pools of black ink. "His son and daughter mean everything to him, don't they?"

"They do." Menakiel's deep voice reverberated through Lilly's chest.

"Maybe ..." Lilly smirked. "But then why would he let me befriend them? Odd, is it not?"

"His ways are not your ways," Menakiel responded. His eyes closely followed the movements of the dark creature in front of him. He was not fooled by the disguise.

"This is my world. His invasion was doomed from the start. It won't work. They shouldn't be here. Neither should you."

"You have one more moon. That is it. You must make your move and do so quickly. Your time ends soon." Menakiel spoke with a focused intensity. "Heaven's armies won't stand by for any longer."

Lilly put her palms up, and the snakes slithered into her fingertips.

"I won't need any longer." Lilly grimaced as the shrunken pythons entered her. She clenched both her fists. Gradually, the pools of black in her eyes faded and their normal coloring resurfaced.

"Where do you think she is?" Adam asked. Eve shook her head. The night had become unnaturally cold for the season, and Adam had not been able to wait longer. In Lilly's absence, Adam had collected wood and started a fire.

"What if we were to lose each other?" Eve's words unexpectedly left her mouth.

"Why would you say that?" Adam responded. "Because of Alatar and Lilly?"

"She can't find him. She said he was taken in the desert by the shadow creatures," Eve quietly responded.

Adam's heart filled with anxiety, and he quickly glanced back at the fire. "I don't know. I can't think about that. I don't want to."

"She said Elohim had told them to also go into the desert. Elohim told them he wanted them to help it look like the garden. Now she can't find him ... she can't seem to find herself either. She seems afraid ... hopeless." Eve gazed into the fire.

"No, she's not. There's a reason she chose to go with us back to the garden." As Adam spoke, Lilly appeared from behind some trees. She had overheard their conversation and saw the small fire they had started. Adam noticed she had brought back no wood. Lilly slowly sat down across from them. The jungle air seemed to grow even colder. Without saying a word, Lilly gazed into the fire.

"What reason would that be?" Lilly finally spoke. The fire crackled in the background as Lilly looked into Eve's eyes. She turned and stared into Adam's eyes. "Why do you think I've chosen to head with you to the heart of Eden?"

"It's not to find Elohim ... is it?" Adam inquired.

"No, it never was," Lilly responded flatly.

"Then why ...?" Eve spoke up.

"The tree of the knowledge of good and evil. I want its

fruit." Lilly paused. "I need what it possesses." There was a coldness to her voice when she spoke.

"Why?" Eve asked.

"With it, I'll be able to find Alatar. I won't need Elohim. Without it, I don't believe I'll ever find him," Lilly responded.

"You don't understand, Lilly. Elohim told us we could eat from any seed-bearing tree, but that was the one tree we weren't to eat from," Eve explained. She looked at Adam. Adam sat in silence, listening. Eve looked back at Lilly. "We could do no such thing."

"And why not?" Lilly asked, looking right at Eve.

"Elohim told us not to eat from it or touch it; if we did, we would surely die," Eve said, an intense concern filling her eyes as she recollected her father's command.

Lilly took a deep breath in and sighed.

"You really believe that? You can eat from any tree ... all of Eden's fruit is yours, but he denies you that one? Why would he withhold that from you? What if you ate it and you didn't die? What if Elohim knows that when you eat it, your eyes will open?"

"What do you mean?" Adam questioned.

"Does the desert look like the garden?" Lilly asked.

"Not yet ..." Adam responded.

"What if it opened your eyes ... what if you were like your creator?" Lilly kept eye contact with Adam.

"Like Elohim himself?" Adam asked.

"Yes! Like the Creator ..." Lilly responded excitely. "What if your eyes were opened and you knew light from dark? What if the wisdom required to turn the desert into another garden of Eden was found within it?" Lilly was full of enthusiasm. "Why does he force you to toil with your hands? Why does he keep secrets from you? What if locked inside of you was a greater power ... and the fruit is the key to unlocking it ...? What if instead of doing hard work, you could speak things into existence the same way he does ... but instead ... he's left you to toil with your two hands ...?" Lilly's voice seemed to fade at the last few words.

Adam peered into Lilly's excited eyes and felt a foreign energy. He was strangely attracted to her, but he didn't know why. He wanted her to tell him more but was afraid that Eve would sense his attraction. He knew he wouldn't know how to explain it to her. What if he wasn't enough for Eve, what if Elohim wasn't enough for him ... what if their work in the desert was in vain? As his mind began to entertain Lilly's questions, his emotions plunged into a darkness he didn't understand how he arrived at or how to get out of.

"Think about it ..." Lilly finally said. "What if you were meant to change the desert into the garden with the knowledge of the dark and the light?" Her question hung in the air.

"And you think it will also help you find Alatar?" Eve asked. "Is this true?"

Lilly nodded. Eve took in a deep breath and looked at the stars above. As she gazed into the night sky, it reminded her of times when she would walk with Elohim. At times, they'd talk about the stars above, their names, and what they meant for her future. At other times, she and Elohim would simply walk together in silence, hold hands, and simply enjoy each other's company. She felt a longing in her heart for those times.

She felt disconnected from Adam. She missed her father. A cool wind blew, and her heart pounded inside her chest. Eve felt a danger descend, and the darkness of the jungle seemed to surround her. All she wanted to do was sleep. She wanted to escape into her dreams.

Early the next morning, Adam opened his eyes and looked toward the east. He saw a light begin to filter through the jungle. The light was emanating from the west, where the sun had previously set. Noticing the abnormality, Adam got up. He gazed toward the west as his eyes looked to follow the normal soft yellows and whites that typically shone from the rising sun. This time, the sun was nowhere to be seen, but there was a soft blue and white light rising from the heart of Eden.

"Eve! Quick, get up!" Adam said. Eve rose from her sleep.

"What is it?" Eve asked.

"The sun, from the east ... it doesn't rise. And look ..." Adam's voice dropped off. "See ..."

Eve followed Adam's gaze as they saw the tree of the light and the dark, the tree their father called the tree of the knowledge of good and evil. Normally, it would have been hidden by a final hill from where they had set up their encampment. Now it towered as the largest and tallest tree in Eden. "How could it have grown so fast …?"

"I don't know," Eve responded with surprise in her eyes. They saw shafts of light flicker in every direction from the trunk, branches, leaves, and fruit. The tree itself seemed to pulse with a soft blue and white light.

From behind them, Lilly got up. A huge smile came across her face as the subtle blue light seemed to dance within her eyes. She walked in between Adam and Eve. She put her hand on Adam's cheek and looked into his eyes. Slowly, she leaned forward and kissed his lips. Adam didn't push back. He sensed all the resistance fade as he felt her soft, warm lips on his. His mind felt intoxicated, and in a near trance-like state, he softly returned Lilly's kiss.

"It's time," Lilly whispered into his ear. She turned to Eve. Eve's eyes showed heartbreak at Adam's betrayal. And in a flash, fear came into them. "It's okay, Eve. I'm here for you as well." Lilly caressed Eve's cheek with one hand. With the other, she took Eve's hand and kissed it softly. Eve's blue eyes locked with Lilly's brown eyes. "When you're ready, come …" Lilly whispered softly.

Lilly gently let go of Eve's hand and began to walk in the direction of the now towering tree of light and dark, the tree Elohim called forbidden. Without looking back, Lilly moved past thick trees and massive rocks and walked over the last hill separating her from the tree. The tree had what she desired most.

Adam took the first steps and then looked back, giving Eve his hand. Eve paused for a few seconds but finally took it. Together they walked toward the tree of the light and the dark, of good and evil.

"It's okay," Lilly said as she held the forbidden fruit in her hands. She brought it up to her nose and inhaled deeply. Lilly looked up and met Eve's eyes; slowly, she handed her the forbidden fruit. "Your eyes will be opened. You will understand everything. You will never lose Adam the way I lost Alatar. You will be protected. You will be like Elohim, the Creator, knowing good from evil."

Eve's heart beat fast within her chest. The words of Lilly cut into her like a knife as questions flooded her mind. You will be like Elohim: Eve thought about Lilly's words. Wasn't Elohim her father? How could she become even more like him? But what if this could help her and Adam with their quest to transform the desert? Maybe they couldn't do it on their own? Perhaps they needed these new eyes to see?

Why was Eden surrounded by a jungle and the jungle surrounded by this barren and harsh world? Why had Elohim created such harsh conditions in all but the garden? Who was Lilly really and why was she here? Why did she kiss Adam? Why did Adam kiss her? Maybe she was just trying to help. Why did she take comfort in Lilly's kiss? She was here, why wasn't Elohim? Maybe Elohim didn't fully understand everything she and Adam faced in the desert. She didn't want to lose Adam, not to the fallen creatures, not to Lilly. Doubt flooded Eve's heart.

"Here …" Lilly interrupted Eve's train of thought. Lilly took the fruit from Eve's hands and quickly took a bite. Lilly's eyes seemed to sparkle with the same light that now emanated from the tree. As she swallowed, she looked directly into Eve's eyes. "See … look …" Lilly looked down at her feet, chest, and arms. Lilly was beautiful, and her body seemed to glow with a seductive allure. Lilly looked back at Eve. "I told you … You will not die. It's okay … take it." Lilly extended her hand and gave Eve the fruit.

Eve looked at the piece of fruit in her palm. The sun had still not risen. The sky seemed to somehow have grown only darker. Even the light from the stars was choked out by the strange and ever-growing darkness. The only source of light was the tree of knowledge of good and evil. The stars were now completely hidden from view.

Eve saw Adam glance at Lilly and then at the fruit in her hands. The dark purple fruit with the bite that Lilly had taken seemed to be pulsating with light. Blue light from the fruit seemed to dance on Eve's face. As her hand held the fruit from the forbidden tree, it felt both as light as a feather and as if it carried the weight of the world.

"I don't know …" Eve quietly said. As she continued to look at it, she felt hunger stir inside of her. The fruit was beautiful and pleasing to her eye. She wanted to make the desert beautiful, and she didn't want to lose Adam. Fear and dark thoughts passed through her mind. She raised the fruit to her lips and took a bite. As she chewed on it, it felt soft and sweet. Its substance slowly glided down her throat as she held it out to Adam. Eve looked into her husband's eyes.

"I'm okay, my love … try it …" Eve whispered. Adam hastily grabbed it. He saw the two large bites Lilly and Eve had taken. An unexamined desire became anchored in his heart … he desired to be one with both of them. Elohim's words from when he was a boy echoed in his consciousness. Adam remembered the eyes of his father as he had spoken instruction to him. He understood he was not to eat from this tree.

But another voice streamed thoughts into Adam's mind. What if those words were meant for a boy and not a man? What if the command his father had given him to extend the garden was too much for him to accomplish on his own? What if the strength this fruit would provide was required to finish his task and please his father? What if he wasn't able to safely partake as a boy, but as a man, the fruit from this tree was not only desired, but it was also needed?

All progress they had made in expanding Eden into the desert faded from Adam's mind; he thought only of the barren ground and the softness of Lilly's kiss. Why was there ground to take in the first place? Why could they not just speak water to flow into existence the way their father did? They had struggled for so long with the desert.

He knew what he wanted. He knew what he must have. The memories of his father faded from his mind, and soon Adam chose to not hear nor recollect the words of Elohim. He stared hard at the fruit from the forbidden tree. He felt Lilly's hand massaging his chest as she nodded approvingly. Adam grew restless. He brought it up to his lips. With a single act of betrayal, he forfeited his dominion of Earth and his very life to the way of the serpent.

BLACK POOLS

XVI

ADAM FELT A SENSE OF VERTIGO AS IF HE WERE falling. To the east, he witnessed the first rays of sun cascade into the garden. As the light from the sun hit the tree of the knowledge of good and evil, all the fruit on its branches dried up and withered. Adam looked up at its leaves. At the intensity of the sun's light, they too wilted, turning from green and traveling through a spectrum of color and ultimately turning black right before him. The branches and trunk seemed to age years in mere moments. It was as if he and Eve had absorbed the life force from the tree.

Adam looked down at his chest, arms, and hands. His veins filled with what looked like a black ink. As his heart beat, the blackness was pumped throughout his body. Adam's skin become almost translucent. He peered down and saw the heart within his chest turn a dark red before it turned black. An explosive pain ruptured in his heart; he clenched his chest in agony. His body began to tremble.

Though his feet were firmly planted, it felt as if he was descending, as if there was nothing beneath him. Adam looked around and saw Eve. Her eyes were wide and filled with terror as she witnessed the black spiderweb of veins that seemed to be taking over Adam's body and protruding from his skin. A single dark vein from above her breast ran up her neck and to her ear. It trailed and spiderwebbed across her face. Fear filled her eyes as it became apparent that what she saw in Adam was also happening to her.

Time seemed to slow down. As if her spirit were stolen from her body, Adam witnessed the color in Eve's eyes turn from blue to gray as she slowly fell to the ground. Adam's muscles ached, and it was hard to breathe. Before his vision faded, he saw Lilly's bright brown eyes turn into black pools as she smiled above him. Adam collapsed into the dust of the earth.

ELOHIM SPEAKS

Eden was never a perfect place. Its purpose was more meaningful. My promise was a world where I could walk with my son Adam and my daughter Eve. It was a world in which I freely chose them, and they could freely choose me.

There's no love without choice, no resurrection without death, no redemption without a fall. There's no true understanding of who I am without knowledge of what I would do next. While my heart ached for the choice they made, I knew what they would do that day. I was not surprised. I too had made a choice, a decision made long before I had ever breathed life into my children, looked into their eyes, softly kissed their foreheads, or wrapped my arms around them.

When my first son, Adam, knowingly followed the way of the serpent, my heart broke. Every night, from that day on, I dreamt of reunion. They had no idea the lengths I would go to give them yet another choice. They had no idea I would upend time and space. I would march through hell itself. I would break down gates of bronze and cut through bars of iron. Nothing would keep me from them. My heart was always to provide a path back to Eden, a path where one day we could find each other and once again walk together in the cool of the day.

ACT THREE

THE NIGHTMARE BEGINS

WHERE ARE YOU?

XVII

3976 B.C. ~ 3 Hours Later

ADAM SLOWLY ROSE. HIS CHEST ACHED WITH A crushing pain. Thoughts of escaping his body darted through his mind as the severity of the pain made him wish for death. Blood rushed down as he stood, leaving him feeling lightheaded and dizzy. Adam looked frantically around and saw Eve. Tiny streams of dark red blood flowed from a nostril and her mouth. It pooled beneath her cheek as she lay on the ground.

Glancing behind him, Adam saw the sun setting. Eden was about to descend into darkness. Eyes of various creatures peered through the deep jungle, watching. Adam felt vulnerable and exposed as if some of the animals were stalking him. He thought of some of the larger, more powerful animals, and fear flooded Adam's being at the thought of being hunted. He knew not from where they came, but violent visions overtook Adam's imagination. He saw terrible images where he was chased, overrun, and torn apart by the beasts in the jungle. Terrified, Adam's heart longed for Elohim. If he could find him, he'd run into the protective arms of his father.

A hawk circled the sky above. Adam took a deep breath in. As he released it, he sent his spirit into the creature to assess the danger and find Elohim. Adam looked down and saw through the eyes of the creature. He pushed further and directed its flight. Adam felt desperation. He knew they were in danger. He flew high above the canopy in search of Elohim. He needed his father now more than ever.

The hawk continued to fly. Adam's vision through the bird narrowed. He saw Elohim roughly a quarter of a mile north of where he was. As the hawk drew closer, Adam saw Elohim beneath a solitary tree, clutching his chest. Adam directed the hawk's flight down so he could get a closer look. He maneuvered the large bird to land on a branch a few feet above Elohim. He wanted Elohim to look up and see him. Another part of Adam wished he hadn't spotted his father.

Fear gripped Adam's heart. He remembered he had violated his father's command. Adam looked down at his father. Elohim wept. Adam could feel both pain and shame overtake his heart as he witnessed his father's body tremble. Time seemed to fade. Adam wished he could escape his own skin and rewind time. It felt as if he was drowning underneath a newfound sense of dread and fear that seemed to cascade through his body. Once again, it became hard for Adam to breathe. Elohim looked up where the hawk was perched. As soon as Elohim looked into the hawk's eyes, Adam's vision suddenly went black.

Adam breathed in deep, and he saw once again through his own eyes. He looked down and saw Eve. The droplet of blood flowed down her chin and onto her neck. Adam felt helpless. He wanted to run but didn't know where to go. As a virulent toxin from the forbidden fruit pumped through his heart, he saw his hands begin to shake uncontrollably. Frantic, Adam breathed in deep and released his spirit once again into the hawk.

He escaped his body and saw through the hawk's sharp eyes yet again. From the air, Adam watched Elohim rise. Elohim began to leave the clearing. Elohim's walk turned into a run as he began to sprint in the direction of Adam and Eve. Adam flew above him as the sun continued to follow its trajectory in the sky. As Elohim got nearer to them, he looked up at the sky where Adam was directing the hawk's flight. As soon as Adam saw the golden flecks in Elohim's eyes, his vision once again went dark.

He breathed in again and saw through his own eyes. The light from the setting sun began to vanish, and Adam heard various animals behind the jungle brush. He felt something stream down his cheek. He brushed it off with his fingers. As he looked down, Adam saw red blood smeared on his hand.

Suddenly, Adam felt a hand grab his ankle. He glanced down and saw Eve. Her eyes were bright and wide, filled with terror. Her finger was pressed tightly against her lips. She motioned for him to be silent. With her other hand, she frantically pointed north. Adam glanced and saw what looked like a large man who was consumed by fire heading toward them.

As it ran with increasing speed, Adam saw it was faster than any creature he had ever witnessed.

Eve inched back slowly as it got nearer, approaching with great speed. Adam's heart throbbed and beat loudly in his chest as an overwhelming sense of dread spread throughout his entire being. Eve jumped up and began to run in the opposite direction. She found some trees and hid. But Adam froze. Fear took control, and he couldn't move a muscle. The being of fire sprinted toward him. Within moments, it stood inches from his face.

"Adam ..." Elohim grabbed his son and held him. Leaning back, he looked into his son's eyes; in an instant, they were gone. His green eyes were replaced by black pools that slowly grew from his pupils until the irises and whites were fully black. "Son ... where are you?" Elohim wept as he held Adam.

He searched his son's eyes as Adam's spirit continued to die. Elohim looked over and saw Eve scream as she hid behind a tree. "Eve ... it's me ..." Elohim's eyes grew more intense as he glanced back into Adam's eyes. "Where are you, son? Come back to me!"

Elohim looked down and saw Adam's hands pushing back at him with all his strength. As Adam's hands touched Elohim's skin, he could see they were being burned by his being. He looked again at Eve; seeing the fear in her eyes, his heart ached. They no longer saw him. When his children looked at him, all they could perceive was an all-consuming fire. He was no longer seen. He was no longer known. Elohim felt the fear in his son and daughter. He felt Adam's rejection and desire to be free from his embrace. With deep sadness, Elohim released Adam.

The flame engulfed Adam, and his mind plunged into confusion. Its heat was intense. He could feel his body burning. If he stayed, he knew the fire would consume him. Adam didn't know how he knew, but somehow, he could sense this place was the being's territory, its home. Adam knew he no longer belonged. He had only one thought: escape!

Adam struggled but finally managed to break free from its strength. He turned around and saw Eve. Her face was somehow covered both in panic and relief at him being released. It was as if she had just witnessed Adam escaping from the heart of the sun itself. Adam glanced down and picked up the Etz Hayim near his feet, quickly putting it into the sling on his back. He ran toward Eve and held out his hand. She reached out and grabbed it.

They ran from the center of the garden into the jungle. They ran so hard Adam thought his lungs would explode and his legs would give out beneath him. They ran as long as they could, as far as they could. They ran in the direction of the valley southeast of Eden.

Adam didn't know how long it took, but finally they got to a place where the column of fire had disappeared into the night. Adam felt safe away from its presence. From that moment on,

Adam knew he could never return to the tree of life nor the garden of Eden ever again, lest he burn.

———————

As Elohim watched his son and daughter, his heart broke. He knew Adam could no longer see him. He saw the panic and fear on his daughter's face as they fled in terror. Exhausted, he sat down and leaned against the tree of the knowledge of good and evil. Lilly had left. The servant of Ba'hal and Lucifer was nowhere to be seen.

The sun set over the garden, and Elohim was left with his thoughts. The birds that normally sang this time of evening were quiet. An ominous silence fell over Eden. From another dimension, a portal in the tangerine sky opened and a bright beam burst through. Seconds later, Menakiel landed in front of Elohim. He kneeled. Elohim forced a soft smile as Menakiel looked up and their eyes met. Menakiel knew that now was not the time for words. He folded his large wings behind him and walked over to sit next to Elohim.

Menakiel put his hand softly on Elohim's shoulder. Elohim breathed in deep. In the distance, they heard the growl of a jaguar ripping apart prey. A tear ran down Elohim's cheek as he heard the flesh of one of his beloved creatures being pulled off its bones as it groaned in agony.

Elohim got up and grabbed the sword strapped to Menakiel's back. Elohim motioned Menakiel to move away from the tree. With a single swift motion, Elohim sliced the tree near its base. The tree's timber groaned. Suddenly, it fell and crashed onto the garden floor. Elohim faced Menakiel and returned the sword to him.

"Lucifer has captured their spirits. He thinks he now has the authority to take their physical bodies." Elohim looked directly at Menakiel's golden eyes. "He is to do no such thing. Go, now. Protect them," Elohim commanded.

Menakiel nodded and got up. He spread out his wings and began to rise off the jungle floor. In a flash of golden light, Menakiel soared into the sky.

THE SHADOW OF DEATH

XVIII

"The Earth turned, and darkness fell. Every creature's eyes turned dark as they gazed into the eyes of their new master. I was always meant to serve the sons and daughters of Elohim. I am the first of the guardians. As I searched for Adam and Eve, I embraced the duty for which I was created."—Menakiel

ADAM TURNED AROUND. HIS HANDS HIT HIS waist as he took in a rapid succession of deep breaths. As he looked back, he no longer saw the being of fire. He glanced over at Eve.

"What was that?!" Adam frantically searched Eve's eyes, hoping for some insight to make sense of what had happened.

"I don't know ..." Eve shook her head furiously. "I saw it ... from deep within the jungle ... it surrounded you. You vanished within the brightness of its fire! I thought you were lost to its flame! I thought you had become like Alatar!"

"Alatar isn't real!" Adam barked. His anger startled him. Eve took a step back in distrust. He breathed in deep to calm his nerves. "He's a fiction Lilly used to get to us. She wasn't telling the truth. Lilly deceived us."

Stunned, Eve froze. She found it hard to breathe. Night had fallen over the jungle. A full moon hung in the sky. As she looked up, the moon's pale light reflected in Eve's large pupils. Slowly, she fell to her knees. Adam rushed over to her and held her.

"I don't understand ..." Eve began to weep. "... you knew?" Eve searched Adam's eyes. Adam wanted to hide. Tears welled up in his eyes. He knew he had failed her. He shook his head slowly but couldn't form words.

"You said nothing ... you didn't warn me?" Eve glanced at the tops of her hands and saw black veins running up her arms. "What has happened to us?" With every question Eve asked, Adam's stomach began to turn. Eve wept. Adam sat with her in silence. "Who are you?"

"I should have said something ... I should have waited for Elohim." Adam paused as he saw the pain in Eve's eyes. "But it is not Lilly or her lies"—Adam lowered his voice to almost a whisper—"it is the fire that I fear most. Whatever that was, we can never go back ... ever ..." Eve looked away; tears streamed down her cheeks.

"If we don't go back, how will we ever find our father?" she asked. Silence hung in the air before Adam slowly responded.

"I don't know."

Eve finally looked into Adam's eyes and nodded.

"If we are to ever see him again, he must be the one who comes out here and finds us ... I cannot go back to the garden," Adam responded. "If I ever faced that creature of fire again, I would be consumed."

Adam looked up at the stars above.

"I need to rest," Eve finally said.

Adam looked around. The jungle was unusually quiet. The only sound was a gentle breeze softly moving the canopy.

"We can rest here," Adam reassured her. Adam leaned in and put his head against Eve's chest. Sporadically, in between moments of silence, they could hear smaller animals being chased by larger ones. The large predators were now controlled by the instincts of the Prince of the Earth. They wished to consume.

"Can you feel that?" Eve looked around. "The animals ... they're afraid ... I feel their fear ..."

Adam held Eve as she wept. After an hour had passed, her cries slowly faded. Adam looked up and saw that Eve had closed her eyes. She had fallen into a dreamless sleep.

In the distance, Adam saw light from a handful of fireflies. The light from these strange creatures was familiar to him. They were present on the days he and Eve were created. Their presence caused a hope to rise in his heart. Drawn to their mystery and beauty, Adam carefully stood. He looked down at Eve; she needed rest. He walked toward their light.

Adam approached a clearing between the trees, and soon their light vanished into the pitch-black jungle. Adam's heart broke as the hope within him disappeared with the light of the fireflies.

"Wait … please … I need you!" Adam frantically looked around, but the light had vanished.

From above, Adam saw a separate golden light descend from the sky. In an instant, Menakiel appeared before him. But Adam could not see his form, only a faint golden orb of light. Adam reached out to touch the light.

"I know you. I can't see you, but I know you," Adam spoke quietly.

"You do," Menakiel spoke softly to Adam's spirit. "Follow me."

Menakiel continued to walk through a clearing. As he walked, he made his way to the edge of the cliff. Adam followed him as the brightness of the moon illuminated the valley below. In the distance, Adam heard various animals fighting each other and was terrified. What happened to them? Why did they shed each other's blood? He saw the light to his side. He looked toward the valley, and his heart broke once again. Purposely, Menakiel revealed himself to Adam. Adam looked at Menakiel's towering wings.

"I saw you … above my father's throne, when Lucifer rebelled …" Adam said quietly. He looked back at the valley below. "What is this place?"

As pale moonlight shone on Menakiel's golden and ivory wings, thousands of eyes began to emerge at the wings' edges. Slowly, the eyes began to open. Adam felt a strange comfort around him.

"The valley of the shadow of death," Menakiel replied. A gentle breeze moved through the jungle.

"What have I done?" Adam whispered.

"Son of my master. Do not be afraid." Menakiel looked into Adam's eyes. "This will be the last time you see me in this form. But know I will watch over you and Eve. The evil one desires to take your life. With me here, he cannot. Though he may try, the fallen will not be able to take your physical bodies before your appointed time." Menakiel paused and raised his right hand, softly putting it on Adam's shoulder. "Guard your heart … who you submit your thoughts and your actions to. Submit only to the King of Heaven. If you adopt the thoughts of the fallen, if you come into agreement with how he sees and thinks—you will begin to destroy yourself, destroy others around you."

Adam gave thought to Menakiel's words. He began to wonder when his appointed time was and the full meaning behind what Menakiel had spoken.

"Can I ever go back?" Adam asked.

"That has not been revealed to me." Menakiel's eyes were intense, comforting, and yet somewhat terrifying to Adam all at once. "You have given your authority to Lucifer. He is now the prince of this world. The Earth that Elohim had given to you is no longer under your rule."

Adam's heart sank. His stomach churned with hunger. In the darkness of the valley below, he heard another animal howl in pain as it fell victim to a predator. He could sense the animals were no longer driven by their spirits but increasingly by their appetites. They no longer saw beyond their own stomachs or survival.

"What am I to do?" Adam asked. He looked into Menakiel's eyes. Adam felt unworthy and exposed. The shame that entered in after his fall rose to the surface of his emotions. He no longer desired Menakiel's presence. As a soft wind blew, all the eyes on Menakiel's wings focused on Adam.

"You are seen. You are known. Heaven's plans have not changed." Menakiel paused for a moment. He looked away from Adam and toward the valley of the shadow of death. "You face a long and difficult path. If it were not so, he would not have sent me."

That night, Adam dreamt. Before the heavenly host, he saw Lucifer accuse his father. Heaven trembled as the scepters of the twenty-four elders crashed into the ground. Angels in every direction fell like meteorites from the sky. Snakes emerged from the thrones of the royalty, but in his dream, they did not crawl. Instead, they flew like arrows as they headed toward Lucifer. They wrapped themselves around his torso, neck, and face.

Between the snakes, Lucifer glanced over at Adam. The Dark Prince smiled as his eyes pierced Adam's soul. Adam sensed Lucifer knew him more than the Creator did. A roaring fire arose from Elohim's throne. Lucifer's smile faded as terror consumed him. The fire from the throne expanded in every direction as it exploded like a supernova that engulfed all of heaven.

DESCENT

XIX

EARLY THE NEXT MORNING, THE SUN'S RAYS FILTERED through the canopy. Eve opened her eyes and found herself in Adam's arms. She breathed in deep and felt safe for a moment. With her second breath, a sense of dread entered into her and a quiet anxiety filled her heart. She could tell that his dreams had gone dark. A foreboding filled her soul. Part of her just wanted to rest, never to open her eyes again. Yet her body yearned for water and food. Slowly, she rose and stretched.

"We need to find something to eat …" Eve said. Adam opened his eyes and looked up at Eve. The blackness in her veins had faded.

Adam got up from his rest and stretched. He looked into Eve's eyes. Her beauty made him feel alive. Her eyes, while not as bright, were still sparkling. He softly smiled at her. She returned his smile, but he felt for a moment that her expression was almost mechanical, as if it were disconnected from any real happiness or joy.

Within a couple of moments, the memories from the previous day crashed into his mind. Adam's heart hurt. He thought about how he had failed to protect her. He knew he had not shielded her from the lies of Lilly. Out of a strange mixture of desiring to know what Lilly knew and not wanting to lose Eve, he had chosen to be silent. He felt great shame. He looked into her eyes before glancing away.

"We need water," Eve said. Her tongue was parched.

"I saw a river in the valley below," Adam said. "We can go there. I'm sure we'll find food along its banks."

Adam picked up the Etz Hayim and placed it into the sling on his back. They walked for a few minutes before they arrived at the place where Adam had seen Menakiel the night before. They both looked at the valley below them.

"Is this it?" Eve asked.

"There's the river," Adam said. He pointed down to the waters a great distance away. A steep cliff face and a long hike down separated Adam and Eve from the refreshment that the waters could bring. Eve glanced back at Adam and saw him lost in his thoughts.

"What is it?" Eve asked. Adam looked down at the distant river before looking back up at Eve. He paused for a moment. The jungle still smelled sweet and fragrant from the tropical flowers. He breathed in deeply before finally speaking.

"I saw Menakiel last night." Adam's voice was low, nearly a whisper.

Eve looked at Adam. Her eyes filled with hope.

"The one with eyes on the edges of his wings?" Eve's voice was very quiet. Adam nodded.

"He called this place the valley of the shadow of death," Adam said with a deep sorrow in his voice.

"What is death?" Eve asked.

"I'm not sure. When I was consumed by the fire, I thought I might die. Maybe the fire is death. Perhaps Menakiel wants us to go into the valley, far from the fire, to protect us," Adam said. "Maybe we'll find safety there."

Eve remembered seeing the being of fire sprint from the jungle and completely engulf Adam the previous day. She had heard Adam groan in pain as he struggled to break free. She remembered how she had screamed in terror, believing that he would be lost. After it had taken him, her fear was it would also consume her. She shuddered at the thought. She wondered how he had been in the fire but escaped without a single hair on his head being singed. When he had broken away and run toward her, she sensed an intention within the fire to consume her as well. She began to lose herself in her thoughts.

"If we are to find water soon, I don't see what choice we have right now," Adam said with resignation. Adam caressed the barely visible bluish lines of Eve's veins along the underside of her forearm. He looked up into her eyes.

"But what about the tree of life?" Eve asked.

Adam removed the Etz Hayim from the sling on his back and looked at it. He felt the hard blonde wood in his hands. The two twigs and the four leaves were still near the top of the staff. He held it up to his eyes and carefully examined the map of Eden carved into its side.

"This is it—you don't remember, do you?" Adam searched Eve's eyes, hoping her memory would confirm his own. Eve simply shook her head no.

"It's a staff ... it's beautiful ... but it's just a staff." Eve struggled to find the meaning.

"It's more than that. When we were young, the first time I took you to the edge of Eden ... that night, he gave this to me. Do you remember?"

Slowly, the memory of that night pushed past the trauma of the last day in Eve's mind and surfaced. Eve looked at Adam and softly nodded.

"I remember that night," Eve responded. "I don't remember what he said." Despair marked Eve's voice.

"He said if we were ever separated, this was his way back to us."

"How?" Eve asked.

"I'm not sure. But he told me not to forget his words," Adam responded. Adam returned the Etz Hayim to the sling on his back. He looked back down on the valley. "We need food and water."

The two of them came closer to the edge and looked at the treacherously steep wall of earth and rock they needed to descend. The mesa they stood on was around one thousand feet above the valley floor.

"I'll go first," Adam said, a wry smile on his face. Eve nodded.

Adam looked for the first foothold in the rocks and began to descend. Eve followed. Adam took each step cautiously, knowing if he lost his footing, he could tumble to his death.

The morning sun was hot overhead, and the climb down was difficult. Drops of sweat beaded down Adam's forehead.

A raven above seemed to be watching as they made their way down. It flew near Eve and landed on a rock adjacent to her left hand. Eve looked at its dark brown eyes. A sense of dread filled Eve as the bird gradually tilted its head and stared at her. The raven squawked and, with a sudden movement, jammed its beak into Eve's hand. Eve howled in pain.

The large, dark bird twisted its beak and shook its head before pulling out of Eve's hand. It turned its head and stared at Eve again. Blood trickled from its beak. With a quick thrust, it pecked violently, digging its bloodied beak into Eve's hand a second time. Eve screamed again. Her right hand gripped another rock, and Eve clung precariously to the face of the cliff. Adam froze, looking at Eve with fear in his eyes.

"Go down! I need to go down! Quick!" she shouted at Adam beneath her.

Violently, the raven snapped its beak out of Eve's hand. Then it drove its beak toward Eve's hand a third time. Eve quickly moved her hand, and the bird's beak hit the rock. Eve moved her left hand down to another rock and slowly lowered herself.

Adam looked above and started moving faster down the cliff face so that Eve could get away from the raven. Blood began to pool where the raven's beak had gashed the top of her hand. As Eve climbed down, blood ran past her wrist and down her forearm and dripped from the bottom of her elbow. A handful of drops splattered on Adam's forehead. He looked up. The raven had not moved from its perch where it had attacked Eve.

It stood motionless and continued to stare at her. Flapping its wings, it took to the sky and flew past Adam. It continued its flight down and darted into the valley below.

"You okay?!" Adam looked up; his hands gripped the rock from the cliff face. He used his forearm to wipe some of the blood from the top of his head.

Eve looked down and shook her head. Fear gripped her heart. Her left hand was now getting weak and slippery with blood. She could feel the strength she'd need to climb down the rest of the way begin to leave her body. There was at least another fifty feet to go, and visions of falling paraded through her mind. She found a foothold for her left foot, and she continued to make her way down.

"You're almost there." Adam looked up. The steepness of the cliff face began to fade, and Adam was able to stand without using his hands to descend. Eve finally found her last footing as Adam helped her with the last few feet of the climb down.

Eve moved her hair from her eyes and looked at Adam with pain surging through her hand. She began to weep. She used her hand to wipe off the remaining blood from his forehead.

"I bled ... how could I bleed?" Eve raised her left hand to show Adam the gash from the raven's beak. "Why would it attack me?"

Adam shook his head in disbelief as he saw drops of sweat move down Eve's face.

"I don't know." Adam looked into Eve's eyes as a combination of tears and fear swelled within them. Adam embraced her and whispered into her ear. "It's going to be okay."

"I don't think so …" Eve's voice was a nearly inaudible whimper. She held her hand; Adam looked down and saw it trembling. "We're not going to be okay …" Eve whispered.

"This is my fault … shhh … we'll be okay," Adam responded gently. Adam picked Eve up and carried her in his arms.

Hours had passed, and they had finally made it to the river. Adam continued to carry Eve to give her time to rest. His legs burned from exhaustion. Both of their stomachs ached with hunger. Finding a large tree, he stopped and gently lowered Eve to the ground. As he lowered her head against the tree, he softly kissed her forehead. Eve slowly opened her eyes and looked around.

"Where are we?" Eve asked. Her voice was weak. She heard in the distance cries from animals as they fought for food and territory. She wanted to cover her ears but didn't. The sound gave her a strange sense of safety as it allowed her to approximate the distance between her and the creatures.

"The valley of the shadow of death," Adam responded softly. "I found water here." Eve turned toward the slow-moving river, and a sense of relief flooded her being. "Have a drink. I will find us something to eat," he said.

"Wait … don't go. I don't know this place … don't leave me by myself," Eve responded. "Please stay."

"We must find food," Adam said.

"Please don't leave me," Eve begged.

Adam removed the Etz Hayim he had been carrying on his back. He carefully handed it to her.

"Take this—for protection," Adam instructed Eve. Hesitantly, Eve reached out and took the staff. "I won't be long; I promise."

THE PROPHECY

XX

ADAM HIKED EAST ALONG THE RIVER. WITH EACH step, he left Eve further behind. He could hear her soft cries fade into the sound of insects, breeze, and the steady flow of water beside him. His stomach ached with hunger. He saw a patch of wild raspberries. He sprinted to the bushes.

Frantically, he picked the berries. He put a berry into his pouch to save it for Eve, then quickly picked another and shoved it into his mouth. He reached for a group of plump berries deeper within the bush. Plunging his hand into the thick bush, he howled in pain. Adam quickly withdrew his bloodied hand and examined it. He looked and saw several hard, dark green thorns embedded in his skin. He took a step back and, with his fingers, lifted a single branch close to his eyes. Slowly, he witnessed the branch grow razor-sharp thorns. Within moments, every branch on the berry bush was plated with the skin-piercing thorns.

Adam picked the thorns out of his hand and right fore-arm. He brushed some of the blood away and looked back at the wild raspberry bush. This time, he was cautious to avoid the thorns. Adam identified another group of bright red rasp-berries and began to pick them. The surrounding berries in the cluster began to age and dehydrate and turned black nearly instantaneously. Adam took a step back and scanned the entire bush. In real time, he saw all the red, ripe fruit turn black.

Adam looked down at his small pouch. It was less than a third full of berries. Exhausted, he shook his head. He closed the pouch, saving just a handful of berries for Eve. He knew this wasn't enough for even a single meal. He sat down on the riverbank and hung his head. In despair, Adam stared at the reflection in the water. The events of the last few days cas-caded into his mind, and a deep sorrow permeated his heart. Eve had almost drowned. Lilly had betrayed them. He had broken trust with his father and couldn't find him. He had almost died by fire, animals were turning on each other, and even plants seemed to have come to despise him.

As hunger pains shot through his stomach, he remem-bered how hungry and now alone Eve was. He had failed himself; he had failed her. Tears formed and ran down his cheek. There was a sorrow in the eyes that looked back at him from the water's reflection. He noticed how his hair was dirty and matted. He watched his tears drop into the water below. As his tears hit, he watched the water ripple. With the rip-pling of the water, he noticed the reflection of himself gradu-ally change.

Adam saw his reflection begin to take on a life of its own. He stared into the water. His face began to wrinkle and age, his hair grew long, he grew a thick beard, and he saw his fingernails grow like claws. He looked at his own youthful hands, then glanced back into the reflection and saw sunspots, veins, and dry patches on his skin become visible.

Haunted by the vision, Adam sprang to his feet. Fear shot through his spine. He wanted to leave the still waters. The image imprinted on his mind wasn't just old age: it was a window into his soul, a revelation of doom. It was a vision of how his body would transform with each step he drew nearer to death. Adam shook his head to get the picture out of his mind. He knew he must focus on survival and on finding his and Eve's next meal.

He began to walk along the riverbed once again. He looked into the distance and saw that all the scattered berry bushes had withered. Their fruit had grown dark for as far as his eyes could see. He glanced down again at the nearby water. He saw the reflection of an old man with a tired gait walking alongside him in the water. Exhausted, Adam stopped to think about where he should go next. If he were to find food, it would no longer be near the river. He decided to leave the banks and head south. Adam smiled at the old man. The old man's smile was more of a sneer. Adam turned from him and walked away.

Adam journeyed, and night began to fall on the valley of the shadow of death. Adam heard various wild animals fighting. It was a strange combination of wolves, jaguars, and panthers fighting for territory. There was confusion. It was as if the panthers had been displaced from the garden and were forced to make a new home for themselves in a foreign habitat. Within their cries, Adam sensed they were establishing territory and fighting over prey.

A full moon hung in the sky. A terrible sense of loneliness and sadness fell upon Adam. He had never been hungry to the point of pain. Eve had never gone hungry. He would have to make sure she could get food quickly. She needed strength the food would bring. He looked everywhere for fruit and nuts, but everywhere he looked, he saw trees that produced nothing edible.

Walking into a clearing, he looked down. Mushrooms were on the forest floor in a cluster. He had never eaten anything like a mushroom before, but the aching of his stomach drove him to his knees. Adam began to pick them off the forest floor. Impatiently, he shoved them in his mouth. His teeth crushed their gamey texture. He detected a vague sweetness as they rolled off his tongue and down his throat.

Suddenly, Adam felt as if someone had taken a dagger to his stomach and twisted it. He wheezed in pain. He looked up from his prone position and saw the moon above. Its intensity appeared unnaturally bright. The moon zigged and zagged, cutting across the night sky. Adam rubbed his eyes with his hands. The moon abruptly halted, then zoomed across the sky and bounced back and forth between the stars. Adam felt he was on the verge of vomiting, but nothing came.

The sound of the wolves in the distance grew louder. As their guttural howling increased, Adam glanced around to see where they were coming from. He cupped his ears. The vibration from their cries seemed to pierce his bones. On his knees, Adam brought his head low to the ground to shield himself from their howling. From the woods, a pack of half a dozen wolves emerged. The wolves were dark gray and closer to the size of a large bear than a normal wolf. As a silence fell, they slowly began to encircle Adam.

"Do you know who we are?" The seething voice of the pack leader hit Adam's ears. Adam looked up. Their ivory white teeth glistened. Coal-black eyes tracked Adam's movements.

"Get back ..." Adam commanded.

"Or what?" The lead wolf's mouth frothed. Suddenly, his dark eyes seemed to glow with a sharp yellow light.

Adam's hands frantically searched for a rock or stick. He went to take the Etz Hayim from the sling on his back, but he quickly remembered he had left it with Eve. He found a stick the length of a walking cane and leapt to his feet. Immediately, Adam felt a sense of vertigo and had to use the stick for balance so he wouldn't fall. Within a few moments, the sense faded, and Adam raised the stick above his head like a weapon. All the wolves besides the leader of the pack moved back a few feet. They continued to walk around him in a circle. The lead wolf growled.

"You come at me with a stick ...?" Its yellow eyes darted back to its pack, then looked at Adam. Its husky voice was coarse with a barbarous cruelty. "I'm not here for you ... I'm here for her."

"For her?" Adam's voice was low as he brandished the stick like a sword.

"Eve will pay the penalty for the death she has brought into your world," the wolf sneered.

"What penalty?" Adam questioned.

"Her life is the penalty." The wolf's bony voice got louder. "Sacrificing her is the only way back to Eden, to the tree of life, to free you of your new union with death."

"Who are you?" Adam continued to walk back until he backed into a tree.

"I have many names. You are not ready to know them." The wolf's voice was stern. The brightness of its glowing eyes increased as it carefully watched Adam. "Know this ... we will spill blood together." The wolf backed away from Adam, mirroring his movements.

"Leave me!" Adam swung the stick in the air as a warning.

"Her blood will be on your hands ..." The wolf paused its walk back. It sprang and leaped. In midair, it dematerialized into dark matter and entered into Adam's body, striking his heart. Adam landed back and fell into the trunk of the tree behind him. He laid on the forest floor with his eyes locked shut. The matter began to pump through his heart and travel through his bloodstream. Adam's body violently spasmed for a few moments before he laid on the ground completely motionless. The wolves cautiously approached. Unsure whether the possession was complete, they began sniffing Adam's limp body. The dark matter reached Adam's brain. Instantly, Adam opened his now sharp yellow eyes.

"I'M HERE!" Adam's voice carried a mixture of his own and the wolf's cruel voice. Adam sprang to his feet with a supernatural strength and speed. His eyes rolled back, and he blinked rapidly. The other wolves took a few steps back.

"I KNOW WHERE SHE IS. I'll take you to her. LET'S GO," he commanded.

Eve looked down at her feet, confused. This was not where Adam had left her. She coughed. Her lungs hurt. She looked up at the dark night sky. The stars, while normally bright, were barely visible. The light of the moon seemed to shine down directly on her as if it were a spotlight. She found herself standing on a flat rock. The rock was in the middle of a large pool of water that resembled a lake. The water was surrounded by a wooded shoreline. She wondered how she had arrived on the rock as she saw no bridge from the shoreline and her clothes were not wet from a swim.

Dazed and confused, Eve used the moonlight to examine the wounds the black raven had inflicted on her hand. She observed that a hard scab had grown on top of the punctures. She pumped her hand into a fist and then stretched her fingers out. Excruciating pain traveled from her hand, shooting through her entire body. She winced in pain. Her body ached. Uncertainty flooded her heart as she started wondering how she got to this isolated place.

"Adam ..." Eve softly whispered.

With every breath she took, she felt vulnerable and exposed. She sensed imminent danger but didn't know why. The large rock was two feet in diameter and rose a few feet above the water. She turned around to examine the shoreline but was careful to avoid falling into the water. The night air was frigid. A breeze blew that began to chill Eve's core.

"Adam!" she whispered louder. "Where are you?!"

Suddenly, a barbarous vision filled her mind. She saw vivid images of a forest floor littered with mushrooms. Large wolves stalked Adam. They covertly followed him as he searched for food. More images invaded her imagination. In a violent and rapid succession, wolves with coal-black eyes stalked, surrounded, attacked, and devoured Adam. Eve heard him howl in pain as they ripped flesh off his bones. After they ate their fill, their eyes began to glow with an ominous yellow hue. Terrified, Eve shook her head furiously to free her mind from the horror of the sight.

She peered again into the woods. Yellow eyes flashed behind the trees. She could feel the presence of evil watching her from the distance. Eve stood alone, defenseless on the rock. There was nowhere to go. She felt a spirit of fear riding on the wind. It approached her as the wind blew across the water. Eve wrapped her arms around her chest to try to stave off the cold air. Waves of emotion bubbled to the surface. A tear moved down her cheek as a series of questions streamed through her mind and landed like arrows in her heart. What if this wasn't just a cruel vision? What if Adam was lost to the wolves? What if she never saw him again? How would she survive the valley of the shadow of death without Adam? Eve felt overwhelmed and alone. Not knowing what to do, she sat down on the rock and started to weep.

"It was your fault."

Eve heard a whisper from the woods and glanced around to see where the voice came from. A smattering of vicious whispers came at her from all directions.

"It's true."

"You will never see him again."

"You're alone."

"You should have known better."

"It's your fault."

"There's no hope now."

Eve covered her ears with her hands. She looked up. The cascade of whispers from every direction slowly died down. Eve's bottom lip trembled; she bit down until it started to bleed. She winced in pain, not realizing what she had done until she felt a drop of blood slide down underneath her mouth. She wiped the stream of blood quickly from her chin.

Eve searched the forest. The intensity of the yellow eyes blinked like fireflies, then went dark. An eerie silence fell over the lake. Under the light of the moon, Eve glanced down. Near her foot, she saw a flat stone with a razor-sharp edge. Eve picked it up with her right hand and looked at the edge. Exhaustion and depression flooded her being. Feeling trapped, she envisioned diving off the rock, swimming to the shore, and running into the woods.

But where would she run to? Where could she find safety? What of the creatures with the sharp yellow eyes who waited for her within the woods? The voices beyond the shoreline, would they not find her and torment her there as well? As the vision continued in her mind, she saw herself being chased by the same wolves that had devoured Adam. She saw herself as they locked their jaws onto her limbs and drew blood. Eve shook her head again, trying to escape the vision. Exhausted and depressed, she began to wish for death. Eve stood up on the rock and looked at the moon. The moon's pale light shined down on her like a soft spotlight.

"It's my fault ..." Eve whispered under her breath. A tear ran down her cheek.

Eve's right hand trembled as she raised the sharp stone and brought its edge to her left wrist. Her hand shook under the stone's weight as she grazed her left wrist with its sharp edge. A small bead of blood surfaced. Eve bent her head slightly as she raised her left wrist closer to her eyes to examine the cut. She stared at the blood as it flowed from her wrist. The bead grew larger and ran down her forearm and dripped into the water below. Hopeless, Eve wept.

As the blood hit the water, it diluted. The light of the moon was bright. She peered down into the water and saw the droplets sink. She was transfixed as she saw how the blood mixed with the water. As they mixed, her blood seemed to come alive and move in different directions. Slowly, she saw it form an outline of an apparition. Eve was startled at the sight of the small ghostly figure. Strangely, she also felt thankful that she was no longer alone. Beneath the water, Eve saw it swim around the rock, looking up at her.

Above the water, Eve made another cut, this one deeper. She pumped her left hand a few times, and multiple beads of blood surfaced from her skin and dropped again into the water below. As the blood fused with the water, the apparition grew until it looked the same size as Eve. Slowly, it rose out of the deep. Eve gazed at the spirit. It looked like a ghastly version of her. The spirit began to encircle Eve, examining her from every angle as it floated in the air.

"You're alone ..." Its voice was soft and caring. "You should have known. You see clearly now. You are not worthy of love. You are not worthy of protection ... unworthy ..."

As it spoke, another tear streamed down Eve's cheek as she took in the words of the demonic spirit.

"Your beauty has faded. Adam is no more. You've seen it yourself. A painful, terrible death. You saw the wolves. They wait patiently for your flesh. You can allow them to devour you, or you can end this yourself ..."

Eve switched the stone to her other hand as she felt a shooting pain from her left hand. She gripped the sharp stone and winced in pain.

"It's okay ... you can escape ... finish what you've started." The voice took on an undertone of kindness.

The spirit rose above Eve. With blood flowing from her left wrist, Eve placed the sharp edge of the stone down on her right wrist. Eve's eyes were vacant. Before she could make another cut, her left hand lost its strength, and the stone dropped into the cold water below.

Eve swayed gently back and forth before losing consciousness. She fell headfirst into the icy water. Blood continued to flow from her wrist as Eve's body descended slowly. As it sank under the blackness of the water, her body eventually reached a depth beyond the light of the moon.

In the distance, a being of white-hot fire bolted through the forest. Surrounding spirits quaked in its presence. The yellow eyes of the demonic scattered as it got closer to the lake. The demonic apparition dissipated like smoke blown by a strong wind. The pillar of fire, Elohim's father, stopped at the shoreline.

From within the flame, Elohim dove headfirst into the water. Elohim's father watched as Elohim swam quickly in search of his daughter. Finding her toward the bottom, he grabbed her around the waist. With speed, he rose to the surface. With Eve draped between his powerful arms, Elohim brought her to shore.

Eve woke. Finding herself in wet clothes and with damp hair, she stared at her left wrist. A scab had formed, and the cut had only partially healed. She turned over her left hand to see the top. The previous scabs had fallen off and left open wounds from the raven's attack. They burned with pain.

Disoriented and dazed, she looked to her right and saw the Etz Hayim leaning against a tree. Adam had left it there for her protection. The morning sun was still hidden behind the mesa, but light was beginning to flood the forest. Above, she heard a crack of thunder. Eve glanced up. The dark blue morning sky split open with a golden orb of light. From within the light, Menakiel flew down to Eve.

His feet hit the forest floor with a thud. Startled, Eve got up and took a few steps back. She looked into Menakiel's eyes.

"Menakiel ...?" Eve asked.

"There's no time to explain. Your life is in danger."

Menakiel's words were measured and direct. "Climb quickly." Menakiel pointed up at an adjacent tree. "Now, Eve."

She nodded. With renewed vigor and strength, she climbed. Branch by branch, she ignored the pain in her body and ascended higher. After climbing for a few moments, she stopped. From high above, she looked down. Eve no longer saw Menakiel. A pack of wolves raced toward her. Eve peered down through the branches. Adam appeared to be leading them. Eve's heart was gripped by fear as she saw Adam's eyes flash with yellow and black.

Adam possessed an unearthly strength with muscles much larger than Eve remembered. His yellow eyes scanned the area as he raced toward where he had left her. The other wolves ran close behind him.

"She's not here?!" Adam seethed impatiently to himself. "Where are you?!" he roared. His head jerked, turning in different directions looking for Eve. Eve held her breath at the sound of Adam's distorted voice.

"Eve! Where are you, my love?" Adam growled. He looked around and moved silently. He picked up a large stone and began to carry it above his head. "I brought us back food!" In the corner of his eye, he saw an image of Eve sleeping with her back against a tree. He moved toward her.

He raised the stone higher and threw it toward her head. The stone hit the tree, but the image of Eve lying asleep remained untouched as if it were a hallucination of Adam's mind. Adam approached cautiously. He reached out his hand to touch her face. As he got closer, his foot was snagged by an above-ground tree root. Adam stumbled. His forehead hit the trunk of the tree in front of him.

Eve gasped from her perch in the branches. Immediately, the wolves looked up and saw her. She peered down and saw Adam lying on his back, unconscious, with his forehead bleeding. Adam's mouth opened. A steady stream of black flies moved from his chest and flew through his throat and out of his mouth. Different streams of flies buzzed in the direction of each wolf. The wolves stopped in their tracks and opened their mouths. The streams of flies entered their bodies. Once the demon fully distributed its strength, the wolves locked their jaws shut. A yellow glow replaced the coal-black eyes of each wolf in the pack.

Eve looked up into the tree to see if she could climb higher, but the branches were thinner and wouldn't support her weight. Terrified, she looked back down. Gradually, Adam regained consciousness and opened his eyes. To her relief, she saw the possession had left.

Adam glanced over and saw the enormous wolves begin to surround the tree Eve was perched in. Near it, he saw the Etz Hayim. Adam quickly got up and lunged toward the Etz Hayim. With the Etz Hayim in his hand, he ran toward the wolves. Adam swung with all his might and hit the closest wolf square in the head. It howled in pain as it flew through the air. The Etz Hayim seemed to invigorate Adam as a newfound strength coursed through his being.

The other wolves encircled Adam, taking an offensive posture.

"You've led us to her," one of the wolves seethed.

"You're no longer needed," another wolf's bony voice bristled with hatred.

A large black wolf jumped toward Adam. Eve screamed and looked away. With his newfound power, Adam smashed the wolf's face in midair with the Etz Hayim. It spun from the force of the blow, landing a few feet away. Adam looked up. Eve started to climb down the tree to help Adam.

"NO! Stay up!" Adam shouted at the top of his lungs.

From the woods, more wolves began to pour into the area from all directions. Another made a move from behind Adam. With a swift movement, Adam turned around and, with lightning speed, smashed the wolf's head in midair. Two more wolves attacked. Adam hit one, but the other locked its jaws around Adam's shoulder. It sank its teeth in. With a quick movement, Adam powerfully thrust the large end of the Etz Hayim into the side of the wolf. It howled in agony. With shattered ribs, its jaws unlocked from Adam's shoulder.

Adam grimaced in pain as the wolf's teeth had punctured his skin. Adrenaline pumped through his system. Adam pounded the wolf's face, smashing its nose and teeth with the Etz Hayim. Looking up, he saw more wolves pouring in from the forest. Exhausted, he watched as a few dozen formed another circle of attack while more flooded in from every direction.

A few yards away, a wolf leapt and latched its jaws on Adam's forearm. Another bit down on his leg. Adam batted them away. He began to lose blood. Adam felt his body's strength begin to diminish.

Sweat and blood dripped down his face as he saw more

wolves come into the circle of attack. Eve watched in horror. Dizzy, Adam fell onto the forest floor, with his back against the tree Eve was in. Breathing heavily and disoriented, he looked up. Eve leapt down and landed next to him. She quickly snatched up the now bloodied Etz Hayim from Adam's hands. She took a few steps forward and raised the weapon, poised to strike. She looked around nervously as the wolves snarled and seethed. Courage surged through her body, but she was clearly outnumbered.

One of the larger wolves' ears perked up. It glanced around, then sprinted away into the woods. Other wolves' ears perked up in unison as they looked behind them. Gradually, they began to take steps away from Eve and Adam. Eve peered into the forest. With the Etz Hayim raised, she took a few steps forward. The wolves had formed two lines that made a path from the distant forest to Eve. Relieved the attack had stopped for the moment, Eve sat down next to Adam. Eve saw him bleeding. She wiped some blood off his face and kissed his forehead.

"You okay?" Eve asked. Adam smiled weakly.

"Forgive me for leaving you … I won't ever leave you again …" His voice was barely above a whisper. Adam's eyes met Eve's. He had given everything he had, all of his strength, to save her.

"It's okay …" Eve caressed Adam's cheek as she returned his gaze. Adam could see forgiveness in her eyes. From deep within the forest, branches broke under the foot of an unknown creature. A deep growl shook the forest floor.

"Panther …" Adam whispered. Dread filled his voice.

Eve looked around. A black panther emerged from the forest. Its sinewy muscles underneath its coat contained explosive strength. All the wolves stopped and began to watch its movements. It had a singular intention.

With its sharp gray eyes, the panther looked past the wolves and stared at Adam and Eve. About fifty yards separated him from his prey. As it continued to move toward Adam and Eve, the wolves made way for the dominant predator. It was there to finish what the wolves had started. The panther let out another low, threatening growl.

As if a portal opened from another world, the forest lit up with yellow and orange hues as a roaring fire appeared fifty yards behind Adam and Eve. Its brightness pierced the forest as it shone in the opposite direction of the panther. At its presence, the wolves fled. The black panther shifted its head as its eyes adjusted to the brightness. Elohim stepped out from the flame. Instinctively, the panther bolted toward Adam and Eve. Elohim began to run directly toward it from the opposite end.

Adam wrapped his arms around Eve to protect her. Closing in, a dozen yards away, the panther jumped in the air. Adam looked up before the giant beast landed. Elohim leapt, meeting the creature in midair. Elohim grabbed its throat, took the creature down, and pinned it against the earth. The panther violently swung its head; its teeth glistened, and its demonic gray eyes flashed with hatred. Eve and Adam each held their breath as their father tightened his grip around the creature's throat.

"Enough. Out—now!" Elohim commanded the creature. The animal shape-shifted. From within the skin of the creature, Lilly emerged. Her jealous eyes stared at Adam and Eve.

"I SAID SHOW YOURSELF," Elohim commanded once again.

Lilly began to convulse. As Elohim applied more pressure to her throat, she gasped. Her skin melted away like wax. Underneath her façade, Lucifer appeared. Lucifer looked aged, weak, and decrepit. His dark wings were crooked and mangled. Lucifer seethed with hate as he looked at Elohim. Elohim leaned down and whispered.

"I AM THEIR FATHER … DO NOT FORGET THIS." Elohim moved back and looked into Lucifer's eyes. Lucifer growled at Elohim. In an instant, Elohim's eyes lit up like fire. Lucifer violently shook his head and tried to avoid his maker's fierce gaze.

"You will strike their heel." Elohim looked back at Eve, then returned his focus to the fallen angel in front of him. "But her offspring will crush your head." With Elohim's words, scales began to cover Lucifer's body. His wings disintegrated into the earth as the scales traveled up to his neck and face. Lucifer howled in terror as they covered his mouth and eyes. Under Elohim's grip, Lucifer was completely covered in black scales. He opened his mouth; his forked tongue darted out and hissed at Elohim. Elohim smashed the snake's head with his left fist, disorienting the creature.

Elohim rose with the snake gripped in his right hand and threw it into the woods. Lucifer traveled through the air and smacked against a tree trunk before slithering into the forest. Elohim turned and walked toward Adam and Eve. The fire extinguished from his eyes. He kneeled and hugged Adam. His hands moved across Adam's wounds, and Adam's broken flesh began to heal. Adam marveled as he looked up and searched Elohim's eyes.

"I didn't know it was you ... all I saw was fire ..." Adam said, his voice trembling with shame. "I'm sorry ... I listened to the serpent." Adam paused for a moment at his father's penetrating gaze. "I knew it was a lie ... but I didn't know what would come to pass. From Eve's hands, she gave me the forbidden fruit, and I ate."

"Cursed is the ground, my son. Creation mourns for what has been lost. From the dust, I formed you, and to the dust, you will return." As Elohim spoke, a tear ran down his cheek. Eve began to weep at her father's words.

Elohim looked at Eve and gently took her wrists in his hands. "You will suffer terribly. When you birth sons and daughters, it will be in great pain." Elohim's lower lip trembled as he continued. "You will desire your husband, and in both his strength and his weakness, he will rule over you." Eve looked down at her wrist and then at the top of her hand in amazement. All her scarring was gone. Her wounds had completely healed.

On Elohim's back were two cloaks made from animal hide. Elohim took them off his back and gave them to his children.

"You cannot return to the garden. You cannot reach out your hand and take from the tree of life—to eat from it and live forever," Elohim said, a deep sadness marking his voice.

At his words, the roaring fire in the distance approached and entered Elohim. Fire rippled through his being. Eve and

Adam backed away and shielded their eyes. The heat of the fire increased, and the light from the fire began to flash as if Elohim were a pulsating star. The flame lit everything around them with a brightness so intense they had to look away. In a burst of light, Elohim vanished from their sight.

ACT FOUR

A TRAITOR'S DEATH

THE BIRTH

XXI

3972 B.C. ~ 4 Years Later

MENAKIEL FOLDED HIS WINGS BEHIND HIM. Gazing between the trees, he watched in amazement.

"Shhh ..." Eve cradled a newborn in her arms. "Shhh ... it's okay ..."

Abel softly cried, letting Eve know he was hungry. She brought him up to her breast. She looked above the campfire and smiled at Adam.

Adam gently rocked Cain, Abel's one-year-old brother, in his arms. He quietly sang a lullaby.

"Beautiful boy ..." Adam whispered into Cain's ear. Cain's chest rose and fell with delicate breaths as he slept. Adam ran his hand over his son's chest and, with a finger, softly pressed Cain's belly button. Cain slowly opened his eyes and giggled. Adam looked up and returned Eve's smile.

"Look ..." Adam whispered excitedly. He raised Cain up

to the light of the campfire. Eve glanced at the small indentation in the center of Cain's stomach. Adam laughed. "Can you believe it? Look at this!"

"Shhh …" Eve couldn't hide her smile. She had the difficult task of quieting both Abel's cries and Adam's observations. All in a futile attempt to help her babies sleep. Though she was less fixated on their belly buttons than Adam, she marveled at their small noses, charming eyes, beautiful hands, and ticklish feet. She would do anything for Abel and Cain. Her heart wondered if the overwhelming love she had for her boys was what Elohim felt in his heart for her and Adam.

The stars above their encampment shimmered in the night sky as Menakiel took in the sight of Adam and Eve's children, Elohim's first grandchildren.

3947 B.C. ~ 25 Years Later

Adam glanced back at his two sons. He planted two fingers firmly to his lips, motioning for them to be quiet. The sun was hot overhead. The three men measured their breaths to be silent. Crouching on the ground, Adam raised two fingers to point ahead. About fifty yards away, a large black panther stopped and sniffed the air. Each man gripped his respective spear.

Cain was an astute hunter. His proficiency, however, had come at a high cost. Scars from deep gashes on his left shoulder and the right side of his rib cage spoke of hard lessons. His past was littered with multiple encounters with creatures whom he had barely escaped. He had faced animals so violent, swift, and deadly that their presence prevented most people back at the encampment from venturing beyond the group or the rudimentary defenses that had been erected. There were many times when Cain had escaped with his life but without meat for the tribe. Cain diligently watched as the creature moved. The panther peered toward the spot where the three men laid in wait. Its sharp golden eyes scanned for threats and possible food.

Abel stepped, and under his feet, twigs cracked. Suddenly, the apex predator stopped in its tracks. Cain lowered his hand quickly, motioning Abel to stop any further movements. Abel had just deprived them of the element of surprise. Cain knew this could be the difference between life and death. Anger swept over Cain's face as he glared at his brother.

Cain looked at Adam and saw that his father had closed his eyes. He again motioned to his brother to wait. Adam breathed in deeply, and through the vision of the hawk flying a hundred feet above the panther, he peered down to see if the cat was by itself or if other equally dangerous predators were in the area. If there were only one panther, they could take a stand and bring food back for the tribe. If there were multiple panthers, it would mean almost certain death. They'd be the hunted, and the only option for survival would be a covert retreat. The animal skins they wore masked their smell and would buy them time. With a short, sudden breath, Adam's eyes opened. His two boys waited as slowly Adam's pupils and irises re-formed within his previously white eyes as his spirit returned fully to his body.

"He's alone," Adam whispered.

A hard smile spread across Cain's face. He nodded at Abel for reassurance. Abel leapt to his feet and let out a cry, "Arrhhh!"

The panther's head turned around. With tunnel vision, it immediately sprang into action. It ran with explosive speed. Its jaws loosened as its nose could smell their masked flesh. When it was thirty yards out, Abel arched his spear above his head and launched it. The spear whizzed through the air. The panther pivoted at the last second, dodging the projectile.

When it was twenty yards away, Adam sprang up. With all his might, he launched his spear at the oncoming predator. This time, the panther had leapt but couldn't change direction, and the tip grazed its right shoulder. Wounded and enraged, the enormous animal growled as it picked up speed.

Ten yards out, Cain read the panther's movements. He waited for it to leap. As soon as it was in the air, committed to its direction, Cain launched his spear. It whizzed through the air and went right through the throat of the dangerous predator. The tip of the spear ripped through its flesh and came out on the other side of its neck. With a loud thud, it collapsed just a few feet in front of the men. Relief flooded them. Big grins spread on their faces. Cain reached out and grabbed Abel, hugging him. As the adrenaline surged through their bodies, the three men laughed at how close they had come to death.

"He was fast!" Adam shared with a huge smile on his face. "Nice work, son." He hugged Cain. He looked at Abel and gave him a hug. "You'll do better next time," Adam reassured him. Abel smiled and nodded, thankful it was over.

"Come on, tie him up." Adam pulled out some vines that were wound up like rope. "Let's not delay. It's been too long since everyone has eaten a solid meal."

Cain and Abel took the vines. Cain tied the hind legs together while Abel focused on the front legs. Once secured, they tied the other ends onto the two spears. They each rested a spear on their shoulders and followed Adam. The large animal hung underneath as Abel took up the rear section and Cain the front. Abel was fixated on the large, vacant eyes of the animal that now faced him as it swung back and forth with the tempo of their footsteps. Both young men eagerly followed their father as they carried the large animal back to the encampment. Tonight they would feast.

A dozen adults a little younger than Cain and Abel crowded around. Led by Eve, they greeted the men like returning heroes. Some of the women carried infants while a handful of children ran up to greet them. Cain and Abel lowered the two spears that held the animal in the air.

"Wow!" said Seth, a five-year-old boy. "What is it?"

"Dinner." Cain smiled broadly. He rustled the boy's hair. "Go start the fire."

Seth nodded excitedly while the other children followed him to the fire pit.

"How'd it go?" Eve gazed into Adam's eyes.

"He was the only one. Thankfully." Adam smiled softly. He kissed Eve.

"Looks like we'll be eating for some time now." Eve gave Cain a hug and kiss on the cheek. He nodded and smiled.

"You can thank Cain for that." Adam put his hand proudly on Cain's shoulder.

"You look lovely," Abel complimented Eve, then gave her a hug and kiss on the cheek.

"Stop!" Eve replied teasingly. "Help Seth." Abel nodded with a big grin.

The fire grew large, and laughter abounded as the large family ate the fresh meat. The panther spun over the fire on a rotisserie. A sharp carving knife was beside the pit so anyone hungry could take off a slice. As the fire burned, its reflection could be seen in the large cat's open, vacant eyes.

"Tell us about him … please!" Luluwa, the young wife of Abel, spoke up.

Cain looked over at her and couldn't help but notice her attractive features and large hazel eyes.

"Elohim?" Adam said softly.

Cain wished she had brought up any other topic. Anything would be better, he thought to himself. Anything but him.

"Yes! What was he like?" Luluwa asked.

A long silence fell over the family. All eyes looked toward Adam. Sensing the tension, a few of the children glanced at Cain with anticipation.

"It's okay, Father ... you can share with us another time," Abel said softly. Eve looked at Adam reassuringly.

"Will *we* ever see him?" Luluwa asked another question. She longed to know if Elohim would reveal himself to her family, not just to Eve and Adam. Adam smiled, but a pain in his eyes was visible to everyone.

"Don't speak of him," Cain said. His voice carried across the fire. "If he no longer wants to be seen, why should we care?"

"Quiet, Cain," Adam said with a flash of anger in his eyes.

"Why should we?" Cain defied his father's order. "He doesn't provide." Cain looked over at the gashes in his shoulder, then back at Adam. "He doesn't protect. What does he do?"

"Enough!" Adam shouted. Startled by the fury in his voice, his family felt the tension rise. "That's enough!"

"You've seen the dangers out there. I've seen them. What has Elohim ever done for us!?" Cain again disregarded the wishes of his father. Anger surged through Adam.

Adam leapt up and charged toward Cain. In a swift and violent movement, he snatched the Etz Hayim and used it to push Cain off the large rock he had been sitting on. He pressed the Etz Hayim tightly against his firstborn's throat. Cain looked up with wide eyes as his father seethed above him in rage.

"Stop!" Eve's cry pierced the night air. Adam looked at the shock on Eve's face, then back down at Cain. A deep bitterness was in his son's eyes.

"Whoa!" Adam looked down and released his grip. "I'm sorry, son! Forgive me."

Cain could feel the cool earth under his back. He watched

his father throw the Etz Hayim on the ground and walk away from the fire. Abel got up and extended his hand to Cain.

"He's sorry, brother …" Abel offered meekly. Cain refused Abel's help and got up.

"Maybe next time my spear will miss," Cain whispered.

MURDER

XXII

3936 B.C. ~ 11 Years Later

G ET!" CAIN TOOK A STICK AND STARTED BEATING the sheep. Abel's flock had been encroaching on his fields, and his irritation had reached a peak.

The sun was at high noon, and Cain sweated profusely. He stooped down and grabbed another large stone from the field. Tossing it to the side, he saw Abel approach. Abel's flock had grown so large that it was routine for them to get into the fields Cain had been planting.

Cain wiped the sweat from his brow. In the distance, he saw Eve with grandchildren. They were under the shade of a large tree listening to stories. As he looked across his field, he felt pride that the crops he was planting would feed many mouths. They had been providing food without the danger of a hunt. He smiled at the thought and looked toward his brother approaching. After putting in hours of work, he wasn't surprised to see Abel there once most of the work had already been done.

"Progress!" Abel shouted.

"You need to keep your animals out of here. They trample and eat the seed," Cain responded flatly.

"The flock has grown, and I don't have enough sons to shepherd them all," Abel joked. Cain stared at his brother.

"I'm serious, Abel," Cain said.

"Okay." Abel nodded apologetically. Abel laid the Etz Hayim he had been using to shepherd his sheep on the ground. Cain didn't know why it was so special. According to his father's story, it was the first gift Elohim had given his father. "I'm sorry," Abel said. He looked at Cain with compassion as he saw his frustration. "Let me help you."

Cain looked over enviously at the gift now in his brother's possession. He didn't want it. Simultaneously, for some reason he couldn't quite explain, it bothered him that Abel had it.

"There's plenty of work that needs to be done. Help me clear these stones," Cain said, pointing at the unfinished rows that needed to be cleared.

The two men started grabbing rocks from the area tilled by Cain and tossed them outside the field. The work was hard. After a few hours, Cain's body ached. He saw Abel sit in the center of the field and take a drink of water from a flask.

Near the corner of the field, a single sheep came over and started eating some seed on the surface of the ground. Cain shook his head. Thirsty, he started to walk toward Abel to request a drink. Distracted by the sheep, he missed a large stone in front of him and slammed his foot against it. Pain shot up his body. Cain clenched his jaw, not making a noise. He hunched over and examined his now bloodied toe. About twenty yards away, he saw Abel drink again from the flask.

Abel held the flask above him and emptied it. Elohim's favorite had left nothing for him. Cain looked at the stone he had walked into. Infuriated, he bent down and started digging around the stone's edges. As he dug, it was clear Abel had missed a massive stone in the area he should have cleared. Finally, he got to the bottom of it and lifted it out of the earth. How could his brother miss a rock of this size? The rage inside Cain grew. Maybe Abel was trying to sabotage his field, Cain thought.

Suspicion and cynicism ran hard through Cain's veins. He walked over behind Abel. Cain's shadow engulfed his brother as the brutal sun beat hot overhead. Over the years, Cain had grown to despise Abel. Abel looked up and saw hatred in Cain's face.

"What are you doing?" Abel shouted fearfully as he saw the large rock in his brother's hands.

Eve turned at the sounds of her sons.

With a swift and violent movement, Cain smashed the rock against Abel's face. Abel was thrown a foot away by the force of the blow and his head split open from the sudden impact.

"No!" Eve screamed. Cain looked up and saw Eve under the tree.

She sprang to her feet and ran toward her two sons. Cain threw down the bloodied rock and began to walk away. Eve ran as fast as she could. Her knees hit the dirt. Picking up her son's bleeding head, she wept violently as she stared into his brown eyes. Blood flowed from his skull and pooled on the earth below. Eve's body convulsed with agony. She arched her back and, with a primal cry, pleaded to the heavens above to return her son's spirit to his body. Pain consumed her as she watched one son walk away while the other died in her arms.

Vultures circled above. The blood that pooled underneath Abel slowly trickled into the crevices of the earth. It flowed past insects and rocks. The deeper it went, the colder and harder the earth became. Moving beyond space and time, the blood found the tips of the roots of an ancient tree. The roots began to soak up Abel's blood; it traveled back in time as it was carried up through the tubes. The higher the roots carried the blood, the warmer and softer the earth became. Finally, it was carried into the ancient tree itself.

As Abel's blood traveled back through time, the roots from the tree of the knowledge of good and evil began to drink. Above ground, a young Eve took her first bite of the forbidden fruit before handing it to Abel's father. Adam took a bite. Their chests grew tight while their veins turned black. A sudden wind blew. They peered into each other's eyes as terror consumed their hearts. Moments later, they collapsed to the earth.

THE RIGHTFUL HEIR

XXIII

3976 B.C. to 131 B.C.

THE DESCENDANTS OF ADAM

Adam	Man
Seth	*Appointed*
Enosh	*Mortal*
Kenan	*Sorrow*
Mahalalel	*The Blessed God*
Jared	*Shall Come Down*
Enoch	*Teaching*
Methuselah	*His Death Shall Bring*
Lamech	*The Despairing*
Noah	*Rest*

L UCIFER DISCOVERED THE HEARTS OF THE SON AND daughter of Elohim were persuadable, even unto betrayal. Their father had abandoned them to a world Lucifer now had dominion over. He would adopt them as his own. Moving through Lilly, he took the spirits of Adam and Eve captive. Advancing through Cain, he spilled the blood of Abel. As their numbers increased, he savagely drank more blood from each generation. Animalistically, he consumed their life force. Each year, he became more dangerous. Through trial and error, he had secured a devasting victory in Eden. After he toppled Adam, the former ruler of Earth was reduced to a pawn on a chess board. Would the son of Elohim survive what was to come?

Heaven held its breath at the turn of events. The possibility that more angels would rebel against heaven resounded within Lucifer's ranks. If part of the angelic armies had already turned, if the son of God could bend under Lucifer's will, why not Elohim himself? But within his growing confidence, Lucifer was haunted by a single prophetic utterance from the Uncreated One.

Lucifer would strike the heel of Elohim's offspring, but they would crush his head. All creation heard the weight of Elohim's word. But in a world of free will, perhaps there was a way to change the outcome of the prophetic declaration. Why wouldn't there be? Nothing was inevitable.

A plan slowly crystalized within Lucifer's mind. Destroy the coming offspring, murdering the one who posed the threat. Enslave all others. By sheer force, he would bend space and time to tilt the future of the world in his favor. But the question birthed from the prophecy still perplexed Lucifer's mind. Which of Adam's offspring would attempt to fulfill the word given from heaven?

In his pride, Lucifer grew confident any future threat

would be rendered impotent. Elohim's throne was his destiny, his rightful place. Within the darkness of his machinations, he saw a way to command his own ascendance. Elohim loved his children. Lucifer would use this weakness against him. Embedded within this idea was a presumption that he understood the nature of the love Elohim possessed. Or did his love possess him? Lucifer was rattled by the question. Which was it?

From the moment Lucifer had seen the young Adam run into the arms of his father in Eden, he hadn't understood it. Lucifer had watched as Elohim tenderly held the hand of his young daughter as they walked together in the garden. He had never been embraced by Elohim the way he embraced his children. What was it about them that so drew Elohim's heart? Within laughter and joy, adventure and play, he saw the looks of intimacy they had shared. There was a glory to it that captivated all of heaven. No matter. Perhaps he'd never understand.

Intoxicated by envy, he knew what he must do. He would drive and twist a jagged dagger deep into the heart of love by destroying what Elohim cared most about. Hell's wrath would descend upon the sons of Elohim. The wages of their sin would be certain death.

Finite energy and resources would be strategically positioned. Each generation would be closely examined and studied. Every spirit from the depths would have an assignment. Nothing would be wasted. He'd work in the heart of man to act out of selfish ambition and fear. Cloaked in light, Lucifer would lull some generations to sleep with prosperity. For them, abundance would be their undoing. He would create a sense that they themselves were gods. Their infatuation with trinkets and tokens of prestige would render them the easiest to manipulate. He would entice them to obsess over little dreams, unable to see beyond the attraction of fleeting wealth or power that not a single one of them would be able to hold on to. Death would take it all. He would take it all. The worship of pleasure would reduce the mortals to mere appetites.

For other generations, he would orchestrate unimaginable conflict, death, and disease. He would convince them they were unknown, unloved, and forgotten. Amid despair, they would convince themselves that Elohim was unaware of their pain or, even better, he was the one causing it. In the darkness of their minds, Lucifer would whisper that the one who breathed the breath of life into each of them in their mother's womb was blind to their plight. More than that, he was reckless and abusive. Subtly, Lucifer would infer control was preferable over free will. Security and comfort were more desirable than freedom. With their spirits broken, they would stare into mirrors and see only orphans looking back. Some would even come to believe they came from nothing and there was no creator. Over time, millions would be enslaved within a carefully constructed web of lies. All affliction imposed served a greater purpose.

Within the depths of the Earth, within the prison called Sheol, the cries of his sons and daughters would haunt the King of Heaven. The collective cry of those on the Earth would add to the chorus of pain. Lucifer understood the consequences. He welcomed them. At some point, the sheer volume of voices would eventually force Elohim's hand. He would come down from his high and lofty place. Elohim would enter into an ambush that would be skillfully set. In Lucifer's cunning, he would entrap Elohim in the same way he had trapped his children. He would conspire with Elohim's offspring to take the life of the one chosen by the prophesy to crush his head. With Elohim defeated on Earth, Lucifer would ascend to the throne of heaven. The victory in the garden was but the start of the real battle he would ruthlessly wage. The prophetic utterance would be nullified. Elohim's throne would be his. It was only a matter of time.

Many nights, Menakiel comforted Adam. While Adam no longer walked with his father in the garden, Elohim still spoke to the patriarch. Menakiel witnessed the prophetic visions Adam received nearly every night. His true father gave him wisdom and warnings. He gave his son insights into the plans of Lucifer. At times, the dreams contained hidden messages meant to be understood by Menakiel alone. As Adam communed with his father in the night, Menakiel would act in the world of the spirit as directed. Other times, impressions were purposed for only Adam to discern. This gave Adam foresight to protect his family from Lucifer's next attack. The spirit world and the world of flesh and blood cooperated.

Lucifer moved in cunning ways. Eventually, through the brokenness in Adam's being, he found a way to join Menakiel in Adam's dreams. After the sun set, Lucifer learned how to cast visions into Adam's mind while he slept. Some nights, Adam had dreams from his father; other nights, he'd have dreams from Lucifer. Understanding both the source and the meaning of the dreams created enormous stress for Adam. If he didn't accurately discern the source, death could visit his family. If he discerned the source correctly but misunderstood the meaning, the lives of his children and grandchildren could be lost to the demonic or natural world. Life and death constantly hung in the balance.

With the lives of his family at stake, tension and pressure on the patriarch increased. Even with foreknowledge, all had to be on constant guard. During the waking hours, the attacks were relentless. Whether awake or asleep, Adam found little rest. Dark clouds of total war loomed on the horizon. Adam saw this within the visions Elohim gave him. Adam was a brilliant strategist, but he felt inadequate for the task in front of him. How could one man protect his family from all threats posed by the entire fallen realm?

Though he was surrounded by family, Adam felt he walked the Earth alone. None but Eve could truly understand what had been lost. None had walked with his father. What happened between him and Eve broke his heart. He had failed her when she had needed him most. He came to believe that somewhere in Eden she had lost the keys to her own heart. That she couldn't have let him in even if she had wanted to. Though rare, at times, he saw a fleeting smile with a hint of joy on her face. These smiles were usually displayed when she held a new grandchild in her arms. These moments gave him momentary peace. But the peace was stolen quickly. A surprise attack or incorrect interpretation could snuff out the life of the child at any time. No one was ever truly safe. Eve's beauty never faded, but occasions for joy became infrequent.

Memories of Cain and Abel as two young boys haunted

Adam. In his mind's eye, he still saw them as children. It was as if it were just yesterday that he had seen them playing in the river. The brothers built forts. They explored. Together, Adam taught them how to hunt. He saw both boys laugh and celebrate as Cain caught his first fish. Beyond Eve, they were the apples of his eye. He would do anything for them.

But something had shifted when they got older. They had grown distant as they pursued different ways to provide for the family. Adam knew Elohim had spoken to both his sons. He could tell within the open heart of Abel that his ways had been pleasing to Elohim. Elohim had also spoken with Cain, but over time, Cain had grown angry. He had despised a world he had no control over. A world where all seemed to suffer. He had blamed Elohim and refused his ways. In his growing rage, he took the life of his brother. The pain of losing his beloved son drove a stake through Adam's heart. That his other son was capable of murder caused questions to arise in his soul. Most questions he didn't know how to ask, much less answer.

When he had lost his son, he knew the serpent's hand was at play. He saw his growing influence manifest in Cain. Adam hated Lucifer for it. But as time passed, a difficult question rose in his heart. The source of the question was unknown to Adam, but it troubled him deeply nonetheless. Why hadn't Elohim protected Abel? Certainly, he was powerful enough. Why would he allow such loss in the world he had created? Adam loved his boy … and now he was gone. Elohim didn't know the pain he felt every single day. He never could. He had never lost his own son. There was no way Elohim could identify with Adam. The weight of this pain Adam alone had to carry.

It was unfair. It was a wound Adam knew he would never heal from. How could he?

Lucifer had caused it, but Elohim had allowed it. Perhaps Elohim's hidden shadow was more grotesque than Lucifer's. Perhaps there wasn't much of a difference between the two. Adam resisted the thoughts, but he was a father who had outlived his own son, and the accusation gradually grew. Eventually, the pain seemed to splinter into a million pieces and a foreboding madness threatened to swallow him whole.

Lucifer continued to cast questions and visions into Adam's mind. Many nights, Adam woke in a cold sweat. He would do anything he could to avoid going back to sleep. He had never wanted the dark visions of the future Lucifer showed him. But he also desired to be free from the weight of the warnings his father gave him. He wanted nothing more than for all the visions to stop. They never did. As years passed, Menakiel witnessed Adam's mind slowly devolve. In the middle of the night, fear would often consume him. Eve would frantically shake Adam to help him escape whatever darkness was chasing him. When he'd wake up, his eyes would be wide and filled with a terror that frightened Eve.

Adam made a vow; he would no longer speak of what happened in the night. He would withhold the insights his father gave him to protect his own family. He knew the life-giving power Elohim possessed. Perhaps withholding the visions would draw Elohim's attention. Adam could force Elohim to finally see and understand his pain. Perhaps Elohim would breathe new life back into his boy. Maybe the two could be reunited. If Elohim didn't see Adam's pain, perhaps he would respond to the pain of his family and for their sake resurrect Abel. As Adam withheld the foresight his father provided, Lucifer slowly took more of his descendants prematurely to the grave. Grief overtook his extended family. There was great mourning among his descendants.

With his silence, the responsibility to protect shifted from Adam to Eve's shoulders. Everyone in the family began to look toward her. Desperate, she asked Elohim for help. Soon, she began to dream. The dreams from her father filled the gap and provided prophetic insight into Lucifer's next attack. The dreams she had were the thin layer of safety her family needed to slow the steady march of death that seemed to be all encompassing. The lifeless bones of Adam's son were never brought back to life. Adam's visions only worsened. Eve watched as her husband slowly gave up hope and his will to live.

To each and every one of his descendants, Adam made the same declaration: prepare for war. Adam taught his descendants what he understood of Lucifer's plan. Earth was a stepping-stone. The skirmishes they now faced were only the beginning. Hell's ultimate intention was to overthrow not just the Earth but the order of heaven itself. They must hold the line. If heaven's order was also overthrown, the hope for Earth would vanish. The weight of the task was too much for Adam and his sons.

Within the dire warnings, however, was a faint glimmer of hope. Face to face, Adam taught nine generations what Elohim had told him the night he had received the Etz Hayim as a young man. If they ever were to be separated, it was Elohim's way back to Adam. It was Adam's hope that it could be his and his descendants' way back to Elohim. It became a sacred and repeated understanding among the patriarchs. As each generation passed the Etz Hayim down, over time, it was something shrouded more in mystery than understanding. Toward the end, most thought of it ritualistically, and its purpose was a hopeful wish rather than anything of true significance.

Adam gave the Etz Hayim to Seth, who gave it to Enosh. Enosh gave it to Kenan, who gave it to Mahalalel. Mahalalel gave it to Jared, who gave it to Enoch. Enoch gave it to Methuselah, who gave it to Lamech. Lamech gave the Etz Hayim to Noah prior to the great rains that flooded the Earth. It quaked with power as Noah held it up to close the ark. Before the waters subsided, Noah used it for balance as the ark was tossed back and forth by the violent seas. Later, Noah would have nightmares as he recollected the screams of thousands outside the boat before they drowned.

On his deathbed, Noah bestowed the Etz Hayim on Shem, who eventually handed it down to Terah, who gave it to his son Abraham. At Elohim's command, Abraham traveled to Mount Moriah. Convinced that his God demanded sacrifice, like all other gods, he took his son to the top of the mountain. Though he hated every step, he would be faithful to the one who called him. He was a child of obedience. Abraham had the Etz Hayim in one hand and a raised knife in the other. Menakiel appeared and put his hand on Abraham's shoulder. Relief and emotion swept through every part of Abraham's being. His hand trembled as he lowered the sacrificial knife, sparing his beloved son Isaac. In that moment, he saw Elohim did not demand a sacrifice but provided one in place of his son.

Abraham eventually passed the Etz Hayim down to Isaac, who passed the staff down to Jacob. Jacob dreamed of a ladder that connected heaven and Earth. He encountered Elohim in the desert and was given a new name, Israel. While Abraham's descendants were in captivity, Amram hid baby Moses when Pharaoh decided to commit genocide against the numerous children of Israel. As an adult, Moses lived in solitude in the desert for forty years. His only inheritance was the Etz Hayim, which most people thought of as an ornate staff or heirloom, if they thought of it at all. While weathered over time, the ancient symbols and the map carved deeply into the wood of the Etz Hayim were still visible.

Moses encountered Elohim in the desert within the roaring fires of a burning bush. Elohim gave a mandate to free the children of Israel from their slavery in Egypt. The most powerful empire would not give up their slaves without a fight. The weight of the task overwhelmed Moses, but he found love and support from his brother Aaron.

Soon after Moses's encounter with Elohim, the brothers appeared in Pharaoh's court. The Egyptian ruler looked on with contempt at the two desert fathers. Aaron threw down the Etz Hayim in the presence of all Pharaoh's sorcerers, and it became a snake. The sorcerers' and magicians' staffs turned into snakes as well. But the snake from the Etz Hayim devoured the half dozen snakes that came from Pharaoh's sorcerers. Then the snake hit the ground with its belly, springing into the air.

When Moses grabbed it midair, the snake transformed back into the Etz Hayim. Pharaoh's court gasped at the display, but Pharaoh's heart grew hard.

After plagues, death, and devastation crippled Egypt, Pharaoh relented and let the slaves who had built much of his empire go. With an ocean in front of the children of Israel and an army behind them after Pharaoh changed his mind, death seemed certain. Moses raised the Etz Hayim, and the staff shook violently with a power from heaven. A mighty wind descended as an army of the angelic led by Menakiel pushed the water back. The Red Sea parted, and Israel's children were saved. Moses found the one behind the burning bush both mysterious and faithful.

The Etz Hayim was eventually given to Joshua and Jesse. They did not see the significance and beauty of the worn staff, but a young man named David did. David used it in combat against bears and lions as he protected his father's sheep. He put it into the hands of his best friend Jonathan to hold before he took his sling to kill Goliath. From David to the wise hands of Solomon, the staff moved across space and time. Solomon eventually gave it to the father of Savah. Savah gave it to his son, the prophet Elijah. Elijah raised it at the top of Mount Carmel, and a bolt of white fire rained down from heaven. It consumed the sacrifice and judged the prophets of Ba'hal.

The prophet Ezekiel had it in hand as he roared a prophecy over a sea of dead bones, calling them to life. Later, the Etz Hayim was taken by the Babylonians with all the temple artifacts they captured in their defeat of Judah. During a night of revelry to celebrate their victories, they witnessed the hand of God write on the inside of their palace wall. Goblets filled with choice wine fell to the floor, and the Babylonians saw the following Hebrew letters written: "לְקָת." After summoning a prophet named Daniel, they discovered that the God of the Hebrews had weighed them on the scales of righteousness and found them lacking. The ones who handled sacred things as common were judged. Not all the Babylonians in the palace that evening lived to see the next day.

Daniel grew in favor before the new king in Babylon. High officials surrounding the king grew envious and conspired against him. Their plot resulted in Daniel being thrown into a den filled with hungry lions. Daniel raised the Etz Hayim above his head, and the lions locked their jaws until the morning came.

After Adam had fallen, the King of Heaven had assigned Menakiel the task of making sure the Etz Hayim would find itself in the right hands. Menakiel had confidence that at the right time, Elohim would eventually reveal who was its next rightful heir. Through wars, judgments, and various conquests, the Etz Hayim became lost in history's brutal tempest. Until one day, it finally reemerged.

VISIONS

XXIV

131 B.C.

A YOUNG BOY NAMED NOAH RAN AFTER HIS OLDER brother Levi. The day happened to be Levi's ninth birthday, and the two boys were excited for the special meal they knew their mom was preparing. Both boys ran from the nearby trees outside the walls of Jerusalem. Noah felt the heat from the midday sun. He and his brother had been playing for a few hours outside the protective walls of the city in a nearby grove of trees. As Noah ran, he saw Levi trip, fall, and land on his stomach. He caught up to his brother and extended his hand to help him up. Puffy white clouds were scattered across an otherwise crystal blue sky. It had rained the previous day, and the air smelled fresh.

"You okay?" Noah asked breathlessly.

"Yeah, I'm okay ..." Levi brushed himself off. "Did you see that?"

"Look ..." Noah backtracked to where Levi had tripped.

Noah's eyes were wide and full of wonder as he pointed to the ground. Lying flat, protruding just a bit above the earth, was some sort of ornately carved wood. It looked as if two-thirds of a staff was buried horizontally. The third that had snagged Levi's foot was covered in a thin layer of dust and dirt.

"What is it?" Levi asked. Noah shrugged.

Trees provided shade as both boys got on their knees. Each started digging around the staff to unearth it. Levi wrapped his hands around the rod. He blew the sand and dirt off it.

"Whoa!" Noah beamed at their newly found treasure.

"Look at this!" Levi gazed at the end.

Though the end had been buried, somehow two twigs with two deep green leaves each had grown from the end. The boys looked at the four green leaves. For a second, they thought they saw a bright green light flow from the bottom veins of the leaves to the tips. The green leaves seemed to shimmer in the light of the sun. Their eyes met and sparkled with excitement.

"What was that?!" Levi said eagerly.

"Look!" Noah pointed excitedly to the intricate carvings on the staff. His eyes gazed at the top of it. "What is it?"

"Carvings ..." Levi handed the Etz Hayim to Noah so he could take a closer look.

"It's a weapon!" Noah lifted the Etz Hayim over his head like a sword. He waved it back and forth as if he were attacking.

"Let me see it!" Levi said enthusiastically.

The two boys played with the staff for a few hours. They smacked stones with it to see how far the rocks could fly. Both boys took turns hitting low-hanging branches from trees. They pretended they were cutting down enemy soldiers. Soon, they heard their mother's voice in the distance.

"Noah, Levi, dinner time!" Rachel called out. The young boys, exhausted, ran toward home. Noah carried the Etz Hayim in his hand.

"Leave that out; we'll play with it tomorrow," Levi said. The boys were just outside the walls of Jerusalem. "Give it to me."

Noah handed the staff to Levi. Levi took the staff and ran the narrower end into the ground a few inches. The end with the four deep green leaves stood up vertically. The light from the setting sun seemed to make the leaves shimmer yet again. The boys looked at it and smiled. To Noah, it looked like they had just planted a small tree. To Levi, it looked like they had hidden a new toy in plain sight. The boys left the Etz Hayim and walked through the south gate of Jerusalem. Tonight was special as Rachel had prepared an uncommon dinner for Levi's birthday.

The two boys found their father, Joshua, outside their house. He gave each boy a big hug and kiss.

"Come, Mom's made something special tonight!" Joshua said as he looked with pride at his two young boys.

That night, each boy had their fill of lamb with hummus and olives. This was their father's favorite meal. Before bed, Joshua sang them a lullaby. According to tradition, it was the same song Adam had sung over his sons Cain and Abel. It was the first melody Adam's ears had heard as his father had sung over him the night of his creation. To hear his father's voice was Noah's favorite evening ritual.

As Joshua saw his boys begin to fall into a deep sleep, he

was filled with wonder. He often thought of what it might have been like for Yahweh, the very first father. What was it like for him to have raised Adam as a young boy, to raise his first daughter, Eve, as a young girl? If he felt such a deep love for his boys, what might Yahweh have felt toward his children? He knew the strength of his love was but a shadow of Yahweh's. The love he felt for Noah and Levi was but a glimmer of the light and love that created the world itself.

While he did not see his creator, he felt Yahweh's presence as he slowly leaned over and kissed each boy.

After they had closed their eyes, both Levi and Noah dreamed about the creation of Adam from the dust of the Earth. In the same way their father Joshua had sang a song over them, within their dreams, they heard the ancient melody sung in celebration over Adam. Though they knew him by a different name, they saw a vision of Elohim. Inside the vision, he had broken off a branch from the tree of life. After carving ancient symbols and a map of Eden into it, Elohim gave it to his first son. In their dreams, each boy looked at the ancient writing, and slowly, the meaning carved into the side of the Etz Hayim was revealed. It read, "Seeing through the chaos of humanity and reaching in with God's strength to shepherd it." The legend became alive in their minds as the boys dreamed of a gift so special that, if Adam were ever separated from his father, the gift could somehow reunite them.

The morning couldn't have come soon enough. As the sun

rose over the city of peace, its rays beamed brightly through their window and hit the young boys' eyes, waking them. They rubbed the sleep from their eyes, stretched, dressed, and then made their way out to help their father with the field he had planted. After a few hours of work, Joshua left midday to go into the city to buy some tools for the work in the field. He suggested his young boys go play.

Levi and Noah grinned broadly at each other. They ran outside the city walls to where they had put the special staff into the ground. As they approached the Etz Hayim, it no longer had two twigs with two green leaves on each twig. The two boys stopped in their tracks; their eyes grew wide. The Etz Hayim had grown two feet overnight. The boys walked around what now looked like a small, budding tree. The two twigs were now the size of two young branches, and dozens of leaves had now grown. Levi approached it and put his hand on its trunk. He felt a surge of energy and life flow from the tree, through his hand, and into his body. He looked at Noah. Not knowing what to make of it, he shrugged.

"Are you sure it's this one?" Noah asked. Levi looked around to see if they might be mistaken. He looked at Noah and nodded. He turned once again toward the Etz Hayim.

"Look!" Levi focused on its trunk and saw the carvings he had noticed the previous day. The carvings seemed to have stretched around its now slightly larger circumference. "It's the same carvings ... Do you see it?" Levi asked excitedly. Noah nodded.

"What do you think it means?!" Noah asked eagerly.

Levi put his hands around it and tried to pull it out of the ground, but it had grown roots that anchored it to the earth. This time, Levi felt no energy. He simply felt the hard wood of the tree under his hands. Just then, they saw their father come out of the gate.

"Boys! What are you doing with that tree?" Joshua looked at his two sons and smiled.

He thought fondly of the days when he was younger and how he'd had adventures with his brothers outside the walls of Jerusalem.

"Come, there's much work to do!" Joshua exclaimed. Speechless, both boys followed their father back out to the field to finish the work they had started in the morning. Noah looked over his shoulder in disbelief at the Etz Hayim.

"Come," Levi said. "Don't worry; I'm sure we'll find new treasures!"

Noah returned Levi's smile and followed his older brother and father back to the field.

The two boys grew into two young men. As young men, they studied the Torah but found themselves going in different directions. Noah discovered that he had a deep appreciation of the oral tradition. He chose to study among the Pharisees and eventually became one. This was much to his mother's delight. Levi took solace in the written word and became a more conservatively minded Sadducee. This was to Joshua's delight.

The young men started families, and eventually Rachel

and Joshua became grandparents. The grandchildren delighted them both.

Though they belonged to different schools of thought on Yahweh, the God of their forefathers, both Noah and Levi loved each other deeply. Their families always remained close. After their father had passed, Noah would frequently take walks outside the city walls.

Occasionally, when he passed by a particular tree, which had grown more than thirty feet in the air, he'd have memories of his brother Levi putting a delicately carved staff in the ground. With time, he wondered if the memory was real or a byproduct of a child's imagination. While at times he swore he could still see the carvings he had seen as a young child etched into the massive trunk, at other times, he was certain he was just dreaming. Either way, whenever he looked at the tree, he felt a sense of peace and belonging. Noah never dismissed the importance of dreams, as he knew they were one of the many ways God had spoken to his forefathers. He understood that dreams tended to shape destinies.

THE WITNESSES

XXV

33 A.D. ~ Jerusalem, 164 Years Later

"His eyes were like a flame of fire, and on His head were many crowns. He had a name written that no one knew except Himself."
—Revelation 19:12 (NKJV)

I T HAD BEEN A STRANGE NIGHT, SIMON PETER THOUGHT to himself. He leaned his back against a tree in the garden of Gethsemane. He looked up at the pale moonlight. Its brightness caused the tree branches above him to cast shadows down below. He looked down at his feet. Earlier, before dinner, he had seen his master get into the position of a servant. He had taken warm water and, one by one, had washed his disciples' feet.

The lesser one was to always serve the greater one, so Peter initially refused Yeshua. He knew he was not greater than his own rabbi. Yeshua had told Peter he could have no part of him unless Peter was prepared to receive from him. He had told Peter that he could not give what he had not received. To learn to love, one must first receive love. After the rebuke, Peter let his master wash his feet. The interaction left Peter feeling jarred and unsure of himself. But the confusion and lack of understanding were no match for the peace he always felt around his rabbi.

The night air was cool, and Peter's stomach was full. James and John were already letting the food in their bellies close their eyes. This was despite Yeshua telling them to keep watch and pray. He had talked about no longer being with them. This deeply troubled Peter. Fear entered his heart, and he forgot about Yeshua's command that they watch and pray. The urgency in Yeshua's voice was displaced by the weakness of his body and the need for rest.

Peter's mind wandered. He thought of the time Yeshua asked him and the other disciples about who people said that he was. Depending on where they traveled, sometimes they heard people say he was Elijah, Jeremiah, John the Baptist, or perhaps some other prophet. But Peter knew differently. He was the Christ, the son of the living God, the anointed one destined to set men free. When he answered his rabbi's question, Peter saw an unmistakable light in Yeshua's eyes.

But Rome was a powerful enemy, Peter thought to himself. Oftentimes between the taxation and laws, he felt like a slave in his own country. What did it mean to be free, and how would this be done? He knew through Israel's history that this had only been accomplished by the sword. Over the years, he had seen his master use his hands to heal; it was difficult for him to imagine seeing those same hands pick up a weapon. But then how would this be done?

As Peter's mind continued to drift, he wondered what else his rabbi might be called. Some Jews had called him a prophet, his mother called him Yeshua, Greeks called him Jesus, and his disciples called him Teacher. Yeshua had eventually called them friends. This deeply touched Peter. Yeshua spoke frequently about his father in heaven. The heart that Yeshua revealed was very different from Peter's understanding of Yahweh. But every time Yeshua described his heavenly father, something came alive in Peter. His heart burned with desire to know even more. He had a thirst for his master's words that was unquenchable. The way Yeshua spoke of his relationship with his father in heaven sometimes both broke and mended Peter's heart in the same breath.

Peter wondered if Yeshua also had a name known only by his father in heaven. Did he have any other names, and what meaning would they carry? For some reason, he felt the names of God himself carried within them the very destinies of the children of Israel. Perhaps even his own. Peter thought if he could know them, then he could somehow also know the future.

As his mind continued to wander, Peter thought of the teaching in the Torah that explained God is one. His thoughts drifted to the ancient writings in Genesis, the first book of the Torah. Within its sacred pages, Yahweh referred to himself as Elohim, which Peter knew to have meant "Us." It spoke of a relationship God had within himself. Peter's mind grew tired.

James and John snored louder. Between the snores, Peter

heard weeping in the distance. He moved James's head off his shoulder and slowly got up. Peter walked past a long grove of olive trees. In the distance, he saw two figures.

Getting closer, Peter observed a girl, maybe twelve or thirteen years old, walk toward his rabbi from behind. Yeshua was deeply disturbed. Peter wanted to comfort him, but he was captivated by the sight of the approaching girl. What was she doing out here in the middle of the night? Peter questioned. Was she by herself? Where were her parents? For some inexplicable reason, Peter's heart began to break, and a compassion overwhelmed him as he witnessed her get closer to Yeshua. A holiness descended. Questions ceased.

Peter stood transfixed as he saw the young girl continue to walk. There was a longing in her eyes mixed with an anticipation that Peter didn't quite understand. It was as if she had come across an old friend she hadn't seen for some time. She was within arm's distance. As she got closer, time itself seemed to stand still. He saw her slowly lift her right hand and reach toward his rabbi's cloak.

Yeshua felt the warm hand of a young Eve on his shoulder. He knew his daughter's touch. She had chosen to witness this moment. He made no attempt to hide his emotions as he turned around to face her. A fierce determination burned in his eyes as he looked on his first daughter with an everlasting love. He smiled softly as he wiped a lone tear that streamed down Eve's cheek. As he gazed into Eve's youthful eyes, he put his other hand softly on her shoulder. She looked up at his forehead and saw a bead of sweat mixed with blood.

She remembered the time in the desert as a young girl. She remembered his victory against his adversary. Her heart stirred with uncertainty. His golden-brown eyes had a gravity that she felt she was about to fall into. She looked into his eyes and saw an expression of agony mixed with deep joy. He was about to go down a road with no escape. Her lower lip trembled with emotion as her heart began to break.

"The time is now. I'm coming for you," her father said as his face broke into a reassuring smile, looking on with a relentless love at his little girl.

~ 2 Hours Later

"And there followed Him a certain young man, having a linen cloth cast about his naked body; and the young men laid hold on him. And he left the linen cloth and fled from them naked."
—Mark 14:51-52 (KJ21)

Adam woke in a small village outside Jerusalem. Gradually, he opened his eyes from a cosmic sleep. Stars hung high in the sky. As he drank in their light, their brilliance mesmerized him. Where were the iron bars? His tormentors, the voices, the stone floor beneath him: all were absent. After thousands of years, now his eyes gazed into celestial light. His heart raced as his mind stumbled to make sense of the situation. The stars twinkled in a tapestry that seemed to veil a hidden code. Perhaps their shimmering light was trying to communicate to him a message, he thought to himself. His heart began to beat faster. Raising his hands to his eyes, he saw smooth, youthful hands. The wrinkles were gone.

Disoriented, Adam slowly stood and looked around. In the distance, he saw the walls of Jerusalem. Somehow, he had been here before. After he had died and entered into Sheol, he thought he had finally escaped the recurring dreams and visions. But much to his dismay, even in Sheol he dreamed. Within the Earth itself, he had been haunted by a nightmare. Dark visions seemed to prey on him nearly every night. They taunted him with the possibility of freedom just for it to be taken away. They lasted for a season, but the scenes within the visions had been burned into his mind.

Nearby was a watering trough for animals. Adam walked toward it and gazed into its cool water. A youthful reflection stared back at him. He ran his hands over his smooth face. The full moon provided a clear view. His beard was completely gone. He looked at his arms and legs. He was young and strong again. Adam looked down and noticed he had white linen around his waist. Dozens of stone structures were in front of him. Voices of people inside the buildings carried through the air. Behind him was a large rock wall about six feet tall. It ran for about twenty feet before he saw a gap. He wanted to escape the village and run toward the trees on the other side of the wall. Quietly, he moved toward the opening. A large man led a single donkey through the entrance. At the sight of Adam, he stopped and stared. The man's dark brown eyes took in the sight of the half-naked teenage boy in front of him. Adam felt uncovered at the man's penetrating gaze.

"Trying to steal our animals?" the man questioned suspiciously.

The man reached into his cloak for a long dagger. Adrenaline coursed through Adam. Quickly, he jumped and reached for the top of the wall. With all his strength, he pulled himself over, landing on his feet.

Adam sprinted as fast as he could, leaving the armed man and small village behind him. Everything felt strangely familiar. The sequence of events from a recurring dream began to run through Adam's mind. He had been in that village before. Every time, he had looked into the water and saw the illusory youthful face from when he was young. Every time, he saw the same rock wall. Every time, he stumbled and fell back. Every time, Adam woke in the dream right after the man with the donkey plunged his thirsty blade into Adam's heart. The blade would slowly slide into his chest. In excruciating pain, he would wake to the comforting familiarity of Sheol. It had always taken a few moments for him to regain his senses and realize he had only been dreaming. But this time he escaped—he escaped! Confused and panicked, he raced toward a grove of olive trees. Adam noticed the steady chorus of cicadas. Finally catching his breath, he looked back. Thankfully, the man with the dagger hadn't chased him. He was still alive.

For a few moments, Adam felt safe. He sat down on the ground, his back against a towering tree. He raised his hands up toward his eyes. He turned them over and saw his youthful skin. He looked at his hands in amazement. What happens now? he thought to himself. A breeze blew, and Adam gazed up at the brightness of the moon. After a few minutes, a faint golden orb of light appeared between him and the light of the moon. Adam rubbed his eyes to make sure he wasn't seeing things. But the golden radiance grew brighter. Adam shook his head, trying to discern the source.

Transfixed by the light, Adam got up. He walked closer to it and slowly reached out his hand. The light seemed to be a strange echo from his past. Adam's heart began to ache with hope. He put his hand out to see if he could touch the source. The orb flashed with an unexpected brilliance. Adam's eyes gradually adjusted. Before him, Menakiel came into focus. Unearthly power and authority shone in the large angel's eyes. Eyes emerged from the edges of Menakiel's wings. Menakiel looked intensely at Adam.

"What is happening?" Adam asked softly. Memories from after Eden began to flood his mind, and emotion began to overwhelm him. "I'm dreaming ...?"

Menakiel saw the youthful Adam and slowly shook his head no.

"You've been summoned from Sheol," Menakiel responded to Adam's question. The eyes on the edges of his wings focused on Adam. "You are to be a witness to your father's betrayal. Time is short. Come."

Turning around, Menakiel began to walk. Adam followed. Gradually, a sense of dread began to filter through his soul. Much to Adam's horror, he heard people in the distance. He wished to hide but found himself obediently following Menakiel nonetheless. Peering from behind a large olive tree,

Adam saw a group of men with swords and clubs. A spirit of sedition permeated the cool air.

"The one I kiss," a man named Judas spoke in a hushed tone to the mob behind him, "he's the one. Arrest him."

Adam glanced back at Menakiel.

"This way," Menakiel spoke in a calm but authoritative tone. Adam began to follow Menakiel as the angel walked down the valley toward the men. They continued to travel through the grove of tall trees. Adam saw the mob halt and stop in front of four men. Adam stopped in his tracks as he saw the man in front.

It couldn't be. Elohim? Why was his father here?! What did these men want from him? He appeared the same way Adam remembered him as a boy. Adam's heart was in his throat. His unspoken question shone clearly in his eyes as he looked back at Menakiel.

"Yes, the King of Heaven," Menakiel spoke. "Quiet—they can see you. You are a witness in the flesh."

A part of Adam wanted to run toward his father. Another part wished to run away. He hoped he was dreaming. He hoped this was real. Adam's soft green eyes continued to peer through the trees. He took a few steps forward, leaving Menakiel behind him. Hiding behind some trees, he listened intently.

"Friend," Elohim asked Judas, "why have you come?"

It had been thousands of years since Adam had heard that voice. The presence of its rich, warm tenor soothed and broke Adam's heart at the same time.

"Greetings, Rabbi." Judas approached Elohim and kissed

him on the cheek. A love and heartbreak for Judas shone in Elohim's eyes.

"Judas, you betray me with a kiss …?"

One of the men reached out his hand to grab hold of Elohim. In an instant, indignation overtook Peter, and he unsheathed his sword. In a swift movement, it cut through the air. The man ducked, but it took off his ear. Stunned, some of the men in the mob took a step back.

"No, Peter. All who live by the sword perish by it. Put that away. Do you think I cannot ask my father for twelve legions of angels?" Elohim looked on with compassion at the man. He picked his ear up and placed it back on the side of the man's face. In moments, the connective tissue regrew. The ringing sound the man had experienced was displaced by perfect hearing. He looked at Elohim, confused. Elohim looked at Peter. "The display of the power of darkness is now."

Adam saw the other men who had been with Elohim flee from the mob. At his father's words, Adam's world grew dim. With hell's black wings, fractured memories rose within Adam's troubled heart. They splintered in every direction until Adam started to fall once again into an abyss. Icy fingers from the darkness wrapped around his throat. It was hard to breathe. His father was betrayed with a kiss? Memories broke down the gate of his mind. The mob grabbed his father forcefully. As they put their hands on his father, Adam felt the warmness of Lilly's lips. He felt the fruit from the forbidden tree in Eden glide down his throat. A sharp pain ran through his body as he clutched his chest in agony. At the sound of his knees hitting the ground, a contingent of men glanced around and saw him.

"Get him!" one yelled.

Adam returned to his physical senses as two men raced toward him. Terrified, he stumbled to his feet. Seeing Menakiel's outstretched hand, Adam ran as the men grabbed him, yanking off the linen cloth around his waist. At the last moment, Adam's hand gripped Menakiel's, and he vanished from the men's sight.

MERE MORTALS

XXVI

Pilate's Court ~ The Next Day

THIS IS HIM?" PONTIUS PILATE GLARED AT THE rebel before him. The Roman governor's patience had grown razor thin. This rebel called Yeshua had seemed to be stirring up problems wherever he went. The Jewish leadership hated him. They envied him. Now they claimed he was threatening loyalty to Caesar and wanted to kill him. The last thing Pontius Pilate wanted to do was get mixed up in their internal squabbles, but they had demanded an audience. As he looked over at the bound man, he thought to himself about a glorious return to Rome. Perhaps in the not-too-distant future he could leave this God-forsaken land and return to a position in the Senate.

"Are you King of the Jews ...?" Pilate looked back at the centurion and smiled. Pilate returned his gaze to Elohim. The man they called Yeshua had a gravity to his being that Pilate didn't quite understand.

"My kingdom is not of this world," Elohim replied.

A smattering of voices from the chief priests of the Jewish people began to accuse the rebel.

"Do you not hear the accusation from your own people?" Pilate asked. This man had claimed to be the son of God, an equal to the one true God. Pilate knew the issues they had with him. Hearing the accusations of blasphemies, the enraged crowd started to roar, "Crucify him!"

Silently, Elohim stood in front of Pilate. The voice that spoke the world into existence uttered not a word. Pilate was beloved by him. The eyes that had seen the creation of the world looked into the eyes of his lost son. Elohim remembered breathing life into Pilate at his inception while he was still in his mother's womb. He saw him as a boy, as a young man, advancing every year. He saw his career as a soldier and politician. He saw his marriage to his first love, his infidelity, his generosity, and his greed and fear. He saw a selfish ambition that was attempting to consume him. Elohim looked with a steely love and determination on a son who didn't know his father.

A golden orb in the spirit world appeared between him and Pilate. Elohim gazed at the orb until it flashed and Menakiel appeared. Menakiel knelt before him. As he bowed his head before the King of Heaven, the eyes on the edges of his wings emerged. They took in the sight of Pilate, his soldiers, the high priests, and the roar of the crowd. The eyes seemed to rest in the fire from heaven.

A chill ran down Pilate's spine. He felt the angelic, but neither he nor anyone else in the courtyard of the palace saw heaven's emissary to Earth. Menakiel stood. He drew his sword and placed its razor-sharp tip on Pilate's neck. Menakiel stared at Pilate.

Between the robes of the religious leaders and the armor of the soldiers that held his father captive, a young Adam stood transfixed. Adam looked at the razor-sharp tip of Menakiel's sword. It impressed itself on Pilate's neck. Sensing his presence, Elohim searched behind him until he found Adam. With love, Elohim gazed into the eyes of his first son. As Adam's eyes met his father's, he wanted to run into his arms, but his feet felt frozen to the ground. Adam felt love flow through his father toward him as Elohim let out a brief reassuring smile before returning his focus to Menakiel.

Adam looked once again at Menakiel with his drawn sword. A holiness exuded from Menakiel's being; Adam felt wave after wave of a demand for justice emanating from heaven's emissary. Within moments, Adam knew Menakiel could end the lives of all his father's captors.

Pilate felt a drop of blood on his neck near the tip of Menakiel's sword. It was as if he had had an accident and nicked his throat while shaving. Menakiel glanced back and searched Elohim's eyes. He awaited his master's order. He had slain tens of thousands. The mortal before him did not know he threatened the King of Heaven himself. This could end now.

"Crucify him! We want Barabbas!" the crowd thundered with an ear-piercing rage.

In a flash, the darkness of Lucifer grew inside of all

those around Adam. At the roar of the crowd, Adam witnessed black pools filling the eyes of all but Elohim and Menakiel, the same black pools that had filled Lilly's eyes at his fall.

They seethed with hate and accusation toward his father. It was as if the crowd began to embody all the pain that every generation had experienced since the beginning of creation. They blamed Elohim. They blamed Adam. Within moments, the hate they felt intensified. Adam tried to hide, but he felt eyes from every direction begin to stare at him. They stared at his father. He couldn't escape. As he gazed back into their hate-filled eyes, Adam felt accusation rise like a giant wave within his own heart. He thought of the loss of his son Abel. He thought of all the loved ones he had lost during his life. What was the purpose and meaning behind it all? He tried to fight the growing rage, but its power was too great. The futility filled him with hate. Why had Elohim abandoned them? What if Adam could make his father understand the depths of the loss? What if he could force his father to feel the pain he knew all too well?

Adam's eyes grew dark. A sound erupted from the depths of hell and from the entire fallen realm. As it moved from the center of the Earth to its surface, the voices of the fallen angels joined fallen man as all roared in unison with one demand:

"CRUCIFY HIM!"

With an unyielding determination, Elohim looked at Menakiel and tilted his head. Menakiel looked at the darkness all around him and his master. Reluctantly, Menakiel withdrew his sword from Pilate's neck.

As if he were awakened from a nightmare, the darkness faded from Adam's eyes. He began to see clearly. Adam saw Pilate wipe the blood off with his right palm. Adam's heart sank at the decree he had lent his own voice to. He wanted to take back his words, but it was too late.

As Pilate wiped the blood off his neck, he stared at his hand. Spirits from another world were here, and he knew it. The sound of the crowd dissipated. He looked away from the man called Yeshua and walked toward a basin of water.

Within the small, dark pool, he stared at his reflection. His wife had warned him this man was righteous. Why did they hate him? An eerie silence hung over the atmosphere. As he breathed in deep, he couldn't seem to get the stories his wife had shared about this man out of his head. Why would they want the life of a man who purportedly healed the sick, raised the dead, and fed those who were hungry? What kind of kingdom was he looking to bring? Certainly, it was nothing that could threaten Rome. He dipped his hands and slowly washed the blood off his palm.

"I am innocent of this man's blood," Pilate said. A certain sadness came into his voice. "Take him away."

There weren't many tall trees outside of the walls of Jerusalem suitable for the task, Octavius thought to himself. The Roman commander looked around.

"Over here!" Titus declared, looking back at his commanding officer.

Octavius walked over to Titus and the nearby tree. His eyes moved from the bottom to the top, taking in its form. About fifteen feet up the trunk, two nearly symmetrical branches jutted out for about three or four feet on each side before splintering into dozens of smaller branches. Octavius marveled. Its form was perfect. It was as if the gods themselves had grown this tree for the very purpose of afflicting terror in the hearts of Rome's enemies. He walked around it and saw long jagged lines that seemed to resemble a map of some sort. Looking closer, he saw within the carvings there was ancient Hebraic pictography chiseled deeply into its trunk. Strange, he thought.

He mostly dismissed the culture of the Jews as inferior to that of Rome. They had but one God; the Romans had many. While he disagreed with the premise and thought their culture was backwards, their ancient writing seemed to harken back to a simpler time. As he gazed at the carvings, he marveled at how someone had managed to engrave the symbols so deeply into the wood. Whatever the symbols meant, one of their own would be crucified on it today. He relished the irony.

"This works." Octavius looked over at Titus. "Clean up the top, but leave the two main branches; they're wide enough. No need for extra work ..."

Titus returned Octavius's smile. At his commander's word, Titus laid his ax to the base of the Etz Hayim.

"Cursed is everyone who is hung on a tree."
—Galatians 3:13 (NLT)
"For the joy set before him he endured the cross, scorning its shame."—
Hebrews 12:2 (NIV)

Elohim hung on the Etz Hayim, the branch from the tree of life, the first gift he had given to his son Adam. Nails pierced his hands where both Adam's and Eve's names were written. He remembered his first son. He remembered his first daughter. Out of the wounds from his crucifixion flowed blood mixed with water. Steadily, it dripped from his body onto the ground below. It pooled beneath the tree he was crucified on.

Elohim trembled under the weight of the world's pain. He felt the brokenness of every heart past, present, and future. All the pain that Adam had brought into the world was put upon him in that moment.

With every breath, a mixture of death, decay, betrayal, sickness, despair, and hopelessness invaded the King of Heaven's lungs. He heaved as anguish and passion coursed through his body. Elohim saw visions of the future. He witnessed a reunion with every lost son and daughter. He saw a restoration of sight to every heart that had been blinded by the prince of the air so they could see how he and his father loved them. A fierce joy empowered him as he writhed in pain.

Dark clouds hung like curtains in the sky. Slowly, they covered the brightness of the sun. A glory beyond light moved like a warm wind over the Earth. It blew from the heart of Eternity itself. It transcended time, space, and every law of the natural world. As it picked up speed, it grew from a gentle breeze into a roar that shook the very foundations of the demonic realm. As it blanketed the Earth, it shifted one last time into a whisper directed toward the heart of man.

Elohim so loved the world he would fight to the death for them. Across every generation of Adam's seed, sin plagued and bound the hearts of his children. Some of his sons and daughters needed a salve for their wounds. For others, the seeming futility and pain produced a blind demand for justice; for others, it was revenge. Regardless of the conditions of their hearts, he would give them a gift so their blindness could be removed.

His children were always meant to be free. Free from every entanglement that bound them. Free from the shame each experienced. Free to receive love. Free to love purely. They were destined to be born once again and, within their new birth, to see for the first time in their lives. He forgave the world for their betrayal of each other, themselves, and him. For they knew not what they did. They knew not from whom they came or the loving arms they were destined to return to.

With his last breath, he cried out in anguish as he dreamt of reunion. Elohim entrusted his spirit to the one who was with him before time began.

A righteous blood traveled down his body, dripping onto the earth below, a cleansing blood that would eventually cover the whole world. The blood on the ground continued to pool. Eventually, it sank into the dust of the earth: the very substance he had formed his first son from. It traveled past rocks and insects. As it dropped deeper, the earth got colder and darker. It slowly cascaded beneath the reach of all light. The blood thinned but continued to flow relentlessly into the darkest depths of the Earth.

NO SHADOWS

XXVII

MY FATHER WAS MURDERED BEFORE MY EYES. Menakiel hid me in the crowd. The evil of that day rendered me hollow. A rage and a steady stream of accusations from the heart of humanity flowed toward my father. Along with the fallen angels, we declared him guilty of all the pain every generation experienced. The brutality in our hearts was poured out on him. Every accusation I had after Eden and the pain after the death of my son was unleashed on him. An abyss was carved out of my soul as I witnessed the one who breathed life into me beaten and scourged. A foreboding madness consumed my mind as I saw nails driven through the strong hands that had held me as a child. Nothing was hidden from my eyes.

I didn't understand. Why would he let this happen to himself? Why would he subject himself to this unyielding violence? No one could take his life. His death was impossible. But I saw it with my own eyes.

When I did, any remaining hope I had for myself—for you—dissipated like smoke in the air. I had failed as a son, and my descendants had taken the life of my father. I was undone. I begged Menakiel to take me from Golgotha. Finally, he relented. I woke once again in Sheol. My hands began to shake as I wrote this letter to you. How could I save you—myself—when all hope was no more? I sat in despair as my last candle burned.

After our time on Earth, Eve and I were taken as prisoners into the depths of the Earth. Millions were to follow in our wake. I wrote this letter to you as a captive. One whose fate had been sealed. I wrote to you in hopes that you may never find yourself in this place. My last candle was almost gone. I thought its dim light could provide me with enough time, enough sight so I could possibly find the right words. Words to save you from this place.

I began to remember the visions of you my father gave me after my time in Eden. He pulled back the curtain of time that separated my past from your present. He gave me a window into your life. I cannot tell you why. I do not know. But he showed me everything. Night after night, I saw you. Your life was beautiful beyond words. But once the dreams were gone, I'd wake up once again. What I saw of your life only added more weight to the guilt I felt. It was crushing me. The pain you experienced was overwhelming. I was undone. I refused to share what I saw. I told no one. How could I? The pain was too great. I wished for death. A futility and despair swept through the caverns of my soul as I thought of your future. The truth was I'm not sure exactly what I could have shared. The burden I felt for what I have caused you deprived me of my strength. I wrote as one lost in my thoughts, lost in the dreaded deeds of my past.

It was then when I felt drops from the ceiling land in the thickness of my beard. For a moment, it felt like slow rain, as if I were above ground once again. Startled, I looked up, and the light of my candle illuminated red drops of blood that trickled from the stone ceiling above me. The drops landed softly on the tan papyrus with its black ink, the same paper that I had been writing this letter to you on.

Suddenly, there was a loud thundering outside my cell and the very ground beneath me shook. A powerful wind blew. I could hear cries in the distance. The light of my candle was extinguished by the gust. I scrambled to collect the pages of the letter I had been writing to you. It was a dark confession of my brokenness and guilt. Terrified, I backed myself into the farthest corner of my cell. I clenched the blood-stained pages. They were all that I had. In the distance, I heard the bending of iron bars and the thunderous cracking of stone. To my amazement, I saw twinkling light from fireflies speeding by. The same creatures were present at my creation. Some came into my cell while others sped past where I was imprisoned. I witnessed a strong hand wrap around one of my bars.

With an abrupt pull, the bars were thrown to the side. Over the years, I had been visited by many demons. Was this a tormenter ... something worse? Fear surged through my being. My heart pounded hard in my chest.

Then I saw him. I saw him, and I could not look away. My father had come for me. He was alive! The moment our eyes met, a rush of wind entered into me. My spirit that had been dead was now alive. A huge smile spread across Elohim's face as he offered his hand to me. It was then I saw where the nail had gone through. The scarring had etched my very name on the palm of his hand. Slowly, I lifted my head up and looked into his golden-brown eyes. I paused for a second, not knowing what to do.

As I looked into the eyes of the one who had breathed the first breath of life into my lungs, his smile only got bigger. He motioned for me to come to him. I felt light as air. My heart felt freer than on the day of my creation. I had come to understand the knowledge of good and of evil. But I knew now that I had seen through a dim glass. I had come to know he who was greater than any knowledge I could possess, greater than any failure or brokenness in my being. I was in the presence of the one who had no shadow nor evil in him. In that moment, his heart became my heart. His life became my life. Death was no longer my master, and it had no hold on me.

I belonged to this time. I belonged to this moment. I belonged to the heavens above and the Earth below. I belonged to the stars, to my family, to all my children, to you. And more than anything, I belonged to him. Slowly, I let go of the pages and put my hand in his.

THE GIFT

EPILOGUE

2033 A.D. ~ Modern-Day Jerusalem, 2,000 Years Later

DURING AN AUTUMN DAY, A TOWERING TREE provided shade to a park outside the old walls of Jerusalem. Children played soccer, swung on tire swings, and slid down slides. The park was large with fountains, fields, scattered trees, and play structures. Various street vendors were throughout the park cooking shawarma and kabobs, serving them with fresh hummus and olives. Some parents looked down at smartphones, some chatted with coffees or food in hand, and others intently watched their children play.

Next to the largest tree in the park sat three people on a wooden bench. As a soft breeze blew, you could hear laughing. They seemed to be talking about old times and exchanging memories as they watched the children have fun. A young boy kicked a soccer ball near them. As the ball neared her feet, the woman rose and picked up the ball. The young boy looked up tentatively at her. His breath was taken away by her beauty. Her eyes seemed to sparkle with joy.

"What's your name?" Eve softly asked the boy.

"Michael," the boy replied.

"You ready?" Eve asked.

Michael returned the smile and nodded. Eve tossed the soccer ball back to him. Adam and Elohim stood.

"Looks a bit like Abel," Adam said. Elohim looked at the young man's features.

"I can see that." Elohim smiled at the boy.

"Beautiful day …" Eve commented as she looked around the park. A warm breeze blew.

"It is …" Elohim took in a deep breath and looked up at the sun. It was just a few hours before sunset. This was his favorite time of day.

As they walked, they watched the children playing freely. Adam observed the countenance of the adults. On some faces, he saw a look of weariness; others had anxiety, while others had sadness. He glanced at his father and saw that he had also been observing the varying dispositions of the people around them.

"Many are tired," Adam lamented. Elohim nodded with a silent acknowledgement.

"They try to earn a love I give freely," Elohim responded. A longing was in his eyes, and a deep sadness marked his voice.

"They've been walking in my shadow," Adam said. Elohim looked over at Adam. He smiled at his son reassuringly.

"There was your shadow; there is my light," Elohim said. "Each and every one I knit together in their mother's womb. I've not given up on any." Elohim gazed at the people in the park and smiled broadly. He put his hand on Adam's shoulder. "They're going to begin to see me everywhere, in everything. In every gift in this life they enjoy, I will reveal my goodness to them. I am making all things new. Come."

Adam and Eve followed Elohim as the three continued their stroll. As Elohim walked, the palm of his right hand gently grazed the largest tree in the park. Eve saw her father's scars, their names etched on his palms. She looked up at the tree and noticed the carvings on its trunk. Emotion began to overwhelm her.

"This was it, wasn't it? The tree of life ... the Etz Hayim?" Eve asked her father. Elohim smiled and nodded as he looked at the tree that had regrown.

"It is," Elohim said. He breathed in deep yet again, a look of unshakeable peace in his eyes.

"It was how you found your way back to us; it was our way back to you," Adam responded in weighty amazement.

Adam saw soft golden flecks of light in Elohim's brown eyes. Adam could feel the deep love and longing his father had for the people around them. A group of young boys and girls kicking a soccer ball ran by them.

"It is my gift," Elohim smiled softly. He watched with fondness as the boys and girls raced by. "Through this, they'll begin to see who they truly are. They'll see who I truly am ... I took all their pain so they could let it go. I took on all their sorrow so they could have my joy. As they look, they'll see and be made whole."

Adam felt a deep love swell inside his heart at the words of his father. These were not words he could have fully understood as a boy. But he believed he was coming closer to understanding at least part of their meaning now. It was as if neither time nor space, nor anything else in all of creation, could come between his father and the ones he loved. Elohim grinned playfully at Adam and Eve.

"Come, there's more who need to see and be made whole," Elohim offered softly.

In the cool of the day, they walked side by side, together once again.

So it is written: "The first man Adam became a living being"; the last Adam, a life-giving spirit. The spiritual did not come first, but the natural, and after that the spiritual. The first man was of the dust of the earth; the second man is of heaven. As was the earthly man, so are those who are of the earth; and as is the heavenly man, so also are those who are of heaven. And just as we have borne the image of the earthly man, so shall we bear the image of the heavenly man.—1 Corinthians 15:45–49 (NIV)

DEDICATION

By Nicholas James Darling

This book is dedicated to my wife, Christine Louise Darling. Without your love and friendship, there would be no Adam. You have shown me a side to God in the way that you've loved me and covered over my weaknesses that has given me a strength and a wholeness I would not otherwise possess. I love you with all my heart. You are the woman within my dreams and the greatest gift this side of eternity He has ever given me. I look forward to wearing a crown of gray with you.

To my daughter, Lucy Rose Darling. Before you were born, your heavenly Father shared with me that peace and joy were going to be your emotional baseline. He also said to me that people would experience freedom just by being in your presence. This is never something you'll have to strive for; it simply flows out of who you are. The world needs to experience the beauty of His joy and His Spirit of peace that you carry within you. Daughter, I am proud of who you are and who you are becoming.

To my son, Noah Price Darling. When you were in your mother's womb, God spoke to me and told me that you would set things right from a place of rest, from a place of strength. You are a fighter. You are strong and brave. Know that

He is the one who goes before you and makes a path for your feet that is firm. The world is at war. It needs the strength and courage you possess so that injustices may be made right. You will take territory. Son, I am proud of who you are and who you are becoming.

The greatest gift will never be found in what you're called to do. Nor is the greatest treasure in this life found after the glory of any accomplishment. The greatest gift is always found in this very moment now, within the time you spend being with your heavenly Father. He is always with you, and He never waits for some point in the future to celebrate you. He enjoys being with you in every stage of your life.

The world longs to know they are not orphans. They long to experience that they are truly seen, fully known, and completely loved. As you learn to receive His unconditional love, it will naturally take expression and overflow to His other children, many of whom do not know their Father in heaven and are in great pain. Do not be overwhelmed by the pain in this world. Partner with the one who is sufficient and longs to bring wholeness to those around you. I love you both with all my heart.

AUTHOR'S NOTE

By Nicholas James Darling

W
E ALL WRITE OUR OWN LETTERS TO THE WORLD around us. In our speech and deeds, people can read our stories like they would pages in a book. Are we willing to see the drops of blood that stain the pages of our own lives? Are we willing to look up into the eyes of love and fix our gaze on the one who could make us whole? Can we release the authorship of our own stories with all the good, the bad, and the pain? What would our stories look like if we were willing to leave the captivity many of us find ourselves in so that we can take His hand? What would our lives look like if we let go of what we knew, to be led by the one who knew us before the world itself was created? What if there was one who would stick closer than a brother, one who was willing to take the heavy burdens off our backs and just be with us?

When you speak with most people about their childhood, it's typically a bit of a mixed bag. Death of loved ones, divorce, abuse, violence, abandonment, and other violations of our worth can leave us with deep wounds. I had some great experiences growing up, but like many, I also had certain things occur when I was young that no child should ever have to face. For me, some of the things that happened earlier in my life opened the door to deep depression and suicidal thoughts in my teens. These things made me feel more alive to pain, as if that was the most real thing in my life.

During some of those more difficult years, I made a vow to God. If I ever made it to heaven, I told God I would kill Adam. Or maybe when I died, if I didn't go to heaven, I'd find him in hell. While I wasn't sure how one would go about killing someone in the afterlife, something within me cried out against pain and suffering. Not just my own, but all the pain I had seen in the world. I wasn't convinced at that time that Adam (or God, for that matter) was real. But in my juvenile way of thinking, if Adam was real, the pain in the world was his fault. I blamed and hated him for introducing suffering into our world. The vow I made in my teens gradually faded from memory. By God's grace, I healed in part and moved beyond some of the things I experienced in my childhood.

Many years later, in my early thirties, out of the blue, God started asking me questions about the Genesis narrative. This was around 2013. I was newly married and was simply trying to provide. My focus was on my wife and a new career. I certainly wasn't studying the book of Genesis. I had a familiarity with the tale of Adam and Eve that I felt was adequate, but that was it. Because the narrative was so far from being an interest of mine, the questions He asked seemed like a bit of an intrusion. I often tried to change the topic back to something I was interested in. But He was persistent.

In the back of my mind, I was curious: why was He asking me about this? He wrote the book, inspired the authors. He certainly didn't need my answers or insight into any of this. He was there, not me. I was reminded of something one of my favorite pastors had once said. Any time God asks us questions, it's not because He doesn't know the answers. The questions He asks are invitations to see things from a higher perspective (repentance in practice). Asking good questions is one of the many beautiful things about how Jesus communicates. The questions He raised were intriguing intellectually and highlighted pieces of the story I had never given thought to. Perhaps one day I will share those questions. Suffice it to say, I gave them thought, then I promptly moved on.

In October 2014, while I was spending time in prayer, God gave me a vision of Adam's creation. By this time, I was somewhat used to God speaking to me in this way (via images). But what I wasn't used to was what He showed me that day. I saw in vivid detail Adam being created as a young boy. I didn't know what to make of it. Seeing him as a youthful and spirited boy somehow changed things for me. It turned this man with an obvious self-control problem from a one-dimensional character who screwed things up for everyone to something more. In some ways, these visions of Adam as a boy in his innocence were a bit of a Trojan horse. They got past my defenses and inspired a series of new questions.

What might it have looked like to have been fathered by God Himself? What might it have looked like for God to have raised a son from being a boy all the way into manhood in Eden? What did it look like for Him to raise a little girl, His first daughter? Through the images I saw, these questions were dropped in my mind like a depth charge that would reverberate through my heart from that time until today. During that same prayer time in October, God gave me an understanding of a three-act structure for a screenplay telling Adam's story from Adam's perspective. I spent roughly eight years, from 2014 to 2022, writing the screenplay initially, then—at the prompting of my writing partner Andrew—writing this book. The third act was subsequently broken into two acts for readability.

When I began writing Adam's story, I was newly married. Now, nearly ten years into our marriage and a father, I'm a much different man. As a father to a three-year-old little boy and a five-year-old little girl, this story took on another, very emotional dimension. To think of how God raised a little boy and a little girl in Eden did something to me that's hard to describe. During the years I was writing, I would see different scenes of Adam's and Eve's lives both as children and young adults. These images would come during worship, prayer, and unexpected times, like when I was driving. I remember pulling off to the side of the road many times to weep, to pray, to process what I was seeing. These depictions filled in the gaps from the high-level three-act structure to what occurred within those three acts. Many of these depictions that God gave me of their story captivated me, while some broke my heart, and others I simply wanted to look away from. Some gave me life; others felt exhausting.

I never sought to write this story. The humor and irony involved with God choosing someone who had previously cursed Adam to write Adam's story is not lost on me. He's the one who calls things that are not as though they were. It's His voice that speaks to us of a brighter future. In some sense, I feel like God has been playing a series of tricks on me. Maybe more accurately, He's just playing a bigger, longer game than we are. Had He told me to put it into a book first in 2014, I would have said no. Not because I wouldn't want to be obedient, but because I had zero faith in my ability as a writer. The insecurity would have overridden my faith. So while most great stories are books prior to screenplays, for this story, the screenplay acted as an outline to the book.

From cursing Adam in my youth, to simple questions in 2013, to a vision of Adam's creation in 2014, He's progressively revealing a path. It's 2022, and while I don't know how it will happen, I believe one day this will be turned into a movie that will awaken people to their worth. That's my heart. It may or may not happen in my lifetime. He's shared with me that at the right time He will surround this project with the right people. One of the ways I've come to understand Him is as a master chess player. You might even say, as King David once did, that God knows how to walk with us through the valley of the shadow of death and from there somehow prepare a feast for us in the presence of our enemies. From a difficult place of death to a place of life and feasting, He knows how to move the pieces on the board and the pieces of our hearts to reveal Himself in ways we can understand.

As I've moved through time, I've always looked to invite people into this story who feel called to it. I'm a layperson. While I've now read many books on this subject, I would never confuse myself with an authority on Adam or the Genesis narrative. I am, however, a disciple of Jesus. I am also a son. He speaks and I hear His voice, imperfectly many times, but I hear it, nonetheless. So, while I'm certainly not an authority, I would also never wish to conflate my lack of a scholarly background with an inability to obey His voice and steward the visions He has given me. This book is a manifestation of an imperfect but faithful stewardship.

I understand up front that there will likely be many varying viewpoints and people of good intentions who will disagree with some, if not much, of what I've written. Many will likely be more educated on the topic than I am. In the gospel of Luke, Jesus says that neither will people say, "here it is" or "there it is," for the kingdom of God is within you. In the testimony of Matthew, Jesus says He will give us the keys to the kingdom of heaven. I believe God has given us all keys. I have some. You have others. God created us for community. We need each other to unlock different aspects of who we are so we can enter into the fullness of our design.

Even if you're not currently walking with Him for whatever reason, there is something that will not be released into the Earth until you receive His love and partner with the one who formed you in your mother's womb. Whatever you're called to do on this Earth is an invitation to discover who you are and who He is for you. God has revealed Himself in ways to others I've never seen or experienced. I need and want to hear from them and others who will have different takes on this narrative. I welcome those discussions as opportunities to learn from others and what they've been shown. Ultimately, to anyone critical of this work, I would simply desire to bless them and invite their thoughtful feedback. It's painfully obvious to me that I've not seen and experienced the totality of God and His goodness. But the part that I have, I give.

I never had a particular aim or agenda to advance when I started this—or frankly, even now. The way the book was written was closer to "show and tell" than an intentional manifesto designed to change people's minds on this or that point. God would show me things, and I'd look to "tell" or share them within what I wrote. Most of the time, I received fragments of the story that only made sense when stitched together with another piece that sometimes I wouldn't receive until years later. That's not to say the book doesn't communicate certain points very strongly—it does. The points that are clear to me, I'll look to outline later. It's simply to acknowledge it wasn't born from a place of looking to advance any particular agenda.

I do not wish to have what I've written confused with the authority of the Bible in any way. Anywhere where this story deviates from Scripture, my desire is for the reader to derive their sense of what's true from the biblical account and understand the deviation as fiction because that is what it is. I am confident that the Holy Spirit will guide you into the truth of the story itself (1 John 2:27). He will guide your heart and mind into the things that are important for you to receive in this season of your life.

Why deviate at all? I offer three directions a story like this might take:

1. Biblical: Something that is clearly within the biblical narrative. As an example, God created Adam. This is clearly articulated in Scripture as well as this story.

2. Extrabiblical: These are things that aren't found in Scripture that also don't violate the Scriptures. An example of this is that within the Genesis narrative, God

tells Adam and Eve to take dominion and multiply. He doesn't tell them how. When the book depicts part of that command being carried out by them redirecting rivers to the desert, that is extrabiblical as it's not clearly stated in the Genesis narrative that this was how they approached obeying that calling on their lives.

3. Antibiblical: These are things that directly contradict KNOWN truth within Scripture. An example would be if in the book it was depicted that Eve was created first and Adam afterward from Eve's rib. This would be antibiblical as it directly contradicts Scripture.

Almost definitionally, a novel retelling focused on just a handful of chapters in Genesis will have elements that are extrabiblical. We did everything we could to seek counsel to explicitly avoid anything that would be antibiblical within the pages of *Adam*. We want to honor the heart of God with this work. This book draws from more than just Genesis. It draws from many books within the Bible.

There was one major decision that I consciously made that was antibiblical and one other decision that is more extrabiblical that I want to address.

1. Antibiblical: In Genesis, Adam and Eve are naked in the beginning. In the story, I have them clothed prior to the fall. There are two reasons for this. The first is with all the sexual brokenness in the world, I thought it would be best if they were clothed instead having the images of naked children or young adults be inferred through the first and second acts. I thought this would detract from the story. The second reason is because

the deeper truth of them being free from shame prior to the fall is present in both the book and the Genesis narrative. In that way, there's no daylight between the narratives.

2. Extrabiblical: Lilly/Lilith is nowhere to be found in Genesis. Why is she there rather than only the serpent? There's a handful of reasons. The first is that as a character who poses the temptation, she's much more believable to a modern audience than a snake. If the serpent was representative of evil and Lilly represents the serpent, then both the book and the Genesis narrative are in lockstep on this. I also saw images in my imagination of her. My imagination doesn't carry the weight of Scripture, but the images I saw did put together a seamless understanding of how they might have been tempted. The last reason for this decision was that when they fell in the Bible, there is a sexual connotation that is present. This shows up in her characterization as a seducer.

Truth is always more powerful than fiction. Instead of defending any other aspect, I want to clearly state what I believe God has given me on the story of Adam that correlates to Scripture:

1. God created the world and His first son and daughter. God is a father and an artist who gives good and beautiful gifts to His children.

2. He loved/loves them deeply: It was His joy to see them play, grow, and mature. This is not unimportant. It was

for the joy He saw within the relationships with His children that He endured the cross.

3. He called them to be fruitful, multiply, and take dominion prior to the fall and sin.

4. Taking dominion was a monumental task that was always intended to be fulfilled by more than Adam and Eve—in fact, by multiple generations.

5. The call to take dominion was given *prior* to the fall, which means there were areas of the Earth prior to man sinning that were under the *wrong dominion*.

6. He introduced choice into their world as an invitation for them to know Him more deeply. Choice not only makes love possible, but it also makes it receivable/ understandable by us.

7. A Luciferian perspective on God was present in the garden prior to the fall. They adopted the perspective, which led to their fall.

8. The fall impacted profoundly how they saw themselves and their Father. The change in perception invited great pain.

9. The fall was not a surprise. Before the foundation of the world, God made a way back to Eden, a way back to walking with God daily. To return to Eden is to return to a relationship with God where we know Him like a friend, and we get to walk with Him in the cool of the day. Eden is available to all this side of eternity.

10. The world we live in isn't God's plan B created in reaction to the mistakes of His children. This is plan A, and the beauty within it is to know what God is

like when we are in violation of our relationship with Him. Without knowing this, we cannot know Him. Nor could we receive His love. If the Bible is to be believed, He was actually crucified before the foundation of the world (Revelation 13:8). It's mind bending but worthy of our minds being bent.

11. While the fall invited great pain and death into our world, it also made it possible for us to know more of God's character than if we never had fallen. There's a truth and beauty to this that's important and deserves further exploration on our part.

12. God cared for Adam and his descendants. When the fullness of that love could be understood and received was when He came back in human form to redeem all that was lost.

This is an imperfect story, but on this side of eternity, what I can tell you is that it has deepened my love for our Father in heaven, the same Uncreated One who even now moves on the Earth, through time and space, and speaks through creation and through all generations. This story has been a gift that has revealed a new vision for who He is as my Father, a father who works past my own brokenness to rescue an otherwise troubled soul. He cleans me up before I deserve it; He loves on me before I can even understand how to perceive it, much less receive it. My hope is that it awakens your heart to the fierceness of His pursuit of you.

DEDICATION

By Andrew Michael Arroyo

This book is dedicated to my wife, Megan, the pearl of my life. Without you, I am incomplete. Thank you for always standing by my side. You are the woman of my dreams.

To my daughter, Emma. I believe God has given you beauty within your spirit that will shine bright for Him. Honor Him by fulfilling His will for your life. Seek the one who will truly make you whole, and carry His message throughout the world. I am forever your biggest fan.

To my son, David. You were born for such a time as this. I believe God has given you a character that will be cherished by many. Seek the Holy Spirit, who will help you develop His character, and carry His message throughout the world. I am forever your biggest fan.

Emma and David: Learn to love finding God's will. Learn to love doing God's will. Learn to love fulfilling God's will. It will become your greatest joy in life. Waking up each morning knowing that you have a purpose, there is a plan, and you have been assigned a specific mission that God has designed just for you to accomplish is a magnificent feeling. Stay humble, reverent, respectful, trusting, loving, devoted, faithful, obedient, and repentant. It will be well with you. Enjoy the journey as you discover the Father's love.

CO-AUTHOR'S NOTE

By Andrew Michael Arroyo

T HE ESSENCE OF ADAM'S STORY IS ELOHIM'S LOVE for His children. It's the first and most important story of redemption ever told: the love of a father conquering death. This foundational part of human history was delivered to us as a gift of forty three verses of Scripture (Genesis 2:7-3:24). The intimate details of Eden remain a mystery.

The journey in assisting my friend and colleague Nick Darling in developing *Adam* from a movie script to a literary novel has been a blessing and lifelong dream. *Adam* was originally written for the big screen. While I was shopping the script to the studios, I asked a successful movie executive what he thought it would cost me to produce the film factoring in the CGI and animation. His response was at least $100 million to do it right. Based on that revelation, the idea of a writing a book was born.

Adam is based on the true story of the first human to ever live. Using artistic imagination, we have sought discernment through prayer and vision to protect the integrity of the Scripture and honor all biblical and historical context while seeking the truth and intent of the limited Scripture around the early days of mankind. Anywhere this story deviates from Scripture, understand the deviation as fiction because that is what it is. Details, locations, timelines, and certain characters have been imagined, and significant dialogue has been added that is not found in Scripture. Readers are encouraged to read the book of Genesis in the Bible.

Adapting a screenplay to a novel is no easy feat. It's usually done the other way around. Nick and I soon realized that this was a blessing in disguise as literature could be an in-depth, more expansive medium to use to explore the earliest days of human history. I believe *Adam* will bring the reader a new, fresh understanding of the depth of God's love. In God's timing, I also believe the right director and producer will be appointed to adapt the book back to the big screen.

There is a deep hunger in our generation for truth and identity that only the origin of love can resolve. Is it possible to successfully share the truth of God's love with today's youth during a cultural revolution that questions our origins? Yes. But how? By revealing the essence of what deep, meaningful love is through storytelling. God demonstrated through the human stories in His Word that He alone is what we desire to completely fulfill our ever-hungry hearts.

Without proper context and storytelling to show there is something to be saved from, how can people believe they need to be saved or redeemed?

How can one consider the redemptive force of a Messiah if you do not accept the first human story as more than a simple fairy tale or glorified illustration?

Creators in this generation are challenged to reveal the

stories of our origin as the unwavering truth, as they were originally presented in all their artistic beauty and light. With the new methods of communication that we have available today, there is no valid reason the truth cannot be elegantly communicated. My hope is that *Adam* is one step in the right direction to accomplish a vision that transforms the hearts and minds of this generation.

Our shared mission with *Adam* from its inception has been to reveal the love of the Father. Our hope, prayer, and desire are that the readers of *Adam* would go deeper in their relationship with God, explore the depth of Elohim's love, and discover the path to redemption through Yeshua, who desires a relationship with each and every one of us.

As Elohim's Word reminds us …
Love never fails.

Contact Information

theadambook.com

Made in the USA
Las Vegas, NV
22 December 2022

63904350R00194